Patch of Trouble

A Southern Quilting Mystery, Volume 6

Elizabeth Craig

Published by Elizabeth Spann Craig, 2016.

This is a work of fiction. Similarities to real people, places, or events are entirely coincidental.

PATCH OF TROUBLE

First edition. May 9, 2016.

Written by Elizabeth Craig.

For Mama and Daddy with love

Chapter One

After a long morning of pulling the impudent weeds in her yard, Beatrice had just tempted herself into the hammock with a tall glass of iced tea and what appeared to be a very promising novel. Her friend, Posy, had thoughtfully given her a quilted pillow in a water-resistant fabric, and the plumpness of the cushion begged to be rested on. Although Beatrice, who was restless by nature, was never one to give into the temptation of resting very often. Her dreams of a life as a relaxed retired woman never seemed to come to fruition.

Admittedly, it was good to stretch out. There was a cool breeze and the shade from the canopy of the overhanging trees provided sanctuary from the heat of the day. Beatrice gave a contented sigh. Her corgi, Noo-noo, seemed content too, lying on her back with her short legs up in the air, fast asleep and snoring lightly in rhythmic puffs.

It was then that her cell phone blared from as deep inside the little house as it could, clear as a bell through the screened window. Beatrice closed her eyes briefly. Naturally the phone would ring when she hadn't had the foresight to keep it next to her. Maybe it wasn't important. She listened stiffly as it rang and rang before stopping. She relaxed. If it had been important, the interlopers would leave a message, after all.

Or call again. Which is exactly what happened. The phone bleated at her again with that staccato, annoying ring that she couldn't quite figure out how to change. This time she struggled from the hammock, startling Noo-noo who struggled to her feet too, looking blearily around her at something to bark at for the interruption she was suffering.

"Hello?" Beatrice demanded a bit breathlessly when she finally grabbed the phone. She pushed a hand over her head to smooth down her platinum white hair as if the caller could see her dishevelment over the phone line.

"Beatrice? It's Meadow."

Meadow was Beatrice's indefatigable next door neighbor who frequently came between Beatrice and relaxation. Meadow was all about quilting, the quilting guild, cooking, and basically not sitting still for half a minute. What was more, she tended to pull Beatrice into her chaos.

Beatrice was about to inquire what Meadow had up her sleeve this time, but Meadow continued on. She was breathless as she said, "Wyatt asked me to call you. Miss Sissy has had an accident and is at the hospital over in Lenoir. I'm on my way over now."

"On your way to the hospital? What kind of accident?" Beatrice was already motioning to Noo-noo to follow her inside from the backyard.

"On my way to your house to pick you up. I'll fill you in in a second," said Meadow before hanging up just as abruptly as she'd called.

Beatrice hurried outside again to find her shoes, put them on, and then started looking for her errant purse. She made a face at her reflection in the mirror. She smoothed down the platinum-white hair that was still sticking up in the back from lying on the hammock. She wore an old pair of khaki slacks with an equally ancient button down baby-blue shirt. It was completely suitable for yard work but not for much else. No time to do anything else about her appearance since Meadow was already in her driveway, tooting the car horn imperiously.

"I'll be back before long," she promised the little corgi that was looking at her with concerned brown eyes. The rushing, the tension that Beatrice felt, it was all felt just as strongly by Noo-noo. She reached down to give her a reassuring pat as she left the cottage.

Beatrice plopped herself into Meadow's van, gripping her purse with one hand as she tugged frantically at the seat belt to secure it around her with the other. One thing she knew for sure—she needed the protection of a seat belt when Meadow was behind the wheel.

Meadow shot backward down the driveway and took off at a fair clip down the road.

"Now *what* is going on?" asked Beatrice. "What kind of accident? Is Miss Sissy in any danger? Because I can't see the purpose in getting *ourselves* in an accident on the way over to the hospital."

At this, Meadow started driving a bit more sedately. "Wyatt didn't give a lot of information, but it sounded like she was probably going to be okay. It was some kind of a car accident, I think. I called Posy, too, but she's working alone today at the quilt shop so she'll check in with us later."

Beatrice wasn't at all surprised to hear that Miss Sissy had been in a car accident. It was something of a miracle that she hadn't been in one before. Miss Sissy was an elderly quilter who confused the sidewalk with the roadway. What was more, she wasn't all that lucid even on a good day. Still, she was the heart and soul of the Village Quilters guild and a fine quilter herself, besides being a good, if unorthodox, friend.

Meadow found a spot in the front of the regional hospital without even going to the parking deck. They hurried inside. Meadow was nearly as disheveled as Beatrice. Her generous frame was covered by a wrinkled turquoise skirt that sat crookedly around her waist and a white tunic top that appeared to have been slept in. She had thrown a disreputable-looking gray cardigan over the top and her long gray braid was caught up in the sweater. Her red-framed glasses were askew. Everything about her suggested that she'd never planned on leaving the house.

Miss Sissy was in a small room on the third floor. Beatrice and Meadow breathed sighs of relief when they saw that the old woman looked cross and even more wildly disheveled than Beatrice and Meadow, but appeared to be all in one piece. She made for a very thin outline under the starched white hospital sheets. Wyatt gave them a reassuring smile and stood from a bedside chair to greet them.

"Miss Sissy!" said Meadow, hurrying over to clasp the old woman's hand. "You scared me to death."

Miss Sissy snarled, "Bad guy!"

Clearly it was one of Miss Sissy's bad days. During bad days, Miss Sissy was not only rather inarticulate, but downright hostile. And perhaps a bit paranoid. Beatrice glanced over at Wyatt. His calm, good-natured, and solid presence was always soothing to her and she felt that he was a balancing force for them as a couple. As usual, he gave her a small but reassuring smile and said gently, "Miss Sissy has had a scary ordeal."

Miss Sissy gave an emphatic nod. "Bad guy in my *house*."

At this point, Beatrice noted that Miss Sissy had a very large bruise and corresponding lump on her head right underneath her wiry gray hair. She suspected that the bump could potentially account for any bad guy. Not that he had *given* it to her, but that he was a figment resulting from her head injury.

Meadow stared, goggle-eyed, at Miss Sissy. "Bad guy in your house? I thought you were in a car accident! Did you call Ramsay?"

Miss Sissy gave her a scornful look. "Course not! No time!"

Meadow's husband, Ramsay, was the chief of police for tiny Dappled Hills. He *would* have been the appropriate person to call, if indeed there had been an intruder in Miss Sissy's house. To Beatrice, this intruder seemed more and more unlikely.

Wyatt said diplomatically, "Miss Sissy, would you like me to find you something to eat? Maybe something light? A chicken broth or a gelatin, maybe?"

Miss Sissy did not even deign to answer this, instead squinted her eyes at him to indicate her disdain at liquid-y foods.

Beatrice decided to cut to the chase. It was apparent that Miss Sissy was not going to progress with life or healing as usual until her story had been completely told. It was just delaying everything to keep it suppressed or to try and change the subject. "So there was a bad guy? An intruder? In your house?"

Miss Sissy nodded vigorously again.

"What made you think he was bad? Was he wearing a mask? Did he break a window and come in?" asked Beatrice.

Miss Sissy snorted in derision. "No mask. Madman! Walked right in."

"Okay. So it's morning, right? This happened this morning, not in the middle of the night? A man entered your *unlocked house*. Is that right? The door was unlocked?"

Miss Sissy pursed her lips and looked away. Ramsay had fussed at her lately, and in Beatrice's presence about keeping her door locked. It was a good idea, even in such a small and friendly town as Dappled Hills.

"I'm calling Ramsay," muttered Meadow, looking huffy as she fumbled in her purse for her cell phone. She was always completely indignant at the idea of anyone committing crime in her beloved town. Even worse that the crime was committed right under the nose of her police chief husband.

Beatrice motioned for her to wait for a moment and then continued, "Why did this madman do this? Did he think that your home housed something very valuable that he wanted?" She wasn't trying to be unkind, but she wanted everyone, including Miss Sissy to think this out. Miss Sissy's home did not even look occupied. It was in exceedingly poor condition with vines growing on and around it that rivaled the thorny ones in *Sleeping Beauty*. The ancient Lincoln parked outside Miss Sissy's house was in completely dilapidated condition. There would be nothing to indicate to any vagrant passing through town that it might be worthwhile to break in. And any criminals living in Dappled Hills would *know* that Miss Sissy's house was not one that would be profitable to rob.

But Miss Sissy was nodding vigorously again, wincing this time as she did it. "Yes! Valuable."

"What was valuable?" asked Wyatt, leaning forward.

"Information!"

They stared at her. The idea of Miss Sissy offering any kind of valuable information to anyone was a rather astounding one to wrap your head around. After all, Beatrice had just been trying, fairly unsuccessfully, to elicit information from the old woman for the last few minutes.

Miss Sissy glared at them all and said, "Information. Asked questions."

"What kinds of questions?" pressed Meadow, hand still on her cell phone.

"About old people!" spat out Miss Sissy furiously.

"What did he look like?" asked Meadow.

Miss Sissy just shook her head. "Ramsay!" she said furiously. "Ramsay, Ramsay!"

Meadow obediently dialed her husband.

After Ramsay had finished talking with Miss Sissy, he joined Wyatt, Meadow, and Beatrice in a small lounge at the end of the hall with a couple of pleather chairs and sofa scattered around a sturdy coffee table.

"Well?" asked Meadow impatiently. "What do you make of it?"

Ramsay, filling a cardboard cup carefully with coffee, put in several sugar packets and gingerly stirred his concoction. His presence, the everyday solidity of it, was reassuring. He was short and balding and heavy from the generous portions of Southern cooking that Meadow pressed on him daily. He took a large sip and then plopped down on the sofa with a sigh. "I've not a doubt in the world that the intruder was 100% real to Miss Sissy. She's not making it up on purpose. But do I believe there's a real intruder? No way."

Meadow slumped in relief in the lounge chair. "That's what I'd hope you'd say. The idea of some bad guy breaking into old ladies' houses to assault them or rob them or something is absolutely horrifying. I simply don't want to think that I'm living in that kind of a town."

"What are you basing your belief on, Ramsay?" asked Beatrice. "Just a gut feeling?"

"It's based on the fact that Miss Sissy has a history of calling me to report wild claims. She insisted that someone had broken in and stolen a ring off of her shower curtain a couple of weeks ago." Ramsay took another large gulp of his coffee.

Wyatt gave Ramsay a sympathetic smile. "I get my share of somewhat panicky calls, myself. Always on pretty odd topics."

"If you think *that's* odd, that's nothing compared to last month's report. She called me in the middle of the night and insisted that a miniature UFO had landed in her backyard and that little fuchsia men had tried forcing her for hours to learn some sort of strange math." Ramsay rolled his eyes.

Meadow said reproachfully, "Now, Ramsay, you know that the little aliens were real to Miss Sissy. I hope you treated her report with respect."

"I'm not all that respectful at three o'clock in the morning. But I did obediently jot down notes. You know. It's Miss Sissy, after all."

Beatrice said, "So you think it's all a figment of her imagination."

"I'm planning on stopping by and checking on her a lot more, let's put it that way. I don't exactly know what's going on, but it usually helps if I step up patrols and check-ins," said Ramsay. He drained his coffee. "And now I'm going to head on out."

Meadow said, "The doctor should be in soon to talk to us. The nurse was guessing that she would probably just stay overnight for observation. Just as a precautionary thing."

Ramsay sighed. "I guess it'll be PB&J for me tonight."

Meadow put her hands on her generous hips. "I think you need to learn how to expand your repertoire in the kitchen."

Ramsay was about to retort when suddenly a tiny, gentle-looking woman peered hesitantly through the lounge door. She smiled when she saw them. "I thought I recognized those voices." Then her blue eyes clouded over. "How's Miss Sissy?"

Beatrice said, "Hi Posy. The good news is that Miss Sissy is going to be just fine. They're just keeping her overnight for observation."

"And I heard something scary about a car accident?" asked Posy anxiously.

Ramsay shook his head. "No car involved. Miss Sissy claims her injuries resulted from an intruder, which is highly unlikely. Maybe Miss Sissy's a little confused from the bump on her head and from being unconscious. Maybe she even saw a door-to-door salesman earlier and just tied it all together in her head. At any rate, I'm not exactly worried."

Posy brightened. "Wonderful news! I was able to get some help with the store for the rest of today and tomorrow, so I'm happy to stay overnight here. In fact, I packed a small bag, just in case. And I've even got brand new cat photos from the store that Miss Sissy hasn't seen yet."

Beatrice grinned at her. "You'll have made her day." Maisie was the store cat at the Patchwork Cottage and Posy allowed Miss Sissy to think of herself as a part owner of the feline.

"And Ramsay won't have to suffer through PB&J after all!" said Meadow with a grin. "A good thing since he manages to destroy the kitchen making simple meals."

Chapter Two

Ramsay left immediately to dutifully investigate a parking place dispute at the Dappled Hills post office. Beatrice, Wyatt, and Meadow told Miss Sissy goodbye and then headed out of the hospital.

Wyatt said, "Thanks to you both for coming all the way out to Lenoir. I was really worried when I first got the call from the hospital. She's been here before of course, and I'm listed as an emergency contact from the last time. They didn't give a lot of information, except that she was agitated. I'd gotten the impression she'd been in a car accident."

"Which was certainly believable," said Beatrice fervently.

"I figured that she'd calm down a lot more if you were both here," said Wyatt. "I hope you weren't doing anything important."

Meadow said thoughtfully, "I'm not sure if I can even remember what I was doing when you called. I've totally lost that thread."

"I was relaxing," said Beatrice with a shrug.

Wyatt and Meadow raised their eyebrows and gave each other a smile. Meadow said, "*Relaxing*? Pooh."

Beatrice said a little defensively, "Well, I was attempting to relax, anyway. Noo-noo was trying to show me how by snoring next to me."

"I'm not sure you completely understand the concept of relaxation, Beatrice. How do you *try* to relax? Relaxation isn't a task to check off your list or a competitive sport. It's a lack of *doing*," said Meadow, waving her hands in the air.

Beatrice pursed her lips. Her inability to relax was something that she'd rather not have spotlighted. It was the one thing she was working hardest on. Could she help it that every time she sat down and put her feet up the dishes from the sink called out to her? The dust bunnies under the bed? The corgi for a walk? Life and her own busy brain seemed locked in a conspiracy to deny her downtime.

Wyatt gently steered the conversation in another direction. "I think I know what Meadow was doing, if it helps. I think you were about to talk to Beatrice about being part of a new group service project at the church."

Meadow snapped her fingers. "Of course! Bravo, Wyatt. Yes, that's exactly what I was doing. I was just mulling over the idea that I could put Boris on his leash and walk over to your cottage and talk about the group."

Beatrice was now feeling an abundance of caution for a couple of reasons. For one, she wasn't sure that belonging to yet another local organization or group of some kind was the right prescription for helping her relax. For another, she was hoping that her quiet afternoon wasn't going to be destroyed by Boris the Great. Unfortunately, his greatness was only evident in his massive size. He was part Great Dane, part Newfoundland, and—insisted Meadow, though Beatrice had yet to find proof of it—part corgi. His size was matched only by his appetite. Boris had claimed Beatrice's kitchen counter as his own personal food trough on more than one occasion.

Eager to escape a future encounter with Boris when she felt least prepared for one, Beatrice quickly said, "Let's talk about whatever it is now, then. On our way back home."

Wyatt gave Beatrice a rueful smile at her efforts to leave Boris out of her afternoon plans. "I'll see you both later," he said as he got into his car. "Thanks again for coming out."

The unfortunate thing about Meadow trying to talk about anything with any degree of focus or concentration was that her driving was all over the place. Beatrice clung to the passenger door in abject terror and slammed an imaginary brake with her right foot all the way back to Dappled Hills. She was sure there must be wide-eyed horror on her face the whole time.

"You see," said Meadow thoughtfully, "I wanted to honor the *social* part and the *service* part of quilting. I wanted to really make the Village Quilters guild current. The wonderful thing about quilting is that it can be a peaceful solitary endeavor, or it can be a bonding social event. Personally, I think we all do plenty of solitary quilting."

"You would," murmured Beatrice glumly.

"So this made perfect sense. And we can tie a lovely service project in, to boot. *And* you have more opportunities to see Wyatt at the church because this won't merely be a *weekly* event. We're going to make it three times a week while we're getting it all off the ground," said Meadow.

"Won't that mess up the ladies who work?" asked Beatrice. "Not everyone is retired or ... well, like you." Meadow did a lot, but nothing that she was officially paid for.

"It's in the evenings!" said Meadow. "We've been very, very careful to make sure that everyone can get there." In her excitement and, to emphasize their caution in coming up with times, Meadow swerved the wheel. She continued on, oblivious, as Beatrice gripped the door that much tighter.

"It does sound like a good idea," admitted Beatrice.

"And we also get time to *meditate* on a lovely scripture-based lesson. Do you *know* the last time I had a chance to do that during the week?" demanded Meadow.

"I'm going to assume it was a while back."

"At *least* twenty years ago! When Ash was in school!" said Meadow.

This conversation, mostly a one-way conversation with Meadow extolling the virtues of their new activity, continued the rest of the way to Dappled Hills. Beatrice responded at all the appropriate times. But when Meadow drove past Beatrice's house, she snapped out of her nodding and murmuring routine.

"Meadow! You're so wrapped up in your monologue that you drove by my house!"

Meadow waved a hand vaguely. "I wanted to show you the fabric I've got. And give you a copy of the pattern for the first quilt we'll be working on so that you can see it in advance. I always like to give the pattern a once-over before group quilting, don't you?"

Beatrice sighed. "Poor Noo-noo probably needs to go potty."

"This will only take a second, I promise. You can take a look at the fabric, grab a pattern and then it's just a quick jog back to your house," said Meadow.

Apparently Beatrice was also about to get a little exercise in the process, to top off the day.

Her mood improved, as usual, when she set foot in Meadow's house. It was a converted barn with lovely old exposed rafters and a ceiling that soared like a cathedral. Quilts hung from every surface and from the ceiling and walls in riotous color. Boris cantered over and sniffed Beatrice's khaki slacks with thoughtful interest. He shot her a reproachful look with his amber eyes for not including Noo-noo in her visit. She reached down and scratched behind the big dog's ears and he flopped onto his back with a grunt for a belly-rub.

Meadow's fabrics for the babies were pretty and the pattern certainly looked doable. Beatrice's favorite had blue and pink dots and fabrics with kittens batting balls and puppies gnawing pink bones that could be cut and incorporated as different panels. But after Beatrice had given her blessing to the fabric, Meadow wasn't quite done with their conversation. "Oh, that reminds me. I also wanted to talk with you about some ideas I had to raise quilting awareness in town."

"Quilting awareness?" murmured Beatrice. She glanced briefly but longingly at the door.

"Oh, you know. Recruiting into the hobby. Or into the Village Quilters guild ... either or both. Here, I could use a little exercise myself today. My poor old ticker got quite the jolt when I heard about Miss Sissy's accident. Or whatever it was. It could use a little exercise. I'll walk you home," said Meadow. "You need to let Noo-noo out, I know."

At the word *walk*, Boris exploded into action, rushing for his harness and leash and intently staring meaningfully at Meadow. She absently put the gear on Boris while saying, "That's right. Quilting *awareness*. Because sometimes I just don't think the quilting community is getting the word out. Posy says younger people think quilting seems complicated. We all know that it's only as complicated as we let it be. Maybe we need to reach the next generation through motion media."

They walked outside and Meadow pulled the door shut without locking it. Beatrice supposed that when one's husband was the police chief that it might be a bit safer than for anyone else.

"Motion media?" asked Beatrice, a bit more politely than she felt. "I don't think I know about that."

"Sure you do! It's like Facespace and Instatwitter and all that," said Meadow. Boris loped excitedly through the woods between their two houses and Meadow dug her heels in to slow him down.

Beatrice said, "Oh, you mean *social* media. And you're right, that would probably be a smart way to reach out to younger quilters. Particularly with one of the apps that centers around photography. The textures and colors of quilting are so vibrant that the excitement might translate better."

Meadow beamed at her. "And that insightful statement is exactly why I want to nominate you as the Village Quilters' social media ambassador."

"*What*? Just because I know what it is doesn't mean that I use it," spluttered Beatrice.

Meadow was starting to huff and puff as Boris picked up speed again. "But you have Piper to help you out. Your daughter would be the perfect resource for you if you got stuck. No, you're The One. I'm sure of it. And then there's just one other thing. One other teeny project."

Beatrice was opening her mouth to heatedly protest when Boris suddenly skidded to a stop, stiffened, sniffed the air, and started baying pitifully. It was a bay: there was no other word for it. Meadow and Beatrice stared speechlessly at the dog.

"I've never heard him make a sound like that. Not ever," said Meadow breathlessly.

"He smells something," said Beatrice. "Let's give him a little lead on the leash."

Meadow loosened up her grip on the leash and they watched the big dog stare into the woods. He took a few steps and then bayed again, looking at Meadow with a sad expression on his broad face.

"Good boy," she said in an encouraging voice. She caught up with him and reached down to give him a loving rub. She turned to Beatrice and whispered, "What do you think it is? Does he smell some sort of strange animal or something?"

Beatrice shook her head. "I don't know. Whatever it is, he's really concerned about it. And that makes *me* concerned about it. I definitely want to get to the bottom of what's making him anxious about our woods."

Meadow made some more encouraging sounds at the dog and he took some more steps forward. And a few more. And then he was leaping forward again, pulling Meadow behind him, barking and baying and jumping up and down in a rocking sort of movement.

"What's that over there?" asked Meadow fearfully. "Behind that bush?"

But Beatrice had already figured out what it was and she knew Meadow had too. It was the body of a man.

"I suspect," she said slowly, "that it might be Miss Sissy's bad guy."

Meadow pulled out her phone to call Ramsay once more and then dropped her phone in a bunch of old, dried leaves as Boris whined piteously beside her.

Beatrice said, "I've got it," although she was a bit shakier than she liked. "Ramsay," she said when he picked up, his voice curious on the other side. "Meadow and I were walking back to my house with Boris and we found a body. Or, rather, Boris found it, I suppose." She tightened her lips as she felt the temptation to be garrulous in her nervousness.

"*What?*"

"A body." Beatrice walked to the other side of the bush, being careful to give a wide berth so as not to disturb any potential evidence. "Actually, I'm going to ensure it *is* a body and not someone in need of medical assistance." She peered over at the figure on the ground. It was a bearded man around forty-five years old wearing a white shirt and khaki jacket with khaki pants. A brimmed hat lay on the ground next to him. And, judging from the state of his head, Beatrice decided that he was *not* a good recipient of medical assistance. "No, he's dead, I'm afraid," she said quickly. Beatrice took a deep breath. "Hope you're finished with the dispute at the post office."

Beatrice could hear sounds on Ramsay's end like he was getting his keys out. He said briskly, "You don't recognize him? He's not someone we know?"

"I've never seen him before. I wondered ... well, it seems so coincidental. I wondered if he might be Miss Sissy's bad guy."

Ramsay said, "Does he look like a bad guy?"

"If bad guys wear safari-type clothing," said Beatrice. "But then, Miss Sissy does frequently get the wrong idea."

"I'm on my way," said Ramsay and hung up.

Ramsay was there in minutes. But it was long enough for Meadow to have worked herself up into a froth. "The *idea* of someone from outside Dappled Hills coming to town, bullying poor Miss Sissy, and dying in our woods!" she fumed.

Beatrice said dryly, "Technically, we don't really know what happened to him. His injuries could be a result of his run-in with Miss Sissy."

"You don't really think that!"

Beatrice said, "No, I don't. But still, I don't think we should make the mistake of underestimating Miss Sissy. Particularly if she believes she's being threatened."

Meadow pulled the still-anxious Boris a bit farther away. "Don't you find it odd that he's here? This *stranger*?"

"I'm not absolutely sure that I could recognize everyone in the town," said Beatrice with a shrug.

Meadow retorted, "Well, I'm absolutely sure that *I* could. And I've never laid eyes on him." She took another fleeting glimpse at him. "Never!"

Ramsay was already pulling off the side of the road nearest their spot in the woods. He was on his phone, likely alerting the state police. He rang off and then said grimly, "So, over there? Behind the bush?"

Beatrice and Meadow pointed wordlessly.

As Ramsay started securing the crime scene, although Beatrice wasn't sure who else besides she and Meadow might happen along through the woods, she spotted something out of the corner of her eye. She frowned and pointed at the bit of whiteness in the bush by the body. "What's that, Ramsay?"

Ramsay carefully reached into the bush and pulled out a notebook. He grimly scanned a couple of pages. "Okay. Looks like our guy had some questions for Miss Sissy. So, despite the look of him, I suppose he was her 'bad guy.'" He frowned at the notebook. "There's something right in the back of my memory on this. But I can't quite get it." He flipped pages until he got to the first page. "This is kind of odd."

Meadow made a snort of frustration. "For heaven's sake, Ramsay! You can't just say things like that to us and then not explain them! What's so odd about the notebook? What sort of questions does the guy bring up? Any clues to his identity? We *know* he's not one of us—that is, a Dappled Hills resident."

Ramsay carefully put the notebook in a plastic bag that he pulled out of a uniform pocket. "And you know this is an investigation."

"You've always let us in on things before," wheedled Meadow. Boris, uneasy at the tone between his master and mistress, gave a corroborating short bark.

"Right now there are some things I need to do with the crime scene before the state police arrive. Taking statements from both of you is one of them," he said briskly. "The notebook just ... I guess it just reminds me of something from long ago."

After the statements were taken, Ramsay waved them off. Meadow left in a huff and Beatrice walked away more thoughtfully.

"Really!" said Meadow, breathing hard as Boris bounded away in his efforts to leave the scene as quickly as possible.

"It's his work," said Beatrice absently as she strode forward to keep up with Meadow and her dog. "But his comments *were* interesting."

"What comments? The fact that he saw 'something kind of odd?'" She gave a sigh of relief as Boris finally came to a stop at Beatrice's front door.

Beatrice supposed that she was now going to be entertaining Meadow and Boris for a while since Meadow was not going to be able to use her favorite cut-through across the woods.

"No, the fact that he said the man had 'questions' for Miss Sissy. Does that mean he was a journalist of some kind? But why would something seem familiar to Ramsay? You say this victim doesn't look familiar to you?" asked Beatrice.

"Never seen him before in my life," said Meadow with a shrug as Beatrice unlocked the door to the cabin and led them inside. Noo-noo gave Beatrice a reproachful look for bringing Boris along and she bent to rub the little dog as she let her outside for a potty break.

"Well, I'm sure Ramsay will get to the bottom of it," said Beatrice.

"Ramsay? I'm thinking that *you and I* will get to the bottom of it. But I'm going to weasel out as much information as I possibly can from him as soon as I get a chance," said Meadow with a smirk. "He'll be worn out when he comes home tonight. Investigations take it out of him, not to mention dealing with the state police. On top of a trip out to question Miss Sissy at the hospital. He'll be ready for a huge meal, a glass of wine, and one of those boring tomes he's always reading. And I'll be there with a chilled glass of red wine, his favorite comfort food, and a few questions."

"What's his favorite comfort food?"

"Meatloaf. And I'm a master of meatloaf," said Meadow with a good deal of personal satisfaction.

It might have been the talk of meatloaf or the talk of wine or the talk of being worn out, but Beatrice suddenly had the longing for her hammock and a nap with Noo-noo close by. "Meadow, I'm feeling some of the strain from the day, myself. But, before you go," she said pointedly, "was there something else you were going to ask me about?"

Meadow stared blankly at her.

"A teensy little project?" prompted Beatrice with a slight edge to her voice now.

"Oh! Oh, that's right. Yes, so besides the hospital project and the social media things, I've another project percolating. It's absolutely fantastic that the Village Quilters are doing all of these service projects, of course. But we're also in need of some, erm, coins in the coffers," said Meadow.

Boris gave a short, sharp bark and looked meaningfully toward Beatrice's tiny kitchen.

Beatrice let Noo-noo back in and heading for the kitchen, saying, "I'm listening. Just getting some treats." At the word *treat*, Boris's tail started pummeling Beatrice's wood floors loudly and Noo-noo grinned at her, brown eyes dancing as she kept a wary eye on Boris. She disapproved of doggie visitors receiving treats in her own home.

Meadow said, "Right. So, money. I'd been thinking what a rich history Dappled Hills has. And a *lot* of it intersects with quilting."

"And the Village Quilters would, I'm imagining, be featured rather prominently and come out looking pretty well in the book," said Beatrice dryly.

"Naturally! There's no other way for our guild to look than utterly amazing. Then we can sell the books in local stores and raise funds for traveling to quilt shows as a group or for introducing others to the craft," said Meadow.

Noo-noo politely received the treat from Beatrice, being very mindful of where Beatrice's fingers were in the process. Boris, on the other hand, gazed ravenously at her as if he might devour her entire hand. Beatrice dropped the treat on the floor and slid it with her foot toward the big dog. No point in losing any extremities over a dog treat.

"The only thing, Meadow, is that I'm wondering how popular this book is going to be. How many people will want to put down money for a Village Quilters guild history that also touches on the history of Dappled Hills? Not that Dappled Hills doesn't have a very rich history and culture. I mean, you and I would buy a book. Posy and Elaine would. All of our guild ladies would purchase a copy. Other than that, though? I just don't think we'd have a massive bestseller on our hands," said Beatrice.

Meadow looked thoughtful. "We could go *more* into the local town history. That might broaden the appeal a little farther."

"Would it? By how much? What you're proposing is a project that would likely take a good deal of time and would be appealing to a limited audience. I'm just not sure it's a good investment of our time," said Beatrice. She gave the dogs another treat and watched as the food disappeared immediately. "Unless ... I may have an idea."

Meadow's eyebrows rose hopefully.

"The appeal for this kind of book will be the photography. The quilts," mused Beatrice.

"Aha! That would help make it more interesting!"

"Except that it would make it more costly to print," said Beatrice.

"Well pooh! I thought you said you had an idea."

"I think we should definitely incorporate more images. From a budget standpoint, they may have to be in black and white. But black and white photography, with the right treatment, can really look amazing. And we need to try to include as many interviews from the older residents of Dappled Hills as we possibly can. Not only because stories will *also* sell books, but because in this town everyone is related to everyone else—and people will want to buy a book with their Aunt Mabel or Paw-Paw or whomever in it," said Beatrice.

Meadow seemed to be unsuccessfully hiding a small smile. "That sounds like an excellent plan. I knew you'd be just the person to figure out how best for us to handle the project."

Beatrice felt alarmed. "Now, I'm only giving *advice*. I'm not saying that this is *my* project. I want no ownership of this project, Meadow. None."

"Think of it! Not only do we capture the thoughts and beautiful old quilts for posterity, we may actually be able to make some good money for the guild in the process!" said Meadow, waving her hand in the air as she warmed to the topic. "And we'll try to include pictures of *people*, too. As many current residents as possible. And dead residents! Because who *wouldn't* buy a book that has a picture of their dearly departed sister in it?"

"Now, Meadow!"

But Meadow was on a roll and warming to her topic. "And who best to capture these lovely old quilts for our book than you? You were a museum curator, for heaven's sake! For folk art! In a very prestigious museum in Atlanta! Just look at you!"

Beatrice didn't think she looked like much wearing the same old beat up khakis and tired baby-blue shirt that she'd been loafing in earlier in the day. And this morning was starting to seem like a lifetime ago. Beatrice's head throbbed. "That's a big project. I'll have to think about it. The whole point about being retired is that I was planning on relaxing."

Meadow rubbed Boris before giving a quick whistle and motioning him out the door. As her parting words, she said, "But that's just the thing, isn't it? You *can't* relax. So you might as well be productive, right? Okay, bye for now!"

Beatrice found that, after her unusual day, she was able to easily doze off in the hammock with the sound of Noo-noo's gentle snoring as a lulling accompaniment.

Not only was Beatrice able to take a nap, she was able to work with great focus on her quilt for a good hour without being afflicted by that all-too-familiar restless sensation. She loved the feel of motion in the pattern with the Snail's Trail blocks in a bold blue and green color wash. She took Noo-noo for an evening stroll, felt more exhausted than she thought she would afterward, ate scrambled eggs with shredded cheddar for supper, and turned in early.

Because of her restful day, Beatrice was wide awake before dawn. She tossed around in her bed in an effort to coax herself back to sleep by somehow lying differently, but couldn't manage it. She rose for the day, ate tomato soup for breakfast since she'd had breakfast for supper, and then headed out to the hospital. Because it was so early, she hoped she might be able to catch the doctor on his rounds and hear firsthand what he had to say about Miss Sissy's injuries.

Despite being acquainted first-hand with Miss Sissy's ravenous appetite, Beatrice decided that hospital breakfast food might need supplementing. Especially considering Miss Sissy's disdain with the idea of chicken broth and gelatin from the day before. She threw in a couple of English muffins, some butter in a plastic container, and a couple of bananas in a plastic bag. As an afterthought, she grabbed a large, finished nine patch quilt full of vibrant reds and blues, and headed out.

When Beatrice arrived in the hospital room, Miss Sissy was having a lively argument with the doctor, who seemed on the verge of losing his patience. He looked relieved as Beatrice entered the room. "Is this your mother?" he asked.

"She's not," said Beatrice briskly. "She's a friend, though. Is there something I can do to help?"

"I'm trying to convince her that it might be a good idea for her to consider moving to a ... well, a senior living community," said the doctor. He removed his glasses and absently cleaned the lenses as Miss Sissy fussed at him.

"No!" she said scornfully.

Beatrice saw that the old woman was worked up which probably wasn't great for any injury-related headaches. She briskly said, "Miss Sissy does have a good number of friends in town. We'll be sure to help keep an eye on her. She spends much of her day at the quilt shop in Dappled Hills."

Miss Sissy's eyes lit up at the mention of the Patchwork Cottage. "Posy is there. And a cat! Maisie."

The doctor gave a resigned sigh. "I only mentioned it because, if she's prone to taking tumbles, she might have a fall at home and not be able to get help for a while. That can be very distressing. Does she at least have a cell phone?"

Beatrice shook her head. She knew that Miss Sissy had even had her *regular* phone service disconnected recently for failure to pay. It had been an oversight on Miss Sissy's part, and it seemed to indicate that some things were slipping past her.

The doctor glanced at his watch. "I've got many more patients to see. Your friend is ready to be released for home. But this is my only bit of advice for you—get her a cell phone. Make sure she knows how to use it and charge it. And that she carries it with her."

And that I receive the bills, thought Beatrice rather glumly. "That won't be a problem," she said. "Thanks for your time."

Miss Sissy glared at the doctor as he walked out. "Mutant!" she hissed.

Beatrice was used to Miss Sissy's random insults or name calling, so ignored her. Although she did spare a hasty glance at the door in the hopes the doctor hadn't heard her. "I brought something for you," she said quickly, in an attempt to salvage their visit.

Miss Sissy's beady eyes lit up as Beatrice pulled the quilt from the tote bag and carefully covered Miss Sissy with it.

The old woman reached out a gnarled hand to gently run her fingers over the fabric. "Pretty," she said gruffly.

Beatrice gave a small sigh of relief. "I'm glad you like it."

"For me to *keep*?" asked Miss Sissy, tilting her chin in determination.

That hadn't really been part of the original plan. And Miss Sissy probably had over a hundred quilts at her house. She'd been quilting for seventy years, for heaven's sake. And she was a far better quilter than Beatrice was. "Of course," said Beatrice stiffly.

Miss Sissy smiled in satisfaction.

Now that she was in a better mood, Beatrice decided to move on to a more sensitive topic. "Do you think you could learn to use a phone like this one, Miss Sissy?" she asked. She pulled out her smart phone and handed it to the old woman.

Miss Sissy glared suspiciously at the device. It wasn't the most expensive phone and it didn't have all the bells and whistles of some others ... but apparently it was alarming enough.

"Maybe one of those basic phones then," said Beatrice with a sigh.

Miss Sissy looked cunning. "One that flips open."

"Oh, so you *do* know something about phones. You want a flip phone. That should be easy enough," said Beatrice. "I'll pick one up and show you how to use it."

Miss Sissy gave her a scornful look. "I use phones!"

"Yes, but this phone will allow you to send text messages. At least, it will if I buy a plan for it, which I guess I should," said Beatrice.

Her thoughts on inexpensive pay-as-you-go phones with hopefully inexpensive pay-as-you-go texting were cut short by a rap on the hospital door as Ramsay poked his rather anxious face around it.

Chapter Three

Ramsay gave Miss Sissy what he clearly thought was a reassuring smile. Miss Sissy snarled in return. Being in the hospital clearly wasn't good for Miss Sissy's temper, nor, apparently, was the hospital breakfast, as Beatrice had suspected. The plastic tray had been shoved as far away from her as possible. The cup of gelatin looked as if it had been ravaged by a wild animal. There were crumbs on the plate that Beatrice suspected having possibly belonged to toast. There was no evidence of any other food. Beatrice reached in her bag and pulled out the English muffins and bananas as Miss Sissy eyed them hungrily.

The old woman voraciously attacked the food. Ramsay said, "Beatrice, may I speak with you for just a second outside?"

Beatrice followed Ramsay into the hall. He absently rubbed a hand across his high forehead. "Brilliant idea, bringing food. That should settle her down a little. I wanted to ask Miss Sissy a few questions, but I needed to feel her out and see what kind of a mood she was in. Is she real agitated today?"

A couple of workers from food service pushed by them with a tall cart for used trays. When several nurses slid past them, Ramsay motioned Beatrice into the lounge where they could talk without being endangered by the swiftly moving staff. They settled into chairs and Ramsay gave a contented sigh as he sat. Since the seating in the lounge was far from comfortable, Beatrice assumed that he'd not gotten much rest the previous night.

She said, "Miss Sissy was very agitated, yes, but I think she's better now. That doctor really got her blood pressure up earlier.

He wasn't the best of people to handle her. But he had a good suggestion about getting her a cell phone. I think I'll take care of that. She doesn't need to be falling down and unable to reach anyone."

"Could just get her a house phone," said Ramsay with a shrug. "She's used to those."

"Yes, but she still goes off *driving*. If she stuck around the house, I could see it," said Beatrice.

Ramsay grimaced. "She *shouldn't* be going off driving. She's a menace to society behind the wheel. But that rickety old Lincoln of hers is bound to suffer a breakdown at any time, with any luck. A cell phone is a great idea, now that I think of it."

"Sorry for the tangent. You wanted to ask me something? Or were you just checking her mood?" asked Beatrice curiously. She was hoping, now that nosy Meadow wasn't around, that Ramsay would let down his guard and talk about the case a little, like he usually did.

Fortunately, Loose-Lipped Ramsay appeared to be on hand. "I was mostly just checking her mood, feeling her out. The state police will want to talk to her, of course, with a murder and everything. And her reported altercation with the deceased. But I want to prepare her for that and also ask her a couple of questions before they do. Will she be discharged soon?"

"Right away," said Beatrice. "Lucky that I was here so I can drive her back."

Ramsay nodded, but Beatrice could tell his mind was miles away. "This case is something else," he muttered. His cell phone buzzed at him and he heaved a tremendous sigh, studiously ignoring it.

"Nobody thinks that Miss Sissy had anything to do with this fellow's death, do they?" asked Beatrice sharply. "He was found a good distance away in the woods. It's not as if she could have dragged herself after him and killed the man after injuring herself. Not a younger man like that. Not an old woman like she is."

Ramsay said, "Technically, no, she couldn't. But that's only because she was in the hospital by the time he died, according to the medical examiner's preliminary reports. He died in the afternoon between the time y'all left for the hospital to see Miss Sissy and when you discovered him. The hospital makes for a pretty solid alibi. Otherwise, not to argue with you, but I'd pit Miss Sissy's wiry strength and utter determination against larger, younger opponents."

"How did he die?" asked Beatrice.

"Blunt force trauma," said Ramsay. "The medical examiner believes it was likely a hammer." He rubbed his eyes this time and Beatrice realized again how tired he must be. "Meadow will flip out."

"I suppose his killer wasn't some stranger passing through town? Like the victim?" asked Beatrice. "No itinerant murderer?"

"There is evidence that points to the fact that it was personal," said Ramsay. "Somebody got desperate when this guy started asking the wrong people questions."

"Wrong people? Like Miss Sissy?"

"And, from what I can gather, others, too. What I'm trying to find out is who he *was* talking to. Since you've done a good job so far today calming Miss Sissy down, maybe you can give me a hand?" He gave her a hopeful look. "All I want to do is wrap this case up as soon as possible."

"Of course," said Beatrice. Besides, it would be a good way to get more information. "What makes you so eager to wrap it up? Have you been reading any good books lately? Penning any poetry?"

Ramsay didn't spend much time talking about his high-brow reading and writing outside his close circle of friends, but he was extremely fond of quiet nights with a collection of Faulkner. And reading and writing poetry.

"Have I told you that I'm trying to get some of my poetry published? That's right. I'm querying literary journals and magazines. I figure that the state is always looking for a poet laureate—why shouldn't it be me?"

Beatrice didn't have a good answer for that one. As a matter of fact, she hadn't read *any* of his work. She wondered if a village policeman living a contented life had good poetry in him. But who was she to say? "I hope you'll find the perfect publisher," she said sincerely.

They walked back down the hall and into the small hospital room. Beatrice stood near Miss Sissy's bed, shaking her head as Ramsay pointed to the metal chair nearby. He pulled it up to sit right beside her. "Miss Sissy, I'm glad to hear you're going to be heading back home today."

She stared suspiciously at him and gave a grunt in return.

"There's no place like home, is there? Especially that cozy cottage of yours."

These genial comments were met with hostility from Miss Sissy.

Ramsay cleared his throat. "I do have a few more questions for you, if you'll humor me, Miss Sissy. You know, about the bad guy you saw yesterday." Ramsay shifted uncomfortably in his seat a bit, likely remembering that he hadn't really believed her.

Miss Sissy grunted again, eyes narrowed.

"You see, your bad guy ran into trouble. He's dead now," said Ramsay kindly, reaching forward to clumsily pat the old woman's crippled hands. "So you shouldn't worry about him anymore. That doesn't mean, naturally, that you should let up your guard at home. Be vigilant when answering your door, don't talk to strangers, that kind of thing. Beatrice tells me that you're going to have a new cell phone," he added in a jolly voice.

Miss Sissy spat out, "FLIP phone."

"Right," said Ramsay, soothingly.

"Who is he?" asked Miss Sissy.

"Your bad guy? His name is Oscar Holland," said Ramsay. He closely watched the old woman's reaction. And there was definitely a flicker of recognition there. Miss Sissy muttered unintelligibly to herself.

"Did you *know* Oscar Holland?" asked Ramsay softly.

She shook her head, and more wiry strands of hair slid out of her loose bun and spilled onto her pillow.

"Are you certain? Because it seemed like he knew *you*. Your name is scattered through his notes. You see, he was quite the note-taker. He had index cards on him in that khaki jacket of his—they looked like the kind of index cards you use when you're interviewing someone. Your name and address and possible questions for you were on these index cards."

Miss Sissy knit her brows and continued dark muttering.

Ramsay continued, "What's more, he had some sort of old notebook in his hotel room here in Lenoir, just down the road here from this hospital. It almost served as a journal. It wasn't his, but it mentioned lots of people—Dappled Hills residents who are now elderly."

Miss Sissy looked at Ramsay and then looked away. "Not me. Didn't do anything."

"I know you didn't do anything," said Ramsay soothingly. "But I need a clearer picture of what *did* happen. And how you're connected to the man you saw."

"Didn't know him!"

"But do you—or did you—know his mother? Because his mother figured prominently in his notes and a bit in this notebook/journal," pressed Ramsay. The old woman gave a croaking sigh. "Mrs. Holland. Years ago."

"That makes sense. Apparently, she just recently passed away in a Lenoir retirement home. Her son was with her. And, judging from the notes we found, she had quite the deathbed confession," said Ramsay.

Beatrice raised her eyebrows. "A confession? Of a crime?"

"That much we really don't know. But we do know that she felt guilty enough or just plain worried enough about something in her possession that she felt she needed to share it with her son right before she passed away. And then Oscar Holland took this notebook she handed him and decided to investigate something, himself. Perhaps he wanted to get answers or some justice? And he was abruptly killed," said Ramsay.

Beatrice asked, "Doesn't that seem especially sudden? He shows up at Miss Sissy's house and then ends up murdered hours later?"

"It looks like he's been in the area for over a week since his mother died," said Ramsay. "I don't believe Miss Sissy was the first resident he spoke with."

"But surely some of that time was spent in Lenoir, going through his mother's things or arranging a memorial service," said Beatrice.

"Still, it does leave some unaccounted-for time for him to poke around in Dappled Hills' past," said Ramsay.

"Didn't know," said Miss Sissy. She seemed rather agitated. "Thought he was bad. Didn't know who he was."

Beatrice said briskly, "Of course you thought he was bad. A strange man shows up on your doorstep? You're right to be careful, Miss Sissy."

"So he shows up at your door?" prompted Ramsay gently.

Miss Sissy stayed silent.

"Did he ring the doorbell or knock?" prompted Beatrice.

Miss Sissy barked, "Knocked. Loud. Like I was deaf."

Apparently, his fateful visit had gotten off on the wrong foot immediately.

"Did you open the door or talk through the door?" asked Ramsay. Miss Sissy stared down at the crisp, white sheets and Ramsay rolled his eyes at Beatrice.

"Opened the door," confirmed Miss Sissy. "Told him to go away. Go away!"

This certainly sounded likely.

"Should have told me. Should've called to say he was coming," said Miss Sissy sulkily. She stopped abruptly when she remembered that she didn't have a house phone anymore.

Ramsay said, "How did you get hurt? Did Oscar do that? Or did you get hurt accidentally, somehow?"

Beatrice noticed that he was being very kind to Miss Sissy. But then, what would you expect from a cop who wrote poetry and loved Faulkner and Steinbeck?

Miss Sissy blew out a large sigh. "Chased him."

"You chased him?" asked Ramsay.

"That's right. With my broom!" Miss Sissy held up an imaginary broom to demonstrate her broom brandishing technique.

"So he didn't hurt you? He didn't hit you on the head at all? Didn't cause the injuries that you have?" asked Beatrice.

Miss Sissy looked mulish. "Did too. Wouldn't have fallen if he hadn't been there."

"So you were chasing him and you fell," recounted Ramsay. "Did you hit your head when you fell?"

"Must've," said the old woman viciously. "Can't remember. Knocked out."

"All right, so the man wasn't *directly* responsible for your injuries. Can you remember if, before you chased him off, he mentioned visiting anyone else in Dappled Hills? Or if he were *planning* on visiting someone?"

Miss Sissy thought hard, putting her gnarled hand to her temple to aid the process along. Slowly she said, "Gwen. Said Gwen."

Ramsay nodded encouragingly. "Gwen. Who still lives here in the area. And is actually still involved in the community."

Beatrice shook her head. She wasn't familiar with Gwen. She was starting to think, though, that if this case dealt with Dappled Hills' past, especially in some sort of criminal way, that the

Dappled Hills history that Meadow was so eager to work on was going to be an excellent vehicle for soliciting information.

"Isn't in the guild!" spat out the old woman.

"Was she in the guild a long time ago?" asked Ramsay.

"*Not* the Village Quilters," said Miss Sissy with a haughty sniff.

Ramsay made a note that Gwen was likely a former member of the Cut-Ups. Then he pulled an old and battered folio-style notebook out of his inside pocket. "There are other names in Oscar's notes. Some of them are familiar to me and some I don't know as well or at all."

He read out a few names and Beatrice surreptitiously jotted them down on the back of a receipt for future reference. "Ida was one. That's an unusual name and I'm thinking it's the Ida who used to do a lot of work at the church."

Miss Sissy was stony-faced.

Ramsay gave a short sigh. "Then there's Jake. There's quite a few Jakes in town. Could he be our baker, Jake?"

Miss Sissy was completely sullen.

Ramsay flipped through the notebook. "Hugh. He's got to be our former mayor, Huey, right? And one of the state representatives. Can't be all that many Hueys around."

Miss Sissy didn't offer an opinion on that one way or another.

"And there's a name on the outside of the notebook," said Ramsay rather thoughtfully. He gave Miss Sissy a sideways look. "Vivian. Vivian Hastings."

"She's *dead*!" snarled Miss Sissy.

Beatrice and Ramsay stared at her.

Ramsay said slowly, "Wait. Is this that Vivian who was in town when I was just a young deputy officer here? Is this what I was trying to remember earlier?"

Miss Sissy snorted belligerently.

"As I recall, she left town rather abruptly. She *did* leave town didn't she?" asked Ramsay. "A reporter of some kind. Always carried a notebook."

Miss Sissy muttered, "People say she's dead."

"People say this? No one told the police they thought she was dead," said Ramsay sharply. "So what do I have here? A cold case from forty years ago?"

Miss Sissy gave an eloquent shrug.

Beatrice asked curiously, "Tell us, Ramsay, what *do* we have here? You have a notebook. You have a victim who was asking questions based on a notebook from long ago. You have various names. How does it all tie together? Maybe that will help Miss Sissy recall some of the events."

The door swooshed open and Meadow stood there, casting a disparaging eye on both her husband and friend. "What's going on in here? You're not trying to keep me in the dark, are you?"

It took a while to fill Meadow in. Especially since she was so indignant at being left out of the investigating.

"*Accidental* investigating," said Beatrice.

Once Meadow was all filled in about the identity of the victim and the various notes, Beatrice repeated, "Okay, Ramsay. Let's go back to my original question. What's the story behind all this? What do you know?"

Ramsay shifted a bit in the uncomfortable hospital chair. "Here's what I know. And keep this under your hat—I'm only really telling y'all this because you might know something or have heard about something in connection with this. Basically, this guy, Oscar Holland? His mother passed away recently, as I mentioned to Beatrice. She clearly felt guilty over something that had happened in the past. She handed over this old notebook to her boy, Oscar." He held up the notebook as if pointing out Exhibit A in court.

Meadow tilted her head to one side. "So ... this notebook belonged to Mrs. Holland." She was leaning her considerable frame against the window sill.

"Actually, no. That's where this gets interesting. The notebook belonged to someone named Vivian. Someone that Miss Sissy says is dead." Ramsay gave Miss Sissy a piercing look. The old woman looked away.

"The whole thing reminds me of something from decades ago. It's on the edge of my memory and I just can't seem to get it. This notebook is something like a diary. Vivian moved to Dappled Hills as an aspiring writer, according to the notebook and she made a lot of notes about people," continued Ramsay. "She was also a reporter at the newspaper."

Miss Sissy suddenly contorted in her hospital bed and they all stared at her. "Miss Sissy?" asked Ramsay tentatively.

Miss Sissy fell into a vigorous coughing fit, face turning quite red in the process. She waved her hand in the air and then clutched at her throat.

"For heaven's ... Ramsay! Get her some water!" barked Meadow.

Ramsay rushed off to get the water. Beatrice was just reaching over the old woman to hit the 'call nurse' button when Miss Sissy's hand gripped her arm with surprising strength. Miss Sissy grunted, "Get it. Get the notebook."

"She was faking!" said Meadow admiringly. "But Miss Sissy, I can't just take the notebook. That's stealing evidence or tampering with evidence or something."

But Beatrice was already using her phone to take pictures of every page, as fast as she could. She was sure that some of the journal entries were going to be completely useless, but she didn't have time to pick and choose what she captured. She fumbled with the old, yellowed pages filled with a flowing longhand and kept her fingers crossed that the images weren't going to all come out fuzzy. "Another diversion, maybe, Miss Sissy?" she murmured under her breath. "I think I'm going to need more time."

"He's coming!" hissed Meadow and Beatrice froze as she heard heavy footsteps hurrying down the hallway.

Beatrice quickly shut the notebook and backed away, shoving the hand holding the cell phone behind her.

Miss Sissy resumed the coughing fit, grimacing most believably. She snatched the water from Ramsay and promptly dropped it off the side of the hospital bed. Continuing to cough, she clutched at her throat, eyes bulging dramatically.

Ramsay turned, dashing off for more water.

Beatrice leaped at the notebook, flipping through the pages until she found where she'd left off.

"Hurry, hurry," whispered Meadow in her usual stage whisper that could likely be heard all the way at the nurse's station.

Beatrice clicked, flipped, and clicked. A few more times. "Almost done," she muttered.

But they could already hear Ramsay's heavy tread returning.

This time Meadow stuck her head out of the door. "She doesn't want the water, after all," she called down the hall before he got to the room. Her hand waved at Beatrice to keep on clicking.

Ramsay's voice gasped, "Not ... the water?"

"No. We decided hot tea would be better. More soothing on her throat."

Ramsay groaned and took off again.

"That should hold him off for a while," said Meadow with satisfaction as Beatrice continued snapping pictures.

"Okay, I've got it," muttered Beatrice mere seconds before Ramsay returned. She closed the notebook and resumed her stance farther across the room. Miss Sissy resumed her rather consumptive cough as Ramsay thrust a cardboard cup at her.

Miss Sissy took several tentative sips of the hot beverage and then lay back peacefully against the pillows again, blinking at them owlishly.

"Miraculous recovery," said Ramsay dryly. "Okay, well, it's time for me to head out. I'll let the state investigators know that she'll be back home in ... what? An hour?"

"With the way that hospital discharges run, better make it a few hours," said Meadow. "You know—they have to get the paperwork together and the discharge instructions and whatnot."

Ramsay left and Meadow said as she plopped down in a chair, "Well, it looks like we have another case on our hands, Beatrice. And how better to investigate than to work on our history of Dappled Hills at the same time?"

Beatrice nodded, "That's what I was thinking, too. Although I'm still not exactly thrilled about being saddled with a big project. Do you remember many of those names that Ramsay dropped?" She pulled up the gallery on her phone to peer at some of the pictures she took.

"Vivian is dead!" said Miss Sissy viciously from the bed.

Meadow raised an eyebrow at Beatrice and said, "Miss Sissy, you seem to be party to information that no one else has. Because, even though I didn't immediately remember Vivian, I did after a few minutes of mulling the name over. As I recall, everyone said she simply abruptly left town."

"Not everybody said that," disputed Miss Sissy.

Meadow and Beatrice waited for the old woman to elaborate, but instead, she appeared to be falling asleep. Beatrice said, "What do *you* remember about Vivian, Meadow? And what time period are we talking about?"

"I figured out why it took me a minute to remember the woman. I was getting ready for Ramsay's and my wedding! This whole thing was a million years ago," said Meadow.

Beatrice said, "How old was this woman?"

"Vivian? Oh, let's see. She must have been about my age at the time. So a girl in her early twenties. Just starting out in life. Attractive, as I recall. Pretty red hair," said Meadow. "She wasn't *from* Dappled Hills, so that made her rather exotic. She was from a city up north, I think."

"And she ended up in Dappled Hills? That couldn't have been usual."

Meadow raised her eyebrows at her friend. "Why not? *You* moved here from a big city."

"Yes, but my daughter was here," said Beatrice.

"Well, this woman was very interested in the arts and Dappled Hills has *always* been a popular place for artists of various kinds settle. Maybe Vivian visited for a short spell, liked the town, and decided to move here. That does happen sometimes."

Beatrice said, "What do you remember about her disappearance?"

"I don't remember anything at all. Imagine how busy I was, trying to get ready for a wedding! Vivian and I were hardly best friends or anything. I wouldn't have had time back then to go around making new friends right before getting married. We were merely cordial. I'm sure I didn't think anything about it when I didn't see her again. I probably figured she'd moved back to whatever city she'd come from," said Meadow.

Beatrice shifted a bit on her feet and Meadow quickly stood up. "Here! Sit here. I'll sit at the foot of Miss Sissy's bed. She's so slight she's not even taking up half of it."

Beatrice sat down on the chair and opened up the gallery on her phone. "Just trying to see what kind of pictures I got during that crazy photo session of mine," she muttered.

"Do me a favor and go ahead and send them to yourself right now. All we need is for you to drop your phone and destroy all our evidence," said Meadow.

Beatrice pursed her lips, but she followed the instructions. She wasn't usually clumsy, but it was certainly easy to drop phones. As she opened each picture, she peered at it before emailing it to herself. "Hugh. Ramsay seemed to know who he is, but I'm struggling to remember. He does sound somewhat familiar."

"Of course you know him! He's always in the town hall. He used to be mayor. Actually, he was mayor for what seemed like a million terms in a row. And he was even a state representative a few times. Bald. Wears a suit all the time, even when he's doing yard work," said Meadow, waving a hand in the air. "We all call him by his nickname, Huey."

"Why on earth would 'Hugh' need a nickname? Especially a nickname that's exactly the same length as his full name? And does he *really* mow the grass in a suit?"

Meadow said, "We're fond of bestowing nicknames in Dappled Hills. And I didn't say he *mowed* in a suit. I'm pretty sure he has a guy that mows for him. But when he's out tinkering in his veggie garden or pruning his roses? He's dressed very formally. I guess he's just old-school."

"All right, so Hugh or Huey." Beatrice sent the picture to herself and then peered at the next one. "This one mentions Ida. I think I must know Ida if it's Ida Calkin. She considers herself the matriarch of Dappled Hills, if she's the one I'm thinking of."

"She does," said Meadow rather indignantly. "Even though she's hardly much older than me. Ridiculous. A *grande dame* should be in her nineties, at least. But she's a sweet enough old lady. Bakes a lot of cookies. Typical stuff."

"Did she have anything to do with Vivian?" asked Beatrice.

Meadow thought about this for a second. "It seems to me that there may have been some sort of terrible tragedy there. Hmm."

Miss Sissy's grating voice made them both jump. "Death!"

They stared at her. Beatrice had been so absorbed in her picture sending that she'd nearly forgotten the old woman was there.

Although Beatrice had assumed that Miss Sissy was just having one of her inexplicable outbursts, Meadow was mulling over Miss Sissy's eruption quite thoughtfully. "Yes. Yes, I think you're right, Miss Sissy. Something involving death, wasn't it? Not Ida's of course. But someone else's. I suppose you don't have any other clarifications for us, do you?"

But Miss Sissy had dropped back into another rather fitful sleep.

Meadow said, "I'm making a mental note that Ida is one of the first people we should interview when we're working on our book project. She'll be so flattered that with any luck she'll spill all kinds of information. And her memory is excellent—it's something she prides herself on. Okay, who else have you got?"

Beatrice finished sending a few more pictures to her email address for backup and then looked closer at the next photo. "There's lots here on Jake," she said. She read to herself for another minute, looking at several of the pictures. "He might have been some sort of love interest of Vivian's. It sounds like we might have to do more digging through these notes to see which Jake might be Vivian's." Beatrice squinted at her phone's screen. "This process will be a lot easier when I pull up my emails on my laptop. This screen is way too tiny for this. Let's see. Gwen? Do you know a Gwen?"

Meadow made a face.

"I can see that you do know a Gwen," said Beatrice, grinning.

"Unfortunately. She's one of those who always gets in the way of our quilting events. She'll go on talking forever at meetings without really saying very much, but tying everyone up. I think she loves the sound of her own voice. Gwen disagrees with our choice of most venues, rejects our ideas on how best to get publicity out about shows, and never agrees on a pattern for a group quilt if we actually try to open up a group quilt to all the area guilds," said Meadow. "What's more, she has a nasty habit of volunteering for things and then either showing up remarkably late and long after the time when she could be useful, or not showing up at all."

"She does sound like a pain. But what does she have to do with Vivian?"

"I can't imagine that she had very much to do with her at all. After all, what would they have had in common?" asked Meadow with a shrug. "Vivian was a pretty, vivacious, and creative young woman. And Gwen?" She shrugged again. "She'd have been older than Vivian and married."

"Did Vivian quilt?" asked Beatrice.

"She was learning, as I recall. It's a vital social skill in Dappled Hills," said Meadow.

"I've noticed. So it sounds as if Vivian and Gwen might have had some social interaction, if Vivian were learning to quilt. We can put Gwen on our list of people to talk to."

Meadow made a face, but nodded.

"All right, so let's get Miss Sissy out of here. We probably should wake her up and get her to change into one of the outfits that Posy brought over. And pack her things. And maybe check with the nursing station to see where we are in the process of getting discharged," said Beatrice, briskly.

Meadow said, "Actually, Beatrice, I can do *all* of those things. I, as a matter of fact, *excel* in doing all of those things. What I'm not so great at is picking out cell phones and teaching the aged and infirm how to use them."

They glanced over at Miss Sissy, now snoring loudly.

"If you take care of that, I'll handle the rest," said Meadow emphatically.

Chapter Four

The cell phone store took less time than Beatrice had feared. Beatrice had thought that maybe the cell phone people wouldn't understand what kind of phone she was talking about since they dealt with such advanced technology all the time. But they quickly found what they called a "basic phone" and she left in mere minutes.

That afternoon, Beatrice pulled weeds near her mailbox. Noo-noo chased squirrels enthusiastically for several minutes before settling down in a sunbeam in the driveway. A few minutes later, a small car carefully pulled in next to Noo-noo and Beatrice's daughter, Piper, stepped out.

"Hi Mama," she said cheerfully, giving Beatrice a warm hug. "The yard is looking great!"

So was Piper, although Beatrice thought that was always the case. Her dark hair, previously in a pixie cut, was now growing out and brushed across her shoulders as she walked. She wore jeans and a black V-neck cotton top that made the most of her slim figure.

"I brought a present for Noo-noo," she said, reaching into her purse. Noo-noo cocked her head to one side, listening intently as soon as she heard her name. Piper pulled out a red bandanna that featured brown dog treats scattered over the cloth. Noo-noo's name was embroidered on the material.

"I love it," declared Beatrice, watching as Piper gently put the bandanna around Noo-noo's neck. I'm guessing that's Georgia's handiwork?"

Georgia lived with her sister, Savannah, and was a teacher like Piper. She'd started an online business supplying cute dog and cat accessories. Beatrice had heard that she was doing quite well at it.

Piper said, "She did. Although I can't figure out how she makes the time. She's teaching and spending time with Tony now."

"She probably doesn't have a spare minute. Speaking of spare minutes, can you spare a few? I know how busy *you* are, too. But I'm now looking for an excuse to get out of the dirt for a little bit," said Beatrice, leaning back on her heels.

Piper gave her a hand up. "I'd love to visit."

Noo-noo trotted in behind them and Beatrice discovered the little dog wasn't nearly as muddy as Beatrice herself was. She sighed and took off her tennis shoes as she realized she was tracking mud in. She nearly suggested coffee, but knew that Piper would almost certainly try to help her make it. And Piper's coffee, which had an unfortunate resemblance to weak tea, was ghastly.

"Milk and cookies?" asked Beatrice cheerfully.

"Oh, why not?" said Piper lightly as she sat on the floor to pet Noo-noo, who wriggled with excitement at the attention. Piper picked up a tennis ball, showed it to the intent corgi and then gave it a small toss. The corgi bounded joyfully after it before picking it up, running it back to Piper, and dropping it carefully back on the floor in front of her.

"Actually, since we were talking about how teachers have so little time ... well, I've sort of discovered that, too," said Piper a few minutes later as she sat on her mother's overstuffed gingham armchair, reaching an arm down to pat Noo-noo, who was still hopeful there might be more time to play ball later on.

"Oh?" asked Beatrice. She had a feeling she knew where this might be headed. Piper and Meadow's son, Ash, had been seeing each other for a while now. In fact, Ash had moved all the way from California to live closer to Piper. But he still lived a good thirty minute drive away. Hardly an insurmountable distance, but when you had a very busy schedule, it certainly made a difference.

"Between my teaching, Ash's teaching, his office hours, and my tutoring after school, I feel like I've hardly had a chance to see him," said Piper. She shrugged a shoulder as if to downplay her words, but her face was worried. "It's almost like every time our relationship takes a step forward, it takes two steps back."

Beatrice nodded slowly. She pressed her lips together to keep any heedless words from popping out. She'd found over the years that she had a tendency to try to fix everyone's problems. It was tough for her to listen to a friend or family member's problem without trying to leap into action to uncover a solution. Sometimes, she knew, people wanted her simply to listen to them.

Piper continued, "It's meant that we've seemed very distant, very disconnected from each other. And I'm just not sure how to grow closer. I don't want to move closer to Harrington College. And it's not as if I can quit my job. I depend on it and I enjoy it, too."

Beatrice nodded again, waiting to see if Piper were done speaking. She said quietly, "That's very hard. I know that you love spending time with Ash when you can. And you're right— it's easy for a sort of distance or wall to spring up when we don't have that regular contact." She hesitated. "Wyatt and I have faced some similar challenges. He is so busy with his work at the church. It's not as if I *begrudge* him that time." She shrugged and then gave a crooked grin.

Piper laughed. "Except you *do* begrudge it! How could you not? It's time spent away from you, even though it's for a good cause. What have you done to make things better?"

"I'm still working on it. I guess it's one of those things that will always be a work in progress. But, for me, the answer lies in doing more things at the church. I've been volunteering more over there, for one. And Meadow has finagled me into spending even more time over there with a quilting service project for children that Wyatt is organizing."

Piper said, "Oh, that's right. She mentioned it to me, too. I said I'd think about it." A frown line grew between Piper's brows.

Beatrice quickly added, "But see? That's just it. You probably *shouldn't* tell Meadow yes. You need to carve out more time for you and Ash. Adding to the amount of activities you're doing, even for a good reason, won't help the situation." She pressed her lips together again, remembering that once again she was trying to help solve a problem instead of being a passive listener. And also realizing that she wasn't doing a good job following her own advice. Maybe if she protected *her* free time better, she could spend more time with Wyatt going out to dinner or going on walks or having coffees.

"But if it helped you and your relationship out to actively seek out more time with Wyatt, it seems as if it would work well for me, too," said Piper thoughtfully. "Although it's a very worthwhile cause, maybe I can skip the meetings and just work on a quilt for a few minutes every night right before I go to bed. It's one of the ways that I relax before I fall asleep anyway, and I don't have a current project."

Beatrice gave her a hug. "That's very sweet of you."

Piper said briskly, signaling that she was ready to change the topic of the conversation, "Now tell me what's been going on with *you*. I know you've been up to all kinds of things since I saw you a few days ago."

Beatrice said, "Well, it's been unexpectedly busy, as a matter of fact. And in a very odd way." She filled Piper in on Miss Sissy's accident and hospitalization as well as the body that had been found between her cottage and the Downeys' house. She took care not to make the account very alarming.

Piper stared at her with wide eyes. "Poor Miss Sissy! That must have scared her to death. And you say the man who died has a connection with Dappled Hills?"

Piper had a tendency to be protective of her mother, so Beatrice was careful to play it all down. And she decided *not* to inform her that she was investigating by means of the Dappled Hills quilting history. "His connection is apparently through his mother, somehow. She may have lived here a long time ago. But who knows how she ended up with Vivian's journal? That seems very odd." Beatrice made a mental note to ask Ramsay what he thought might be the reason behind it.

"I'm sure Ramsay will get to the bottom of it." There was the slightest of emphasis on *Ramsay*. "Well, I hate to say it, but I should get going. I've got some papers to grade and then I'm supposed to go back to the school later to help at a bake sale they're having," said Piper.

"And maybe give Ash a call?" asked Beatrice.

Piper's eyes twinkled. "Yes ma'am. I guess it's my turn to call, anyway. What have you got for the rest of the day?"

Beatrice shut her eyes briefly. "I believe I'm going to head over to Miss Sissy's and show her how to use her new phone, now that it's charged up. That should be fun."

Piper said quickly, "I can help you with that."

"Oh no. No. You're so far advanced with technology that you'd be enthusiastically showing her how all the little bells and whistles worked. No, it's better for me to do it. I think I can get down to her level, technologically speaking, anyway. I'm only going to show her how to take and receive calls and how to take and receive text messages."

"All right. Well, call me if you need back-up," said Piper, giving her mother a quick, tight, hug.

Miss Sissy glared at her brand-new cell phone as if it were an instrument of the devil. "No!"

They were sitting in the dim light of Miss Sissy's kitchen. The paint was peeling in chunks from the dilapidated, dusty, and cluttered table they were sitting at and Beatrice was very much afraid that she might fall through the fragile caning of the chair bottom. She sat as delicately as she could, holding the flip phone in front of her as Miss Sissy eyed it warily.

"Miss Sissy, remember we talked about this? At the hospital? The doctor was worried about you having an accident, whether it was here at home or away in the car." Beatrice gave a small, involuntary shudder at the word *car*. "This way you can feel free to come and go as you like without having to worry about not having someone to help you if you run into any trouble."

Miss Sissy glared furiously at the device.

Beatrice took a deep breath for the sake of her patience and showed her how to make calls on it. Miss Sissy, who had apparently reverted to her teen years, rolled her eyes through the explanation.

Beatrice said tightly, "Okay, so it seems as if you know how to make phone calls on a cell phone. Let me show you how to send text messages."

This time Miss Sissy appeared more engaged in the process. Her beady eyes gleamed as Beatrice pulled up a list of contacts that Beatrice had added to the phone and demonstrated how to send and receive a text message. Beatrice followed up by making Miss Sissy engage in a texting conversation with her until the old woman fully caught on.

Beatrice had just finished up when there was a tap at Miss Sissy's door. The old woman responded by drawing back in alarm. Beatrice frowned. "Maybe we need to update your locks, just to help you feel more secure."

She rose cautiously from the fragile wooden chair and walked to the door, peering out a small window that looked out on Miss

Sissy's front porch. She smiled and waved at the figures there and turned to say, "Miss Sissy, it's Savannah and Georgia, here to visit with you! And it looks as if Savannah brought a furry friend."

Miss Sissy beamed at the prospect of having visitors and immediately hopped over to a small, smudged mirror to try to fix her hair, which rather resembled a squirrel's nest in appearance.

Beatrice opened the door to the two women. The sisters couldn't be more different, although they shared a love of quilting and of the Village Quilters. Georgia was soft, pretty, and crafty. She taught with Piper at the same local school and loved setting up and supplying her own online pet boutique. Savannah, on the other hand, was a lot more uptight in appearance and demeanor. She wore her thin hair pulled up in a bun and high necked floral dresses. Beatrice had found that, although Savannah could seem very prickly, she also had a warm heart. And nowhere was her warm heart more evident than in her love for animals.

Georgia took a seat gingerly on one of Miss Sissy's living room chairs. The chair, like the one in the kitchen, desperately needed re-caning and Georgia was trying her best not to end up on the floor. Savannah decided to take a shortcut and just go ahead and sit on the dusty wood floor. Besides, it made it easier for her to take Smoke out of his cat carrier.

"Miss Sissy, we were sorry to hear about your accident. I thought that a visit from Smoke might help raise your spirits," said Savannah gruffly. She opened the door to the carrier and the deliciously fuzzy Smoke came prancing out, preening as if he knew he was going to be admired. Georgia had obviously been outfitting him for Savannah, and he wore an adorable green polka dot bow tie. The little gray cat with the beautiful green eyes glanced around him quickly before spotting Miss Sissy. As soon as he saw the old woman, he padded over to rub against her legs. She gave a delighted exclamation and plopped down in a low chair to give Smoke a lap to sit on. "So cute," she muttered.

"Are you feeling better now, Miss Sissy?" asked Georgia politely.

But Miss Sissy apparently couldn't be less interested in regaling them about her health. She was way too absorbed in the cat. She pulled a piece of string from the unraveling nearby sofa upholstery and moved the string around as Smoke hopped off her lap to play intently with it.

Savannah, who was usually fiercely protective over her little pet, seemed more relaxed today and also genuinely concerned about the old woman. She and her sister both looked to Beatrice for more information.

Beatrice cleared her throat. "Yes. Well, as you can see, Miss Sissy is fortunately much better. I think the worst part was the scare of it." She looked toward the old woman but she was blissfully playing with Smoke with a pencil she'd grabbed from a nearby table when the little cat had tired of the string.

"The scare?" asked Georgia.

"Miss Sissy got hurt from chasing away a man who she thought meant her some harm," explained Beatrice. She hesitated for a minute before continuing, "And then Meadow and I discovered him dead later on."

Savannah stared at her and Georgia gasped. Miss Sissy, oblivious, laughed as Smoke pounced on the pencil as seriously as if it had been its prey.

"What did this man look like?" asked Savannah curiously. She tilted her long neck inquiringly, giving herself a birdlike appearance.

Beatrice thought for a minute. It was hard to get much of an impression when he was dead. She instead thought about his outfit, which did make him stand out. "Well, he was wearing quite a bit of clothing, considering the weather. It made me wonder if he'd come from a place with a colder climate."

Savannah squinted at her. "Did he look like he was going on a safari?"

Georgia nodded. "I remember that guy! We were biking down the street and saw this man we didn't recognize. That's weird enough, but then we saw that he was really overdressed for the weather. He had a brimmed hat and a white shirt."

Georgia paused and Beatrice jumped in, "And a khaki jacket."

"Like he was going on a safari!" said Savannah emphatically.

Smoke thought his owner sounded agitated and padded over to rub against Savannah. She petted him, absently, until Miss Sissy clicked her tongue to call the little cat back up on her lap.

"Did you see what he was doing?" asked Beatrice.

"I certainly did," said Savannah. "I thought maybe he was selling something. You know how that happens sometimes? There will be a salesman in town and he'll make the rounds knocking on everyone's door and driving us all crazy. Usually I make calls to everybody I know to let them know not to answer their door or to peek out first."

Georgia smiled at her sister. "Savannah is the unofficial neighborhood watch president."

"Someone has to be!" said Savannah hotly. "You know how you'll open the door right up. And even buy something, Georgia!"

Georgia gave a low laugh. "I can't help it. I feel sorry for them because I know it's such a bad job to have. I couldn't imagine slamming the door in their faces. And then they usually look so hot and discouraged and out of sorts that I end up giving them some lemonade. By the end of the visit, I've usually bought whatever it is they're peddling. But like I said, it's a bad job for them."

"But it's a bad job for us to have to deal with it! And then, who knows? The salesman might not even be a salesman at all. He might be a bad guy. That's what Ramsay said that day, remember? He told us not to open the door," reminded Savannah. "Said that sometimes bad guys will pose as salesmen or repairmen and they're actually casing the joint!"

Beatrice coughed pointedly and the sisters turned to look at her again. "What I was wondering while thinking about this is why the safari man looked like a salesman to you, Savannah. What gave you that impression?"

"Because he was knocking on doors," said Savannah simply. "When Georgia and I were biking out to the store, he was visiting Huey. Or trying to. He was knocking at Huey's door, anyway. When we were biking *back* from the store, he was going inside Gwen's house."

Savannah and Georgia didn't drive, but they didn't have to in a town like Dappled Hills. Since they biked everywhere they went, they were definitely more likely than most to spot a stranger in town.

"So, if he wasn't a salesman, what was he doing here?" asked Savannah sharply. "Up to no good apparently. Especially ending up dead like that." Savannah made it sound as if he had really used poor judgment indeed.

"As a matter of fact, I think he *may* have been up to some good. At least, I think that maybe he was trying to right a wrong," said Beatrice slowly.

Savannah sniffed.

Georgia said, "What sort of wrong? And why did he visit people we know to do it?"

Beatrice said, "Apparently, it's all connected to someone who lived here a long time ago. He had a notebook belonging to someone named Vivian Hastings."

The women both looked blankly at Beatrice.

"The name isn't familiar to you at all?" asked Beatrice, disappointed.

Savannah and Georgia glanced at each other and then shook their heads.

Beatrice snapped her fingers. "Well, of *course* it isn't. You must not have even been born. This happened forty years ago."

Savannah and Georgia laughed. Georgia said, "Then I feel better about not being able to offer any help or information. I was wracking my brain trying to figure out how I could have forgotten anyone who lived in Dappled Hills!"

Chapter Five

July 4th

Dappled Hills has been interesting. It's both everything I thought a small town would be, and something very different.

I've met a lot of people here already. If I want to meet more, I probably need to start joining clubs or other activities. Quilting is really popular here. I never thought of myself as a quilter, but there are women here who are eager to show me how to do it. It might be a good way of making friends.

One thing has been sort of odd. I'm sure that one of the people I met isn't who they say they are. I'm not going to write anything down until I'm sure, since I carry this journal along with me to serve as my writing notebook, too. But I know this person is a criminal, no matter what kind of story they've concocted about themselves here in Dappled Hills. My aunt would usually tell me that my imagination is running away with me, but in this case? I think she'd agree with me and would recognize this person on sight.

It was early in the morning as Beatrice read Vivian's notebook over a cup of coffee. Beatrice reread the first journal entry again, looking for more clues as to what might have been going on in Vivian's head when she was writing it. It appeared she had made it as inexplicable as possible, which was most annoying. But Vivian seemed to have figured out that a small town like Dappled Hills could be rather nosy. And if she were carrying around her journal, she likely was trying to keep her thoughts private, even if someone managed to read some of it.

A rap at her door startled her and her gaze automatically flew to the clock. Seven o'clock was early for a visit. This meant it was probably Meadow, who frequently didn't conform to strict visiting hours. She peered out the window by her front door and saw that it was indeed Meadow. Unfortunately, Boris was out there, too, tongue lolling out and a grin on his massive face at the prospect of visiting his neighbor, so generous with giving treats. But she would have expected Boris to accompany Meadow at this point in the morning. Meadow, despite her determination to work in more minutes of exercise each day, found it quite an uphill battle. Most of her walking centered on exercising her massive dog.

Noo-noo gave her mistress a long-suffering look as if she knew who was at the door. Beatrice murmured, "I'm rewarding you in advance," and tossed the corgi a cookie. "Coming!" she called to the door and Boris gave an excited yelp in response, his tail drumming the porch floor in excitement at hearing Beatrice's voice.

"I saw your lights on," said Meadow beaming at her friend. She turned to Boris, loudly yelping, and said fondly, "Shush! Shush, Boris! No crying!" She turned and walked inside with Boris loping after her. "So I thought we'd pop by. You're going to the organizational meeting tonight, aren't you?"

"Organizational meeting?" asked Beatrice, her heart sinking. Why was everything sounding like work now?

"I made it sound quite corporate, didn't I?" laughed Meadow. "It's not as serious as all that. It's the first meeting of our children's blanket project. And the meditation, which Wyatt will be in charge of, of course. It may take a *little* longer than the rest of the meetings. You know how it is just starting out: you have to hand the materials out and you talk about your purpose then you give deadlines and the process simply takes a bit longer. But then the meetings get more focused and honed and all."

As Beatrice's face apparently continued to look blank, Meadow said, "Mercy! Didn't I tell you the first meeting is this evening? I swear I'm getting so forgetful in my dotage. And here I am prattling on about first meeting logistics and inefficiencies!"

"Must have slipped your mind," said Beatrice. She tossed Boris a couple of treats so that he would calm down a little. He snapped them up with his great teeth before they hit the ground. She slid Noo-noo another couple more for her sweet patience. Although she was feeling as if *she* should get a treat, herself for her patience in dealing with Meadow's madness and her ravenous Boris at a very early hour in the morning. "You only mentioned that we'd been meeting in the evenings because everyone was working."

"Right. And then I guess I got distracted. Which is hardly a wonder considering our dramatic day!" She glanced over at the table to see Beatrice's phone. She nodded toward it. "Have you been looking at the journal? What does it say?"

"I haven't gotten too far yet. Actually, I just started. I was exhausted last night and turned in without even taking a look at it," said Beatrice. Her phone suddenly dinged and she and Meadow stared at it. "Someone *else* is trying to get in touch with me this early?"

Meadow's phone dinged as Beatrice was reaching for hers. "What on earth?" muttered Meadow.

Beatrice sighed. "Miss Sissy is apparently up."

"I seriously underestimated her ability to text," said Meadow, blinking at her phone.

"Your message was from Miss Sissy, too?"

"Unfortunately," said Meadow.

"She appears to be in an adventurous type of mood," said Beatrice. "When it comes to technology anyway."

"I'm surprised she even knows my cell number," said Meadow, still staring at her phone.

Beatrice flushed. "I added it to her contacts. For some reason, I thought that she might only use it in the case of an emergency."

"Well, you know Miss Sissy. Perhaps she *thought* this was an emergency," said Meadow.

"Unlikely. How could '*Reprobates!*' be considered an emergency?" Beatrice sighed again. "This may be even worse than the whistle that Wyatt gave her to help her feel safe."

"*Nothing* is worse than that whistle," said Meadow emphatically. "Now let's see. What were we talking about before? I've lost my train of thought. Oh, that's right—the journal."

Beatrice shrugged. "I haven't gotten very far, as I was saying."

She showed Meadow her phone and Meadow pulled reading glasses out of the front pocket of her bright red shirt. She pulled off her regular glasses and put on the reading ones. "I've got to get another pair of bifocals," muttered Meadow. She read the journal thoughtfully, finally giving it a "phish!" as she finished and handed the phone back to Beatrice.

"This reads like a bad novel," said Meadow, making a face. "She's so determined not to disclose the identity of the *person* that she goes way too far."

"I gather that she was carrying this notebook around with her? Do you remember her doing that?" asked Beatrice. Noo-noo plopped down on Beatrice's foot to let her know she would protect her from Boris, who was now making loud slurping sounds as if he might consume anything in his path.

Meadow threw up her hand, nearly throwing Beatrice's phone with it. "Who knows? I remember very little about Vivian. I'm thoroughly ashamed of myself for being so clueless."

Beatrice kept hoping that the information she was looking for must be buried somewhere in Meadow's memory, if she could only find a way to unlock it. She prodded, "Were you one of the 'women who were eager' to show her quilting?"

"Heavens no! All I was interested in at the time were china patterns, which wedding dress I was going to attempt to stuff myself into, and which florist or even semi-talented friend could do Ramsay's and my flowers on the cheap. I promise you, recruitment into the Village Quilters wasn't anywhere on my mind," said Meadow.

It was hard to believe. Meadow was such an ardent recruiter for the guild. It may even qualify as conscription instead of recruitment. "The notebook, though? This journal? Do you remember seeing her walking around with it?"

Meadow frowned in concentration. "Not really. Although I *do* remember that she wanted to be a writer. It was that time when everyone was trying to figure out what they wanted to do with their lives, you know? And Vivian wanted to write. I assumed she wanted to go into journalism."

Beatrice jumped on this. "But why? Why did you assume that?"

"Well, she was a cub reporter at the local paper. And she certainly seemed as though she needed to make some money." Meadow snapped her fingers. "And, yes! Yes! Because she carried around a notebook. I remember talking to her about my wedding, spotting the notebook in her hand, and saying something coy like *are you going to quote me on that?*"

"What did she say back?" asked Beatrice, hoping to get more information on what Vivian was like. Was she someone who could engage in light conversation? Was she serious? Did she think too highly of herself?

Unfortunately, Meadow seemed to have few insights. "I have no idea what she said. I did think she was nice, so she mustn't have been very rude. But I was busy at the time."

"Did she have any other friends?" asked Beatrice.

"You mean any *friends*. Because, sadly, I wasn't one of them. I seem to recall that she hung out some with ... oh, what's her name." Meadow tilted her head back and stared at the ceiling as if the answer were up there. "Sam Holland."

"Was he a boyfriend?"

"No, he was a she. Samantha Holland," said Meadow. Her eyes opened wide. "Wait a minute! That must be the dead body's mother. Oh, my word. I can't imagine why I didn't make the connection."

"The woman that Miss Sissy was talking about? She was married at the time?" asked Beatrice. "And if she was our victim's mother—well, wasn't she a lot older than Vivian?"

"She was. So I suppose that she was a bit of an odd choice for Vivian to make friends with, but then she probably didn't have a lot of choice, either. Perhaps Vivian looked at her as more of a mentor. Or maybe Vivian was learning more about quilting from her, if she were so interested in quilting. Sam was a very proficient quilter. But how did Sam Holland get hold of Vivian's journal? And why, if Vivian were a friend of Sam's, did Sam feel guilty enough over Vivian to give her son Vivian's journal as she lay on her deathbed?" Meadow thumped the table next to her and Noo-noo jumped. Boris, who was now taking a nap, merely opened one eye to gaze at Meadow with outrage before closing it to fall fast asleep again.

Beatrice said, "If they were friends, maybe she knew about the notebook and decided to grab it. After all, it probably has some personal information that Vivian wouldn't have wanted getting out. So she could have been protecting Vivian's privacy. Perhaps she didn't even look at the journal until years later. Maybe she only *suspected* that something had gone amiss with Vivian and was unable or just unwilling to invest the time in investigating. Then, when she approached the end of her life, maybe she realized or accepted that something bad had happened to Vivian. That could have made her feel guilty enough to turn over the diary—a belated hope for justice for her friend."

"Which is all well and good, Beatrice, and certainly inventive of you. Very good ideas. We should share them with Ramsay. But here's the flaw in your theory. At least, *I* think it's a flaw. I would accept your theory better if Vivian were *dead*. But as far as we know, Vivian merely left town to get a job somewhere else. Or maybe she was disappointed with life in Dappled Hills. It seemed like she had some reservations about it when she was writing," said Meadow. "Although I can't imagine that. She would have had more friends than she would have been able to handle if I hadn't been so tied up with the wedding planning. And if she'd gotten fully involved in the quilting community, she'd have found a ton of friends, too. I mean, we even consider Gwen and *Ida* our friends because they're quilters. And I don't even think they're likable people at all."

"Getting back to the journal entry, who do you think she could have been talking about?" asked Beatrice.

"Who? You mean the person who resembled a criminal?" Meadow snorted. "Who knows? Although I guess it makes sense if it's one of the people she kept mentioning in her journal. Let's hope she got more lax with her reporting as she went on. Otherwise, it's not going to be a very helpful read for us." She considered the ceiling again, thoughtfully. "Criminals. Criminals. Maybe Gwen."

"You really seem to have something against this Gwen," said Beatrice. "I'm looking forward in horrified anticipation to meeting her."

"Oh, she's not all that bad. And she'll be at the quilting meeting tonight, or at least she said she would. Sometimes she doesn't show up for things," said Meadow.

"Charming." Beatrice, always on time, had very little patience for people who weren't.

"It's very annoying, I'll agree. That's why we never allow her to take any important roles. She's simply not dependable," said Meadow.

"Undependable. But a criminal?" asked Beatrice. "We're talking about an old woman who quilts."

"She wasn't always old. And she wasn't always a quilter. She could be anything in a former life," said Meadow.

Beatrice was beginning to suspect that Meadow was purposefully throwing Gwen under a bus at this point, metaphorically speaking. "You bring up a good point, Meadow," she said to redirect her.

"Do I?" She replied with some surprise.

"You certainly do. For Vivian to suspect that this person even *had* a former life as a criminal of some kind, would necessitate the person either originating from another town, or leaving Dappled Hills for some time before returning. Which of the people listed in the journal would have done such a thing?" asked Beatrice.

Meadow said, "I know Gwen went away to college," said Meadow. "And then ... let's see. Who are the other suspects? I forget."

"We don't know if they're suspects or not. They're just people Vivian listed in her journal. And we don't know if Vivian was even killed or if she just left to peddle encyclopedias in the Midwest or something," said Beatrice.

"Yes, but we do know that Oscar was murdered. Ramsay was most clear on that point. And Oscar was going around asking questions of all the people in the journal," reminded Meadow. "It doesn't look good for our Vivian, I don't think."

"Good point. So on to the suspects. We have Hugh and Gwen, starting out."

Meadow said, "Huey. I can't wrap my head around calling him Hugh. It seems to me like he's been in Dappled Hills for forever. He was mayor here briefly and he was a state representative. Everyone did his banking with him for ages and ages."

"So he's from here?"

"He's from here." Meadow frowned thoughtfully. "Although I believe he went away for a while when he was young. His parents were very strict types. They sent him to a military school or something. And then he went away to college."

"Well, I doubt at a military school he'd have the opportunity to engage in much criminal conduct. Unless he found a way to escape. But if he went away for college too, that means he was gone for quite a while. Maybe he had a chance to get into some trouble," said Beatrice.

"Mayyyybe," said Meadow doubtfully. "He just seems like the upright type. You know—the typical politician."

"Ida?" asked Beatrice, looking through the notes.

"She's also been in Dappled Hills for more years than I care to count. If she were involved in any criminal activity, it would have to be something white collar. I can't see her doing anything else," said Meadow.

"But has she left *town*?" asked Beatrice. "Did she have the opportunity to commit a crime?"

"She also went away to school. I guess she could have done something while she was away." Meadow made a face. "It's very disturbing to think of all my neighbors as potential criminals."

"And we still have Jake to consider."

"There are a few of those here. Who knows?" said Meadow.

"Who is it most likely to be? Someone older, right? Our age or older? Who might not have grown up here?"

Meadow sighed. "I suppose that could be Jake Hunter. But this is becoming seriously depressing. He was always such a cute guy. I had a crush on him, myself. He's a widower now, but still pretty cute." She gave Beatrice a sideways glance.

"Don't be looking at me. I've got Wyatt, remember? Save your matchmaking for someone who needs it," said Beatrice.

Boris, now sleeping, rolled over onto his back, feet in the air. Noo-noo gave him a disgusted look.

Meadow stood up. "All right, so let's start seeing some of these people once it's later in the morning. What do you think ... eleven o'clock? Something like that? And of course we'll use the history as our excuse."

"To really make it a good excuse, we'll have to make sure to see other people, too," said Beatrice glumly. "Otherwise, we'll be just the same as Oscar. And you know what happened to him."

Chapter Six

They made plans for Beatrice to pick up Meadow at eleven. That gave Beatrice plenty of time to get dressed and ready for her day and even take a short walk with Noo-noo before picking up Meadow.

Meadow hopped into her car, a bit breathless. She smiled at Beatrice and then frowned, glancing around the seat and floor of the car. "Where's your camera? You haven't managed to stuff it into your pocketbook, have you? You always keep such a small purse. I don't know how you manage. I'm like Mary Poppins—I've got everything stuffed in my bag but a coatrack."

"Oh, right. I'd forgotten that I'm there to take pictures for the book," said Beatrice with a sigh. She kept forgetting that she was actually at the start of a potentially massive project, not just an investigation of a mysterious death.

"It's okay. Let's just run by and get it real quick before we head out," said Meadow, putting on her seatbelt. "So who is first today?"

Beatrice drove back home again. "I thought we'd go in the order of the names mentioned in Vivian's journal. Which means Hugh, Huey, or whatever he's called should be first." She paused. "Actually, it didn't occur to me that he might not be a fit for our cover story. How might he fit into the Wonderful World of Quilting?"

"Pretty easily, actually. He was the mayor when the Village Quilters approached him about having a craft festival. He was surprisingly gung-ho. I believe he was trying to think of ways to draw visitors to our little hamlet—you know—a revenue-raising device of some kind. The fair was heavily attended and we continue to have it today—and we're about to have it again, of course."

"So it's basically the same fair that the town puts on each year? Not the huge spring one, but the smaller craft-oriented one?"

"The very one. It got popular enough that we needed to bring in some outside craftspeople to make it work. We have vendors from all over the South. Huey helped to jumpstart it. He will probably have all kinds of ancient festival artifacts," said Meadow.

"What's he like?" asked Beatrice curiously. "Is he very much a politician?"

"He can be. Or he can be very empathetic and genuine. Unless the empathy and the genuineness is part of his being a politician, which it might very well be," said Meadow. "Is it okay if I take a look at your phone while we're on our way? I want to read the next entry to be ready to see Huey."

"Read it aloud, while you're at it," said Beatrice. "It will be good to refresh my memory."

Meadow cleared her throat and then read in a storytelling voice that seemed greatly at odds with the content of the journal entry. "She says: '*The problem is that I suspect I have something of a crush on Hugh. He's a nice-looking guy and seems smart and driven. I need to resist. But he seems keen on me, too, and he looks to be the kind of man who always gets what he wants. The only problem is he's involved with someone else.*'" Meadow raised her eyebrows. "I suppose I remember a time when Huey was an irresistible force, but time does force unwelcome changes on us."

"All right—so takeaways from this," said Beatrice. "I suppose the main takeaway is that Huey *knows* Vivian. That they had some sort of relationship. Perhaps he can give us more information on her."

With Meadow's guidance, Beatrice pulled up to an attractive brick home filled with old trees, vines climbing on stone walls, and a full rose garden. "Apparently, banking and the political life have served him well," murmured Beatrice. "That's Huey in the garden, I presume?"

"It is indeed!"

Beatrice parked and the two women walked up to a bald man wearing a pair of freshly-pressed khakis and a white button-down shirt with rolled-up sleeves. Beatrice agreed with Meadow that he hardly looked like a leading man in a romantic story. He was briskly dead-heading the roses and throwing the debris into a brown paper grocery bag. "Hi, ladies," he called in a booming voice. "To what do I owe this unexpected pleasure?"

Meadow beamed at him. "So good to see you, Huey. As usual, it's quilting business. Do you know Beatrice Coleman?"

Beatrice and Huey shook hands. Huey's handshake was very firm and he looked intently into Beatrice's eyes like a person who's learned from experience how important eye contact can be.

"Nice to meet you," she said.

"Well come in, come in. I can fix you both up with a coffee." He eyed Beatrice's camera and said, "Uh-oh. Do I need to look presentable, or is that thing just for show?"

"I think you need to look presentable," said Meadow. "Although you look just fine to me the way you are right now. You tend to want to look even spiffier, though, as I recall."

"Let's just say that I'd rather not be in my yard clothes for any pictures," he said with a twinkle in his eye. He held open the front door for them and Beatrice gave an appreciative sniff. The house smelled of old books, which was always an alluring scent for her. The dim light in the house was shot through with sunbeams. In one of the sunbeams was a German shepherd, whose tail began beating the floor in earnest as he spotted them.

Huey led them into a formal living room with damask covered chairs and an old settee. He returned in a few minutes with coffee.

"If you'll excuse me," he said, "I'll just run upstairs and change. Suit and tie or something more casual?"

Beatrice put up a protesting hand. "Please—no suit and tie. That will really be overkill. This is just a picture for a quilting history of Dappled Hills that Meadow and I are putting together."

He left to change and Beatrice said under her breath to Meadow, "He takes formality to a whole new level."

She shrugged. "It's just the way he is." Meadow leaned a bit closer and said in her loud stage whisper, "Can you picture him as a killer, though? Or a criminal in a former life?"

The German shepherd whined as if he somehow gathered his master was being slandered in some way.

Beatrice waved her hand at her. "Keep it down!" she hissed. "I don't know. But there have been plenty of bad guys who didn't exactly look the part. Let's try to keep the questioning more conversational, all right?"

They resumed sipping their coffee as Huey walked back in wearing a blue button-down with a tie and khaki pants. He carried a canvas tote bag.

"I thought we said no tie," said Meadow with a smile.

"I decided that a tie would be nice, even if we'd skipped the suit," said Huey with the same smile. He put the tote bag on a chair and started pulling things out. "Let's see. So I gather that your quilting history is intersecting with the craft festival. How about if I pull out an old newspaper clipping, this old box of award ribbons, and a banner we used to advertise it?"

"Perfect!" said Beatrice. She picked up her camera and started adjusting its settings.

Huey set some of the things around him and held the banner. "How about this?" he asked. "What should my expression look like?"

He was certainly a former politician. Considering things from every angle. "Oh, I don't know," said Beatrice. "A pleased smile?

A warm look? Nothing serious, for sure. This is going to be positive coverage of the festival—it's not like we're covering some sort of scandal with it."

He gave a light laugh, but Beatrice sensed a bit of withdrawal from him. Did he have something to hide, with the festival or otherwise? Is that why the subject of scandal provoked a response?

Meadow seemed eager to start investigating. As Beatrice snapped pictures from various angles, Meadow said, "Beatrice, you shouldn't even bring the word *scandal* up. You know how upset I've been."

Beatrice stood back and looked at the playback on the pictures she took. "These look great, thanks," she said to Huey as they all resumed their seats.

Huey was looking at Meadow. "What scandal is that? Did I miss some local news?"

"I'm afraid so," said Meadow, looking anxious. And, knowing Meadow's rather extreme reaction to any crime that took place in her beloved Dappled Hills, she probably didn't have to fake it. "You see, Beatrice and I discovered a body in the woods between our properties. So disturbing!"

Huey was either very surprised to hear this, startled that Meadow would broach the subject so abruptly, or else he was ... like many politicians ... an excellent actor. His eyes opened wide and his mouth made an O of surprise. "A body? What? In the woods? *Here?*"

"Here. In Dappled Hills. It's scandalous," fumed Meadow. "Imagine arriving to town and getting yourself killed here. As a visitor!"

"Now I know why I didn't hear about this. I went out of town to visit some old friends and missed all the excitement here. But it sounds as if you can update me. You know something about this person?" asked Huey. "This visitor?"

"Only what Ramsay has told us. He was here in town asking questions about a person who lived here long ago," said Beatrice. "But, actually, someone mentioned they'd seen him talking to you. Here at your home. Maybe you got the date of your visit wrong?"

Now his gaze was wary as if he wondered if he might somehow be caught up in something he didn't want to be involved in. "Someone was mistaken, then. I couldn't have spoken to this man if I were out of town at the time. You say he was asking about a person who lived here long ago?" he parroted.

"How did you know it was a man? We didn't mention that," said Beatrice.

Huey made a flustered gesture. "I just assumed that. Are you trying to twist my words? Who is the person who lived here long ago that he was asking about?"

"Vivian Hastings," said Beatrice, closely watching the older man's reaction.

There really wasn't one. His face was carefully blank with only the slightest hint of polite interest. "Does Ramsay know who this Vivian was?"

Meadow chuckled. "I bet he's going to visit and ask *you* who Vivian was. As I recall," fibbed Meadow, "you were dating her at the time she lived here. This was something like forty years ago."

Huey stiffened. "I didn't date her. I was far too old for her."

"So you *do* remember her," said Beatrice quickly.

Huey sighed and shifted uncomfortably in the antique chair. "I suppose I do, although I didn't when you first mentioned her. Reddish hair, right? A pretty girl."

"The very one," said Meadow. "And, if you may recall, she disappeared."

Huey gave her a sideways look. "I wouldn't have used the word *disappeared*. I believed, as did everyone else, that she simply left town to live somewhere else. Small town living isn't for everyone. Residing in Dappled Hills sometimes doesn't work out the way people think it will." Seeming very interested in changing the subject, he turned to Beatrice to politely inquire, "How are you enjoying Dappled Hills so far? Since I don't know you, I know you didn't grow up here."

"I've loved it," said Beatrice, surprising herself with the admission. "But then, my daughter lives here and that may be one reason I've settled in so well."

"That and the Village Quilters!" reminded Meadow stoutly.

Beatrice tried to return to the subject. "Going back to Vivian. What if she didn't move away? What if she was murdered?"

Huey gave an unamused laugh. "Why on earth would someone want to murder the girl, though?"

"Maybe she knew something, or heard about or saw something, that someone else wanted to keep quiet," said Beatrice. It certainly seemed likely, considering the fact that Vivian wrote down everything in a notebook and was fairly nosy. "Maybe she knew someone had a criminal past, for instance."

Huey's mouth thinned. "I think you're engaging in speculation."

Meadow said, "What if we're not? Can you think of anyone would might have wanted to do Vivian harm?"

Huey gave a short laugh. "Certainly not. She was a very nice person. And it was a very peaceful time here in Dappled Hills."

Beatrice said, "It wasn't the 1950s, Huey. It wasn't some idyll. It was still a small town with small town irritations and small town envy. Wasn't there someone who might not have liked her? Might have been jealous of her?"

Huey shifted again in his seat. "I suppose, if we somehow assume that Vivian met with foul play of some kind, any type of investigation would have to start with Ida. She had quite the bone to pick, you know."

Meadow frowned. "Ida and Vivian. Wait. When Miss Sissy was talking to us, she mentioned something about death."

"Miss Sissy is always harping on death," pointed out Beatrice.

"Yes, but it jogged something in my memory. A tragedy of some kind. It's a pity I was so caught up in my own wedding plans that I can't remember more than that," said Meadow in frustration.

"Involving, perhaps, Ida's sister?" asked Huey.

Meadow snapped her fingers. "That's right! Now I remember. Vivian Hastings was driving a car with Ida's sister, Fiona, as a passenger, wasn't she? I'll have to ask Ramsay more about it, since my memory is so dodgy. But I think it was an accident, wasn't it? It wasn't something like drunk driving. It was more minor."

"But still fatal, no matter how minor it was," said Huey.

"Maybe you could remind me about it, Huey," said Meadow.

"There's not much to tell, since I only really knew what people were saying at the time. Vivian was driving; a deer leapt out at her car; she was a city girl who hated the thought of killing a deer; she swerved to avoid the animal. Fiona, Ida's sister, didn't have a seatbelt on. Very tragic," he said in a flat voice. He glanced longingly out the window at his rose garden.

Chapter Seven

Huey didn't have anything else to really offer them in terms of the case, so they spent the rest of the time asking him questions about the origins of the craft fair. Beatrice dutifully took pictures and Meadow took notes.

On their way out, Beatrice murmured, "This will have to be written in quite a lively style or else it will be as dry as toast."

Meadow laughed, "But it's history. I'm not sure how lively we can make it without embellishing the truth. Anyway, it will still be interesting to people who enjoy quilting or want to know more about the town."

"I suppose," said Beatrice doubtfully as they got into the car. "Maybe I can work some magic with the photography. So where are we heading now? Am I driving you back home?"

"Can we run by the Patchwork Cottage first? I have a few things to pick up there for the service project," said Meadow.

Beatrice said, "Of course. I'm glad to get back to a feeling of normalcy at the Patchwork Cottage. I don't think I've ever spoken to anyone who tried to lie as much as Huey did while we were talking to him."

Meadow shrugged. "What did you expect? He's a politician, Beatrice."

The Patchwork Cottage was buzzing with activity when they arrived. Meadow made a face. "I was hoping to talk to Posy. Maybe it will die down a little bit soon."

Beatrice, who had been hoping Meadow's mission lay more along the lines of grabbing some fabric or thread before heading back home, stifled a sigh. It wasn't that she didn't enjoy talking to

Posy, it was just that she was hoping to have at least a bit of quiet time before she went to the meeting at church that night.

Meadow did seem poky about finding her fabric and other supplies. Beatrice took the opportunity to sit on a sofa that fell right in a sunbeam. Posy had soft folk music playing in the shop and it was soothing to listen to. The shop itself was always a mood-brightener to be in with the visual feast of fabrics and soft textures and the cheerful gingham curtains in the windows. The store cat Maisie, looking a little on the chubby side, climbed sleepily in her lap and she absently stroked her, nearly falling asleep in the sun.

Finally, Meadow seemed satisfied with her fabric choice. This moment coincided with Posy's store suddenly becoming quiet. Posy sat down in a soft armchair directly across from Beatrice and Meadow plopped down next to Beatrice, reaching a hand out to mindlessly rub Maisie.

Posy relaxed into the chair, a smile on her face. "This is heaven," she said. "I may not be able to get up again."

Her cell phone went off across the room on the checkout counter and Posy's brow wrinkled. But when Beatrice's and Meadow's also started going off, Beatrice groaned. "Ignore it, Posy. You can stay seated. I'll break the suspense for you ... it's Miss Sissy. She's the only one sending out gobs of group messages. I don't even know how she figured out how to do it."

Posy laughed and relaxed again. "Oh, is that who it is?"

Beatrice pulled out her own phone and glanced at it. "It is." She grimaced and quickly put the phone away again to the relief of Maisie who awakened to give Beatrice a reproachful look.

"What's the urgent message this time?" asked Meadow, a brow raised.

"It's: *vagrant*!" said Beatrice dryly. "Miss Sissy is clearly omniscient and sees that we're finally taking a load off our feet today."

Meadow said, "Maybe she knows you're petting her cat." She bobbed her head at Maisie, snoozing happily again.

"She's only a *part* owner of the cat, after all," said Beatrice.

Posy's brow wrinkled again. "How's Miss Sissy doing, though? Apart from excessive texting? Is she feeling all right? I haven't been able to check on her as much as I'd like to. It's been so very busy at the shop lately."

"She seems to be feeling great. I'm not sure I'd be nearly as lively after the experience she had. She's not even as worried as she was when she was convinced that the man at her house was a 'bad guy,'" said Beatrice with a shrug.

Posy said, "Oh, I didn't hear about that. So her intruder ...?"

"He wasn't an intruder at all. He was a man who was in town to interview a group of people that were mentioned in an old journal that his mother had." Beatrice explained what had happened to Posy, who listened with thoughtful interest. Meadow chimed in from time to time to help embellish the story.

Posy nodded thoughtfully at the end. "So the bottom line is that someone murdered this man for trying to find out information about something that happened forty years ago?"

"Exactly. He meant no harm to Miss Sissy," said Beatrice. "And she had nothing to do with his death. Not that we'd like to think she would anyway. But she was already in the hospital from her injuries when he was murdered. Although I'm not sure what he was doing in the woods near our houses. Maybe he'd gotten turned around. Unless he was planning on speaking to Meadow."

Meadow said sadly, "I doubt Vivian would have written about me. I barely knew her. Maybe Oscar got turned around when he was trying to talk to the next person. Or maybe he was trying to lay low because someone had scared him."

Beatrice said, "Posy, do you have any memories of Vivian during the time she lived here? Did you even have the shop back then?"

Meadow said, "Well, of *course* she had the store back then. It feels like she's *always* had the store."

Posy said thoughtfully. "Let's see. Vivian was a young woman. Attractive. Red hair, I believe?"

Meadow nodded encouragingly.

"Of course, we were all young then, weren't we? I remember that she was very enthusiastic about learning how to quilt. She was driven, I think. That kind of personality that really takes something on full-force. I remember being delighted that she was throwing herself into it. But then, I'm always glad to see someone young taking on crafting. That means there's a future for quilting. Vivian bought a lot of fabric, notions, thread. She worked very hard on learning, too. Attended a class and asked lots of questions." Posy came to a stop, looking as if she might be tapped out on any more information on Vivian.

"What did you think when she disappeared?" asked Beatrice. "First of all, is that what it felt like? A disappearance? Or was she simply just not around one day and no one really thought about it?"

"I did think about it," said Posy. "After all, she'd invested a good deal of money into quilting and gave every impression that she was going to stick around and keep quilting. I thought it was very strange. I talked with a couple of other customers about her just disappearing like that. But they seemed to think there was nothing out of the ordinary about it."

Beatrice said, "But there had to be some kind of a police investigation or something. What about her house? Didn't she have all kinds of clothes and stuff left there? Wouldn't that have looked suspicious?"

"The only thing was, she was in a furnished apartment and lived pretty much like a monk. She didn't have a lot of personal belongings to begin with," said Posy. "At least, that's what I heard at the time. She'd left a note saying something about making a fresh start. You see, *some* of her things were gone. So I think

Ramsay and the police chief at the time probably thought that she had gotten fed up with the town, thrown a few things in a bag, and left."

"What if she was still here, though?" asked Beatrice. "What if someone wanted everyone to think that she'd left town but they actually murdered her and got rid of some of her stuff to make it look like she'd gone of her own free will?"

Meadow scoffed, "What, drive up to her apartment and load their car full of her things? Wouldn't that have looked a little suspicious?"

"It would have if someone had seen it," said Posy in her gentle voice. "But Vivian lived in a rented duplex apartment. A small house that was bordered by woods on all sides. No one was in the other part of the duplex—I remember Vivian saying how nice and private it was there. Someone could have taken things out of her apartment without being seen."

Meadow said, "That's very disturbing!" She thumped the arm of the sofa emphatically. "So while I was happily planning my wedding, someone *my age*, who could have ended up in *my guild*, and been a quilting friend, may have been brutally murdered!"

"I think you're taking the little amount of information that we have and running away with it," said Beatrice dryly.

"Where could her body be then?" asked Meadow, ignoring Beatrice. "Say that someone needed to silence her. They went to her apartment ... probably at night. She *knew* them and let them in. They killed her and grabbed some of her belongings. And ... did what with them?"

Beatrice shrugged. "Well, if I were a killer, I'd probably weigh down the victim and the belongings and throw them into that small lake near downtown."

"You're right. That's what I'd do, too," said Meadow, snapping her fingers. "I'll tell Ramsay that he has to drain the lake."

"I'm not even sure it would have to be *drained*. It could be that he could send some divers down there or maybe even drag the lake," said Beatrice.

"At any rate, this is a lead he can't miss," said Meadow. She was already pulling out her phone.

"Except this is all circumstantial," reminded Beatrice.

But Meadow waved her away. "Ramsay?" she said when he picked up. "Listen. I think you need to search the lake somehow. There might be a body down there." She squinted her eyes, listening hard. "What? What's that? Okay." She hung up again. "What do you know? He says they're already on it."

"I guess he's reached a similar conclusion," said Beatrice.

Posy said, "But such a sad one. She really was a *nice* girl."

"It sounds like her only fault was that she might have been too curious. Too observant," said Beatrice, thoughtfully. "How is Ramsay going to search it? I know it's not a huge body of water, but it could be fairly deep. I wouldn't think he would have the resources to search it."

Meadow said, "He's called in some help from the sheriff's office and the state police are assisting, too. It sounded as if they were dredging." She shivered.

Beatrice said to Posy, "You're always so good about making friends with your customers. How much did you know about Vivian? Who were her friends? Did she talk about any specific people?"

Posy said sadly, "I think one of the reasons she was pursuing quilting was because she was trying to *make* friends. She wasn't exactly what I'd call a loner, but she didn't have a lot of people she hung out with, either."

"How about Gwen?" asked Beatrice.

"Gwen? You mean fellow quilter Gwen?" asked Posy. She looked confused. "No, those two weren't what I'd call friends. But then Gwen was older than Vivian. And married, too."

"Maybe they weren't friends. But Vivian did mention Gwen in her journal," said Beatrice.

Meadow said with a sniff, "Probably because Gwen was being unkind in some way. You know how Gwen is. Vivian's entry probably read: *I sure would like Dappled Hills better if Gwen didn't live here.*"

Beatrice said, "I'm wondering how Gwen and Vivian even became acquainted. Gwen didn't ever work at the newspaper, did she?"

Meadow snapped her fingers. "No, *Gwen* wasn't there, but her husband was. Or, rather, her husband was the editor of the newspaper that Vivian wrote for."

Posy's eyes opened wide. "You don't suppose that Vivian and Gwen's husband were involved somehow, do you?"

"Maybe the journal will give me some hints if that's the case. Or maybe Gwen was just jealous that her husband was working with a nice-looking woman like Vivian," said Beatrice.

Meadow said to Posy, "Do you remember if Vivian was dating someone? It seems like an attractive single woman in Dappled Hills wouldn't get very far without someone asking her out. Just so we can maybe get some idea if Gwen was really off-base with her suspicions."

"We don't know that Gwen *was* suspicious. We're just guessing," reminded Beatrice.

Posy said, "I—well, I'm having a hard time remembering. I want to say that either she was seeing someone or else someone was interested in seeing *her.* But I don't think I can quite remember."

Beatrice said, "There's no point in trying to force a memory. Maybe it'll just pop into your head at some point if you mull it over gently." She saw that Posy's sweet face still seemed puckered in concentration, so she changed the subject. "Are you able to make the first meeting tonight?"

Posy smiled. "Yes, and I'm looking forward to it. I love the fabrics that Meadow picked out and the blankets for the preemies are going to end up being so sweet. Did you find the extra materials you were looking for?" she asked Meadow.

"That and some more!" said Meadow ruefully. "I tend to get myself in trouble when I come to the Patchwork Cottage. Well good, I'm glad you can make it. Beatrice, did Piper say anything about being able to come?"

Meadow was sometimes practically an immovable force, but Beatrice knew one thing that she prioritized even over her love of quilting. "She said she wishes she had time for the service project, but she wants to spend some more time with Ash."

Meadow's face softened. "Of course she does. What a dear. And I know Ash loves her for it. It's hard, isn't it, both of them teaching and living in different towns? I'm glad she's going to make plans with him instead." She sighed. "Well, as much as I feel like I could sit here on the sofa all day in the middle of beautiful fabrics, I guess I should go get checked out so that Beatrice and I can head back home."

"If I can extricate myself from the cat," muttered Beatrice.

Chapter Eight

July 8th

Sometimes I wonder if anyone in this town really likes me. It's been harder making friends than I thought it would be. Somehow, I thought in a small town where everyone knew everyone else it would be easy meeting people. It may be easy meeting *them, but it sure isn't easy to establish relationships. Maybe they're just a little suspicious of outsiders, or maybe it's the fact that I've got a different attitude, coming from a big city.*

And then sometimes I wonder if they don't like me because someone is making sure *they don't like me. Gwen is one of them. She's already confronted me because of her own jealousy. She hates that I spend so much time with him and is sure that I've been as bewitched by his blue eyes as she has. I told her we were only friends and she didn't believe a word of it.*

What's more, she's been talking about me. I was walking out of the quilt shop a couple of days ago and saw Gwen looking my way with the meanest expression as she was talking with Ida Calkin. And then, the very next time I saw Ida, she pretended not to see me.

After Beatrice had dropped Meadow back home, she did some light housework and laundry. Then she regretted having done it because she realized she was going back out again for the service project meeting and she really hadn't taken any time to relax. She sighed. At least her house was clean.

Her cell phone rang and Wyatt was on the other end. "Looking forward to the meeting in a little while?" he asked.

"I was just thinking about it," said Beatrice dryly. "Actually, it's been a busy day so I might not have a lot to say at the meeting."

"Sorry. Maybe tonight isn't the best time then," said Wyatt slowly.

"Best time for what?"

"I was thinking that after the meeting, we could spend some time together," he said. "But we don't have to, especially if you're tired out."

Even though Beatrice usually leapt at the chance to spend time with her elusive boyfriend, this time she hesitated. There was part of her that also relished the idea of recharging and spending some time alone. Thinking about her own advice to Piper though, she said quickly, "I'd love to see you. What were you thinking about doing?"

"Whatever you'd like to do," he said pleasantly.

And, although Beatrice knew perfectly well that Wyatt was simply trying to be amiable, the fact that she needed to make a decision didn't make her any more relaxed. Making a split-second choice she said, "How about if you come over here and we can cook supper together?" She rather surprised herself at this, considering she wasn't much of a cook and rarely did a lot of cooking.

"Perfect!" Wyatt said in a happy voice. "Want me to run by the grocery store to pick up some ingredients?"

"No, let's not make things complicated. I'm sure you've had a busy day too." Beatrice's phone beeped at her and she pulled it away from her ear to see who was texting her. As she suspected, it was Miss Sissy. She sighed. "How about if we plan on cooking breakfast for supper? That's always been a favorite of mine. Scrambled eggs, bacon, pancakes, and whatnot."

"Looking forward to it," said Wyatt.

And this time Beatrice realized she agreed with him. It would be the perfect way to close the day.

Beatrice was able to fit in a few minutes of putting her feet up before she walked down the road to the church for the service project meeting. And the walk to the church was rather nice, too. There was a cool breeze and the air was fragrant with some flowering bush or tree. The sun was going down and Beatrice realized there was going to be a full moon later to light up her return walk.

The church's basement activity room was buzzing as the ladies pulled out materials and caught up with each other. The preemie quilts were going to be adorable and Beatrice loved seeing the cheerful fabric colors. Wyatt gave Beatrice a warm smile when she entered the room. Meadow said, "Beatrice! You're here! Listen, I had a great idea on the way over here. Why don't you be in charge of community updating for our service project?"

Beatrice frowned at her. "Community updating? Is that a thing with service projects now?"

"Oh, I just thought it would be a really good way to help get the word out about how active the Village Quilters are," said Meadow with a small shrug as Wyatt joined them.

"But there are other guilds represented here, too," said Beatrice, glancing around the room.

"Hmm. I guess you're right," said Meadow a bit deflated.

"Even better, right?" asked Wyatt lightly. "That way you can play up quilting in the community. It's not an exclusive club. It's for everyone—and it's not just a solo activity. It can be used to really make a difference."

"Has quilting ever been thought of as an exclusive club?" asked Beatrice in a doubtful tone. Then she waved her hand quickly. "Never mind. Long day. It's a great idea, Meadow. I wasn't sure I wanted to take on something else right now, time-wise, but I can probably update our social media. Somehow I didn't even realize we had a presence there."

Meadow flushed a little and Beatrice said quickly, "Wait. You mean ... we *don't* have a presence there?"

"It'll be easy as pie to set it up, Beatrice," said Meadow enthusiastically. "And you know how good you are with that stuff from your time in Atlanta. Promoting the gallery."

"Museum," said Beatrice faintly. Her quiet retirement definitely remained elusive. She was thinking of ways to mount a suitable defense when the meeting abruptly came to order.

After Wyatt said a few words thanking them for coming and for their time and explained a bit about how the project had come to be and who it served, Meadow stood up. She explained the pattern they'd be working with, handed it out, and showed some of the fabric and supplies that she'd picked up.

"But these are just guidelines, of course. Well, not with the pattern, but the fabric. And Posy has offered to give our group a lovely discount since this project is all in the name of service to others!" said Meadow, beaming. There was a round of applause from the collected quilters and then Meadow added. "Now I want Beatrice to stand up and tell us a little about how she's getting the word out on social media about our good deeds and other activities."

Beatrice shot her a look, which Meadow completely missed the point of. Or maybe Meadow was just deliberately playing dumb. She knew, after all, that the best way of cementing something was to announce it at a meeting.

Beatrice slowly stood up and gave a short smile to the gathered women. "Unfortunately, since I've just—taken on—this responsibility, I don't have a lot to say about it yet. I did do something similar at the craft museum in Atlanta that I worked for. The idea is to show that quilters are not just creating amazing art in a solo environment, but that it's a way to collectively enjoy ourselves too, through service to others, gatherings, and guild meetings."

There was another burst of enthusiastic applause. As Beatrice took her seat again, she took the opportunity to glance around her at the other women. There were mostly people that she knew very well there—Savannah and Georgia both gave her a small wave, Posy was there, of course. But there were also women who were part of the other quilting guild in Dappled Hills, the Cut-

Ups, and some who didn't appear to be part of a current guild and were reaching out for this particular project.

There was one quilter who looked particularly sour and hadn't really been very quick to applaud. Judging from what others had said, Beatrice wondered if she might be Gwen. It was also someone who asked a good number of questions, even asking about things that had already been explained previously. From what Beatrice had gathered, this sounded like something Gwen would do.

After all the information had been given, questions asked and answered and the pattern discussed, Wyatt gave a short devotion about how service benefits the volunteer.

After the meeting was finished, Wyatt was chatting with some of the quilters who were leaving, which suited Beatrice fine since she wanted the chance to speak to Gwen before she disappeared. And disappearing seemed to be what Gwen had in mind as she gathered up her things and looked purposefully at the door, unfettered by anyone wanting to talk to her. She was perhaps in her late sixties with a somewhat dumpy appearance that wasn't helped by the shapeless cotton pants and bright purple tunic she wore.

To waylay her, Beatrice did the only thing that popped into her head. She promptly dropped everything in her hands directly in front of Gwen. "Mercy!" said Beatrice, hand to her chest in a gesture that was perhaps too dramatic, "Why am I so clumsy today?"

Gwen sighed with gusto and bent to assist Beatrice. Meadow winked at Beatrice and left her conversation with Savannah and Georgia to join Beatrice.

"Gwen, have you met Beatrice?" asked Meadow in a jolly voice.

Gwen, thrusting Beatrice's papers and purse at her, gave Meadow a rather sour look. "Don't remember," she muttered.

"I don't think I've had the pleasure," said Beatrice brightly. She put out her hand and Gwen gave her a limp handshake in return.

"I should be going," murmured Gwen.

But Meadow was continuing as if Gwen hadn't spoken at all. "Isn't it nice that Beatrice is going to help us to put the word out about quilting in Dappled Hills? You and I have been quilting for so many years here that it sure would be nice to see some fresh faces, wouldn't it?"

Gwen furrowed her brow as if she wasn't at all sure that it would be nice. As if, maybe, she would rather not even see some of the old faces.

"Speaking of having been in Dappled Hills for a while," said Meadow, making quite the conversational leap, "It seems a name from the past keeps appearing?"

Gwen blinked several times before maintaining her rather truculent expression with some effort. She didn't give Meadow any sign of curiosity.

Meadow continued, "Do you remember Vivian Hastings?"

There was a flicker in Gwen's eyes, but she stayed silent.

"It was a long time ago when she was in Dappled Hills. Forty years ago—can you believe it? But it was at a time when we didn't have a lot of people who were new to the town, so she would have stood out." Meadow chuckled. "She would have stood out anyway, since she had red hair."

Gwen pursed her lips for a second and then said in a clipped voice, "I don't say that I do remember. But my memory isn't very good."

Beatrice injected smoothly, "What about Oscar Holland? Do you remember him?"

A telling bit of red crept up from Gwen's purple collar. "Who? Was he also someone who lived here a long time ago?"

"No. He's someone who was visiting here recently. Until he was killed. You couldn't miss him. He looked like an explorer.

Tall, thin, had a beard? Wore a khaki jacket and a brimmed hat?" asked Beatrice.

Gwen shook her head quickly, but she didn't look at Beatrice.

"Are you sure?" pushed Beatrice softly. "Are you sure that he didn't knock on your door and ask you a bunch of questions about Vivian? Someone mentioned he was at your house."

Gwen glanced furtively around her as if the entire group of service-oriented quilters were giving her the third degree. Satisfied that no one else was listening, she whispered furiously, "I've already talked to Ramsay and his group of policemen. I understood that he was being professional and keeping this *quiet*."

Meadow said quickly, "Oh, Ramsay has nothing to do with this. You see, I *do* have an excellent memory and I recall that you were friends with Vivian back then. So it's only natural we should ask you what you remember."

Beatrice hoped that Meadow had her fingers crossed as she fibbed.

"Friends with Vivian?" scoffed Gwen. "Your memory clearly stinks. I said the same thing to that man." She stopped abruptly, looking irritated with herself for having acknowledged Oscar.

Meadow said in a chatty voice, "Well, you know, Vivian and I weren't really friends either. Not that I had anything *against* Vivian. It's just that it was a very busy time for me then. I was engaged to Ramsay and planning a wedding is *so* time-consuming. Do you remember how time-consuming it was?"

Gwen's face was grim. "I don't think back on my wedding planning or marriage with any warm, fuzzy feelings."

Meadow looked momentarily startled before quickly moving on. "Still, who knows? Maybe I wouldn't have even been friends with Vivian if I *had* had the time to get to know her. What made you upset with her?"

Gwen took a deep breath as if she were hanging onto her patience by a thread. "What upset me was her complete and utter lack of morality." Her lips tightened into a stern line.

Beatrice asked, "Can you be more specific than that?"

"I don't want to talk about it," snarled Gwen.

Wyatt was free from chatting with the quilters and was moving in their direction. Beatrice said in a rush, "If you're not willing to talk about what *you've* got against her, can you speak on who else might not have liked Vivian?"

Gwen pulled the strap of her purse up onto her shoulder. "Jake had good reason to dislike her," she said in a catty tone.

"Jake? Jake who?" asked Beatrice desperately.

"Jake Hunter," said Gwen before pushing past them and resolutely heading up the stairs to exit the church.

Meadow and Beatrice stared at each other for a second. "You'll have to fill me in on that marriage," said Beatrice under her breath.

Wyatt joined them and said brightly to Beatrice, "Ready to go eat?"

Beatrice was relieved that Wyatt had been in cooking mode when they arrived at her house. She mainly watched as he put together an omelet and flipped pancakes. She filled him in on her conversation with Gwen.

Wyatt gave her a sympathetic glance as she set the table for them. "Gwen can be a difficult person sometimes," he said. "Although I believe beneath that gruff exterior is really a loving person with a heart of gold."

Beatrice said, "Well, she certainly hides it well. And I do think that you tend to think the best of everyone."

Wyatt smiled at her. "Not as much as you think. But I might know more about the behind-the-scenes people in the community, including Gwen. Sometimes their public faces are different from their private ones. Take Gwen, for instance. She was at a service project meeting for the sole purpose of doing good. She doesn't particularly enjoy being around other people."

"I noticed," said Beatrice dryly.

"So her only motivation was to do something nice for someone else."

Beatrice said, "Have you got any insight on her marriage? She seemed not to want to talk about it."

"I can't talk about anything I know through my pastoral care. But it might be enough for you to know that she and her husband divorced many years ago. He's passed away now, as a matter of fact. But that's all public knowledge," said Wyatt, carefully putting the omelets, bacon, and pancakes on plates for them.

Beatrice wasn't sure that she bought this generous portrait of Gwen, but decided to give herself some time to digest the idea. And time to take a few bites of Wyatt's meal. The omelet and pancakes were perfectly fluffy and the bacon was just the crispiness she preferred.

"This is delicious," she said, smiling at him.

"Thanks. I enjoy cooking, I just don't get a lot of opportunity to experiment as much as I'd like." He took a sip of his wine and then said, "I'm trying to remember everything I knew about Vivian Hastings. It's been a while. Ramsay was asking me to try and come up with small details."

Beatrice raised her eyebrows. "Does this mean that he thinks Vivian has met up with foul play? After all, I hear that he's planning on dredging the lake."

"At least he thinks it's an option, I suppose. Maybe his efforts to locate Vivian weren't fruitful. All I could remember were personality traits. I can't recall any specific reasons why she might have been or felt threatened in any way."

"What were her personality traits?" asked Beatrice.

"She was nice. I liked her," said Wyatt. "But I could also see where her appearance in town could have been jarring to some people. She wasn't used to the pace of life here. She was brisk and forward. She said what she thought in an open way that was likely off-putting to some residents. I could tell that she was having a hard time fitting in here and so I invited her to come to church."

Beatrice polished off her pancakes. "How did that go?"

"Vivian seemed to me to be fitting in all right," he said slowly. "I'd encouraged her to not just attend services, but to attend some smaller groups like Bible study and Sunday school. I'd thought that she was starting to make connections with people."

"Maybe she was," said Beatrice. "But maybe they weren't good ones."

Chapter Nine

Jake is starting to be another problem. He's not a bad guy, of course. He's got a fun sense of humor, even if it can border on goofy sometimes. He makes me laugh—a good thing because lately I could use some laughter.

But what he doesn't seem to understand is that I need a friend. I've tried to hint that I'd love to go out with him ... as a friend. I always see a flash of hurt in his eyes before he resolutely continues on just as flirty as before. I guess I'm just going to have to make it clearer to him.

Beatrice called Meadow first thing the next morning. Meadow had apparently been sleeping in.

"Sorry," said Meadow, yawning. "It was a disruptive night last night."

Beatrice frowned. "Were there any more developments last night? Did Ramsay come and go?"

"Oh, gosh, I forgot to tell you, which is hard to believe. But then, I guess I didn't find out about it until much later, when Ramsay checked in with me."

Beatrice kept her impatience in check with difficulty. "Find out about what?"

"While we were having our service project meeting, Ramsay's team discovered a body in the lake. It was weighted down with bricks. So sad," said Meadow. "I guess that's why her body never came to light, even when we had a drought. Because the lake got pretty low during the droughts, you know."

"The body was Vivian's?" asked Beatrice, suddenly feeling breathless.

"We're guessing. But there will have to be confirmation on that. Her dental records are still at the dentist's downtown, so it should be easy to check out. That dentist has been here for a million years. Anyway, it was probably after ten o'clock when Ramsay finally got back home and told me. It just stuck in my brain and I couldn't fall asleep to save my life. Just kept tossing and turning."

"What's he doing now?" asked Beatrice. "Is he contacting Vivian's relatives?"

"The whole thing is sort of sad. She really didn't have any relatives. She had an elderly aunt that she was close to, but the aunt passed away before she moved to Dappled Hills. I guess that's why the murderer was so lucky. No one reported her missing. No one missed her birthday or Christmas phone call, or insisted on checking in with the police at her last address. We all thought she'd gotten tired of the town and left, and she was here all the while," said Meadow.

She sounded like she was getting choked up. Beatrice said quickly, to keep her from breaking down totally, "It was foul play, though? At least, that's what the police are thinking so far?"

"That's right. Her skull was fractured and that appears to be the cause of death. So it wasn't as if she went for a dip in the lake and accidentally drowned." A gusty sigh on Meadow's end.

Beatrice said, "I'm sorry, Meadow. I know it's hard to think that someone here in town could do something like that. Let's stay focused on finding out who might be behind it all. I was reading more of Vivian's journal entries. The next person on our list to talk to should be Jake Hunter."

"Sounds good. Let's do it after breakfast," said Meadow. "Although we can't use our quilting history premise to talk to him. He's got nothing to do with quilting."

"Uh-oh. Then how are we going to be inconspicuous and still have a chance to ask a few questions?" asked Beatrice.

"He's the baker downtown. We could go get our breakfast down there and then ask him a few questions during a quiet period. Shouldn't be too hard."

Beatrice said, "I'll pick you up in thirty minutes."

The bakery was right in the heart of downtown Dappled Hills. It was in an old stone building with two tables and café chairs outside. A customer opened the door as Meadow and Beatrice were outside and Beatrice took in a deep, appreciative breath. It smelled of fresh-baked pastries, muffins, and breads.

Jake Hunter had apparently decided to take the old world approach to being a baker. He had a white, double-breasted chef coat and white pants, over which he wore an apron. You could barely see a few strands of still-blond hair under his white chef toque. He had a dimple and dancing blue eyes. He gave a jaunty greeting as they entered. "Hi, ladies! Know what you want?"

Meadow said with a smile, "Hi Jake! We'll browse for a minute, thanks."

"You can go ahead and browse," murmured Beatrice, "I think those blueberry muffins are calling my name."

Meadow said, "I'm overwhelmed by all the choices. Somebody pick for me."

Jake just smiled politely so Beatrice stepped in. "Why not have the banana nut muffins? Then you and I can mix and match."

"Perfect!" said Meadow, looking relieved.

"Are you taking these home or eating in?" asked Jake as a group of women walked in the door.

"Eating in. Definitely," said Beatrice. "And can we also get a carafe of coffee?" Because it was starting to look like it was going to be a while before they would get a chance to talk to him.

"Isn't he adorable?" asked Meadow under her breath.

Meadow and Beatrice decided to sit inside by the front window. Everything in the bakery was spotlessly clean, including the large plate glass window with "Jake Bakes!" on the glass and the pristine white tablecloths. Beatrice was sure she was going to dribble coffee or crumbs on theirs. But then, as neat as everything was, Jake would likely swoop down and fix the problem with a clean tablecloth.

The group of women didn't appear to be in any hurry, so Meadow and Beatrice slowly ate.

"Ash said he loved seeing Piper last night," said Meadow, looking pleased herself. "It's too bad that she isn't doing the service project, but I love that she's spending more time with Ash."

"I'm glad they had the chance to catch up," said Beatrice. "It's not easy with both of them teaching."

Suddenly both Beatrice's and Meadow's cell phones went off. They looked at each other and shook their heads. Beatrice reached out and glanced at it. "Apparently, she's figured out how to use emojis." She showed Meadow the screen, which had a long line of smiley faces, frowney faces, and devil faces with horns.

"Nice," said Meadow with a sigh. "At least last night she didn't send a text in the middle of the night like she did a couple of nights ago. That was going to get old."

Finally the women left, toting their baked goods. Jake came by Beatrice's and Meadow's table to check on them. "How are you ladies doing?"

"Fine, Jake. Everything is delicious, as usual. Do you know Beatrice Coleman?" asked Meadow, waving a hand in her direction.

He reached out a hand a flashed a really charming smile at her, showing off his still-excellent teeth. "Pleasure to meet you," he said.

It seemed like flirting might come second nature to him—as if he didn't think a lot about it. But he was definitely one of those people that you didn't mind having flirt with you. He had a certain charisma that was difficult to resist.

Meadow was blinking in the force of his smile, so Beatrice took over the conversation from there. It was going to be more of a clumsy interview, but that's because they might not have enough time to slowly develop the questions in a more natural way. She took a deep breath and plunged right in. "I haven't met you yet, so this is a pleasure. Although I've heard of you. I've been doing some work into the history of Dappled Hills on a project that Meadow and I are doing and your name has come up."

He raised his eyebrows until they almost shot up into his chef's hat. "That makes me sad that I'm showing up in ancient historical documents."

"Well, you have to delve into nearly everything when you're working with history. This isn't *that* long ago, though, if it makes you feel better. It's forty years ago, actually," said Beatrice, leading into the topic cautiously.

Jake immediately reacted, though. His peaches and cream complexion blanched. "Vivian," he said softly.

His reaction was so immediate and so extreme that Beatrice and Meadow glanced at each other in alarm. Meadow reached out a hand to Jake, laying it on his arm. "Why don't you sit down for a minute," she murmured.

It was a good thing she did, because Jake looked weak on his feet. Beatrice said, "I've asked several people about Vivian and you're the first one to even directly admit that you remember her."

Jake nodded, looking at the still-pristine tablecloth as if trying to gather up his strength. "Oh, I remember her. Still miss her to this day. I still feel as if she's my soulmate." He sat up straight in the café chair and put his hand in this jacket pocket. He pulled out what looked to be a laminated picture of an attractive young woman with luxurious red hair and a grinning younger version of himself.

This was the first time that Beatrice had seen a picture of Vivian. Seeing her as she was when she was a vibrant young woman made her come to life and made her murder more real.

Meadow leaned over Beatrice to look at the picture, too. When she saw it, she gave a small sob. "So sad!" she said, nearly knocking over her cup of coffee to grab her purse for a tissue.

Jake was looking intently at her. "You remember her, too?" he asked intently.

Meadow nodded. "At first I couldn't remember very much. That's because I was planning my wedding. You know how much goes into planning a wedding? Especially a wedding on a low budget. But seeing her face, it brings it all back to me." She blew her nose loudly.

Jake said sadly, "I wanted to be planning *our* wedding then."

This had the unfortunate effect of making Meadow cry even harder than before. Beatrice contributed to her tissue fund by handing over an entire travel pack to her. She said to Jake, "You and Vivian were sweethearts?" It was an old-fashioned word, but seemed to fit the wistfulness she saw on Jake's face.

"I wanted to be. More than anything," he said in a heavy tone. "But apparently, it wasn't to be. Vivian and I had such a great time together, but she was determined to keep our relationship friendly."

Meadow, turning blotchy from the crying, said, "She was just *too* sweet. So interested in quilting. And she had a little stray kitten that she'd rescued. She loved that little thing so much."

"Mittens," said Jake with a reminiscent smile.

Meadow boo-hooed in earnest.

Beatrice wanted to try and plumb Meadow's memories more later on. At this point, it seemed like it would be more useful to try and learn more from Jake while they had the opportunity. "Was she dating someone else, maybe, then?"

A flash of hurt crossed Jake's face, but then he regained his composure quickly. "I don't think there was anyone special. Of course, plenty of people would have *liked* to have dated Vivian. As you can tell from her picture, she was absolutely beautiful—both inside and out."

Meadow said, "She wasn't dating *Huey* then, was she?"

Jake's eyes shuttered. "Huey was way too old for her. And engaged." He looked out the window as if somehow still waiting for Vivian to come through the bakery door. "I've never gotten over the loss."

"The loss?" asked Beatrice quickly. Meadow sopped up the rest of her tears and listened intently. Did Jake know that Vivian was at the bottom of the lake?

"That's right," he said, a slightly puzzled expression on his face. "She got sick of Dappled Hills. Oh, it's hard for those of us who've lived here and loved the town to believe it, but that's the way she felt. It can be tough for new residents to get used to living here. And, maybe, for others here to accept them. It's a close-knit group."

"So you think that Vivian eventually just decided to move away?" asked Beatrice slowly. "But didn't she leave her things here behind her?"

Jake looked curious. "No. That is ... yes, in a way. She did take some things with her and then left behind the things that she didn't care about or that didn't matter. That would include me, in a way," he said a touch bitterly. "But she also left a typewritten note for whomever might be looking for her ... saying that she had left for better things. Something like that. I've never stopped looking for her online."

Beatrice and Meadow looked at each other. Should they broach this topic? How could they bring it up in a gentle way?

Meadow still had her hand on Jake's arm when she said quietly, "There's a tragedy you need to know about, then. Ramsay just learned. Vivian never did leave town. She was murdered."

Jake's face was a mask of shock. "What?" he asked, numbly.

Beatrice said, "Someone murdered Vivian. Her body has been concealed for years and only just discovered now."

"But why now?" asked Jake, holding his hands out, palm up, beseeching them. "Why would Ramsay discover her? Why would you be asking questions about her? It's been decades."

"It's because of a man—a stranger—who came to town and was asking questions," said Beatrice, watching him closely.

He betrayed nothing on his face but grief, though. "The man who died? The one they found in the woods?"

Meadow said, "That Beatrice and I found, yes. He came to town for the express purpose of asking questions about Vivian. Until he was murdered."

Beatrice said delicately, "I don't suppose he came to speak to you? It sounded like he was speaking to everyone who knew Vivian." Or, at least, anyone who had a strong reaction to Vivian—either positive or negative. Because those were the only ones listed in her journal.

Jake's expression was unreadable as he said firmly, "I only saw him when I was out a few days ago. He was at Ida Calkin's door, talking to her. I made a mental note to myself that there might be solicitors out and I should peek out before opening the door. That's all."

"Are you able to leave the shop?" asked Beatrice, lifting her eyebrows in surprise.

He looked at her silently for a minute before cautiously saying, "I can. But I don't often."

"Do you have someone to watch the shop for you while you're out?" asked Beatrice.

"I just put a *back soon* sign up. It's the kind that has a clock with arms where you can show the time you plan on being back," said Jake.

Beatrice thought wistfully that she would have loved to be able to use such a device in Atlanta when she'd been alone at the museum. It wouldn't have gone over as well with patrons as it apparently did with Jake's customers at the bakery.

"Were you out a couple of afternoons ago?" asked Beatrice, trying to sound offhand about it.

Jake's eyes were wary, though. "Was that when that guy was killed? No. That was a very busy day here. I was at the shop all day long. Had a couple of birthday cakes to make."

Which were presumably made in the back of the shop. Where no one could corroborate if he was there or not.

"Why do you think the man was talking with Ida?" asked Meadow curiously.

Jake said brusquely, "I told you—I thought he was a door to door salesman or something."

"No, I mean, what do you *think* he was doing now that you *know* what he was doing?" asked Meadow in her usually convoluted way.

Jake shrugged. "If he was asking questions of people who knew Vivian, I guess he was asking Ida about the accident. You'd remember that, Meadow. Ida couldn't seem to get over the fact that it was an *accident*. It wasn't a matter for the courts. Ida's sister should have been wearing a seatbelt. Vivian wasn't under the influence, wasn't speeding, and wasn't driving recklessly. It was an *accident*. And, if I were looking at people who might have something to do with Vivian's death," he swallowed hard at the word *death*, "then I might logically want to start with Ida. She held quite the grudge against Viv."

Chapter Ten

More customers came in the bakery and Jake left their table with a relieved expression on his face. As Beatrice and Meadow walked out, Beatrice intoned, "All roads lead to Ida."

"It certainly appears that way," said Meadow. "Are we heading that way, then? Here, pull out your phone and let's see what Vivian has to say about Ida before we go."

Beatrice obediently pulled up the journal entry involving Ida.

July 9ᵗʰ

Of course, one reason no one may like me is because of the accident. That accident still haunts me so much that I can't stand to write about it. I would never have wanted anything to happen to my new friend. Never. I wish I'd made her wear a seatbelt ... she just hated them so. And I wish that deer, bounding out in front of my car, hadn't startled me the way it did. I guess I'm too much of a city girl still. I couldn't sleep, couldn't eat for weeks after it happened. My doctor recommended that I start a journal as a way to not only practice my journalism skills, but also as therapy in a way.

She was my only friend here—a new friend, but still ... a friend. Ida, of course, blames me. I can see the hatred in her eyes. It makes me feel like I must watch my back at all times.

Meadow said, "Poor Vivian. Clearly, it was just a horrible accident. Even the police didn't press any charges, which they certainly would've if they thought it was some sort of vehicular manslaughter. I guess Ida just never got over it."

"Ida and her sister were very close?" Beatrice asked.

"Yes. Although there was a huge age difference, as I recall. I think Ida might have been more like a mother to Fiona."

"Sure," said Beatrice. "Sounds like an easy set-up. What's she like, by the way? I've met her a few times, but I don't know her."

"Oh, she's very nice. Sweet old lady. The kind with twinkling blue eyes and cookies constantly coming out of the oven," said Meadow as they got into the car. "Although the way she thinks of herself as matriarch of Dappled Hills annoys me."

"That's all I need. More baked goods. Maybe we should walk to Ida's house on second thought," said Beatrice.

"We can if you want to. It's a beautiful day. Let's just leave the car here and walk back to it later on," suggested Meadow. "It's not that far of a walk."

Perhaps Meadow was remembering that Ida's house wasn't so far of a *drive*. Because it was over four miles later up steep hills that they finally arrived at the old woman's gingerbread style house, which was surrounded by dense woods.

Meadow was huffing and puffing and Beatrice was rather breathless herself. "It didn't seem that far away," gasped Meadow.

"Never mind," said Beatrice. "We probably could use the exercise after all the muffins this morning."

"Then we double it on the way back," moaned Meadow. "And I just realized you don't have your fancy camera with you. We won't look very convincing."

"I think we'll be fine. As far as Ida knows, my cell phone has the best camera around. That's what we'll tell her, anyway."

Meadow said, "I wouldn't bet on it. If even Miss Sissy is now technologically advanced, who knows how far along Ida might be?"

At first glance, the gingerbread house was a confection from a fairytale. On closer inspection, however, there was quite a bit of chipping paint, and some floorboards on the verandah looked as though they could prove dangerous. There was a menacing thicket of thorny bushes waving at them on the side of the verandah. The thorn bushes were nearly as scary as Miss Sissy's.

Meadow noticed, too. "Maybe Ida has fallen on bad times," she said in her stage whisper that could probably be heard back at the bakery.

Beatrice saw a flutter of lacy curtains in a downstairs window. "Shh! She's right there."

Meadow immediately rang the button of a doorbell.

And no one came.

Meadow stared at Beatrice. "You saw her, right?"

"Perhaps she thinks we're trying to sell her something and doesn't want the embarrassment of telling us no," murmured Beatrice. "Understandable. We should have phoned first."

Meadow wasn't one for giving up, though. She decided that the bell must be malfunctioning and tried knocking on the door instead. Or, rather, pounding. "Ida!" she hollered. "It's Meadow Downey. I want to feature you in a quilting book!"

"She's not deaf, is she?" asked Beatrice, wincing at the pounding.

"Who knows? It's been a while since I've talked to her. A lot can go wrong with a person in a short period of time at our age, you know." She put her head even closer to the door, bellowing, "A quilting book, Ida! You! In the *book*!"

"She's going to think you've been drinking in the middle of the day," hissed Beatrice.

But whatever the reason, Ida did open the door. And, perhaps, one *could* consider her a sweet little old lady. She had the appropriate crocheted shawl, likely created by Ida herself. She had the bright blue inquisitive eyes. She wore the slightly faded floral dress with a pair of sensible orthopedic shoes. Although she could only be a few years older than Beatrice and Meadow, she had the part of being the storybook old woman down pat. Still, though, there was something in those blue eyes that wasn't quite so inquisitive. The dull gaze she turned on Beatrice was indicative of *something*. Beatrice just wasn't sure what it was.

Meadow made a hurried introduction. "You know Beatrice, don't you, Ida? Um ... may we come in? We stupidly walked here and I for one am completely exhausted now."

"Oh dear," said Ida automatically and without much inflection in her voice. "Yes, of course. Come on inside."

She led them into a dim interior with peeling interior paint, some weathered furniture, and creaky floors and past an old cat in a sunbeam who gave them a scathing look. Meadow raised her eyebrows at Beatrice. The only decorations in the whole place were quilts. Quilts were either hung or draped everywhere. There were also some old photos in dusty frames that were scattered about on equally dusty tables.

"I suppose you'll be wanting something to drink?" asked Ida stiffly.

Meadow said in a meek voice, "It would be nice. If you have something."

"I've got water. I just don't have ice," said Ida. She left them in the dim living room as she headed to the back of her house, presumably to her kitchen.

Beatrice lifted her eyebrows at Meadow and Meadow shrugged. "I guess she's not one to appreciate the unexpected visit."

"Perhaps," said Beatrice, "there's more of an art to the unexpected visit. Perhaps we should have brought something with us from the bakery. Because the air here certainly isn't permeated with the scent of freshly baked goods."

"I guess she's been under the weather. Or something," said Meadow with a frown as she considered the matter. "I'm trying to remember the last time I saw her. I believe it was at the church picnic. She seemed like her usual, jolly self at that point."

"That was only a few weeks ago. Maybe she's just in a bad mood. Or maybe," Beatrice said archly, "she's in a bad mood because of Oscar Holland poking into her past."

Ida returned with the two waters which she sat on a rickety coffee table in front of the equally rickety sofa they were perched on. Beatrice and Meadow were just about to take a sip when Ida quickly said, "Now then. What exactly is all this about a quilting book?"

Meadow greedily gulped down a few sips before explaining what they were trying to accomplish with the quilting history. Ida didn't want any pictures taken of herself, but she certainly had ideas about which quilts she might want to have featured. Beatrice found herself taking numerous photos. She also found that Ida was quite the control freak and demanded to see each picture that Beatrice took, telling her which ones she wanted redone. Beatrice felt like she was an actress in a bad Hollywood movie with a demented director.

Meadow tilted her head to one side, considering the photo shoot. "Don't you see how it will be more effective, more appealing, with *you* in at least one of the pictures, Ida? It's good to have a human element. You can take the time to change or spruce up, if you want to. Beatrice and I have all the time in the world."

Beatrice gave Meadow a sour look, which Meadow studiously ignored.

Ida looked doubtfully down at her faded floral dress and the sensible shoes. She put a hand up to her white hair which certainly hadn't been combed either that day or probably the last few. "Do you think so?" she asked.

Meadow beamed at her. "Absolutely! It'll be darling. We'll wait."

As Ida disappeared upstairs, Beatrice settled in more comfortably on the groaning sofa. "I better make this water last. I have a feeling this is going to take a while."

Surprisingly, however, it didn't. Ida returned wearing an old, but still serviceable pair of black slacks and a stiffly starched white blouse. Her white hair was pulled severely back in a bun. But, overall, she looked so much better than she had minutes ago that Beatrice blinked.

Beatrice said, "You look wonderful, Ida." And she meant it. It was quite the transformation in a short period of time. And maybe this was a lesson to Beatrice to keep her appearance in mind, even on those days when she'd rather not. Which was nearly every day.

The compliment, which Meadow immediately echoed, brought the twinkle back to Ida's eyes. The next few photos that Beatrice took, in a couple of different rooms, were much better than the first. Especially since she opened the blinds and curtains to bring in even more daylight for the pictures. She figured the grouchy cat in the other room would thank her if she could. And Ida's general temperament had improved and she was no longer trying to direct every picture that Beatrice took.

After ten more minutes, they were finished. It was definitely time to work in questions about Oscar and Vivian while Ida's guard was down. The trick was to work them in naturally so that she wouldn't immediately put a wall back up.

Meadow started heading in that general direction. "You know, working on this history had reminded me of so many things, Ida. It made me realize how much I've seen and experienced in this small town over the years. Sometimes people think that nothing happens in a small town, but I'd beg to differ."

Ida gave her a faint smile and nodded.

Beatrice cleared her throat and took her cue. "Meadow's been good to fill me in on a lot of the things that happened. It's tricky, of course, for me to help out on a history when I've so recently moved to Dappled Hills."

"Yes," said Ida with amusement, "how did you get roped into doing that?"

"Just luck, I guess," said Beatrice, making a face. "Actually, my part has mainly been photography since I used to do a good deal of it for my job back in Atlanta. One thing I've noticed as Meadow has filled me in on the history is, it has a way of reaching from the past and impacting the future."

Ida was listening closely now, no longer nodding in agreement. But she definitely had Ida's attention. It was almost as if she knew what was coming.

So Beatrice took a deep breath and plunged right in. "One interesting tale I came across was the disappearance and reappearance of Vivian Hastings."

Now the corner of Ida's mouth turned down in a sneer. There was no pretense here that Ida didn't know who Beatrice was talking about.

"What do you mean by *re*appearance?" asked Ida after a moment. "Couldn't have reappeared."

"I meant only that Ramsay unfortunately discovered her remains in the lake," said Beatrice. "Why do you think she *couldn't* have reappeared? Did you know that she was dead all along?"

But Ida, the twinkle now long gone, stared stony-faced at her. She silently shook her head. "I was merely thinking that Vivian certainly wouldn't return to a town that she disliked forty years ago. She wouldn't have any fond memories. Why would she bother?"

Meadow said gently, "As I remember, you had reasons to dislike Vivian. One of the reasons had to do with that picture over there, doesn't it?"

Now Ida's eyes flashed in fury. It was almost like the grudge she carried was as fresh now as it was then. "Vivian killed my little sister, Fiona. So, no, I don't have any reason to mourn her. But I had no idea that she was dead. I figured she was so unhappy in town that she simply decided to leave." She paused. "Why did Ramsay think she was in the lake?"

Beatrice said, "It has to do with another recent death. The death of a man named Oscar Holland."

Ida muttered under her breath, repeating the man's name to herself as if to jog her memory. "I give up. Who's Oscar Holland?"

Beatrice affected a look of surprise. "Oh, I thought you'd know him for sure. Everyone says he came by your house to talk to you the other day."

A blotchy flush crawled up the side of Ida's neck. "Everyone sure seems to know a lot about my business," she snapped. "I suppose I did have a visit from him. I didn't know his name. If he was a young fella wearing a safari hat and a khaki vest. He was most insistent in his nature. Yes, I do remember him."

Beatrice and Meadow both found themselves leaning forward slightly. "What did he want? What did he ask you?" Were they finally going to get some answers on this question?

"Very impertinent," she said. "Almost as if *I* were at fault in some way or as if I had a secret of some kind." The flush was more prominent on her neck.

Beatrice and Meadow just waited, allowing her to tell the story her own way.

"He asked me if I had been angry with Vivian. If I had any idea what happened to her when she left town. Of if I knew if she *hadn't* left town. He also asked me about other people in town and if I knew them and if I thought *they* were angry with Vivian, too." She snorted. "Clearly, he didn't come from a small town if he asked whether I knew the other people or not."

Beatrice said, "And you told him about your sister?"

Ida gave her a sharp look. "It's no secret that I found Vivian at fault in a crash that took away someone who was very dear to me. I never married, never had children of my own—only the schoolkids I taught. My little sister was as important to me as if she had been my own daughter."

Meadow said in a curious voice, "How did you treat Vivian after the car accident? I mean, did you approach her in private about it?"

"Now you sound like the young man!" said Ida. "He asked something similar, so I'll tell you what I told him. As soon as I saw Vivian out shopping in town after the accident, not a scratch on her, I told her exactly what I thought of her. I didn't think I could live in the same small town with her and not give her a piece of my mind. They say that keeping anger bottled up in you can kill you over time. I simply let that anger out."

"What did Vivian say?" asked Meadow. "I'm sure she was mortified. You ranted at her? In the middle of downtown?"

Ida could easily hear the censure dripping from Meadow's voice. She drew herself up tall in her chair. "Did it matter? I felt like maybe she was one of those people who was always able to get away with things her whole life. Never held accountable. It wasn't as if I put her in a public stockade in the middle of the town. I just told her off. That's it."

Beatrice said, "How long did Oscar stay here asking you questions?"

"Not nearly as long as you are," observed Ida dryly.

"But we're not here to ask you questions. We're here for the Dappled Hills history," said Meadow.

"Whatever you say," said Ida.

"Did he mention anyone else he was going to see?" asked Beatrice.

"We weren't exactly having a pleasant chat. He wasn't going to give me an itinerary. And before you ask, I had nothing to do with his death. Why would I? I was here at home, like I usually am."

Meadow jumped in, "How do you know exactly when he died? We didn't give any specifics."

"I know because your husband has already been by asking questions," said Ida, looking at Meadow sideways. "I've been quizzed and quizzed on this thing."

"But you don't know anything," said Beatrice.

"Don't I?" said Ida scornfully. "I guess that's for me to know and for you to find out."

Chapter Eleven

"What a fun person," said Beatrice as she and Meadow left for the long trudge home.

"And she didn't even offer to drive us back," said Meadow a bit huffily. "And I dropped plenty of hints."

"You did everything but order her to drive us back," agreed Beatrice.

Both Beatrice and Meadow's cell phones started buzzing and ringing at them.

"I declare, Miss Sissy is going to be the death of me!" said Meadow, fishing out her phone from her large pocketbook. "I have half a mind not to even look at the message."

"Which, of course, would be the one time that she actually does need us for something," said Beatrice.

Meadow stopped in place on the sidewalk as she opened the message. "This one sounds dire."

"Don't they all?"

"This one simply says *help*," said Meadow. Her brow wrinkled in concern.

Beatrice groaned. "I don't think that I could possibly sprint over to Miss Sissy's. I may barely be able to make it at ambling speed."

"It's okay," said Meadow, peering closely at the phone. "She copied Ramsay on this one and I see that he's already sent her a message back."

"Just to be sure, let's head to her house before we go back to ours. I was planning on checking in with her today anyway," said Beatrice. "And not only to see how she's feeling. I wanted to fill her in on our investigation and see if she has anything to contribute about any of the people we spoke with."

"Or maybe it will jog her memory," said Meadow brightly. "It sure has mine."

It took a while for them to reach Miss Sissy's house and both were out of breath by the time they got there.

"Yet another house where cold drinks are likely not to be in residence," muttered Beatrice as she tapped lightly at Miss Sissy's front door.

"Oh, let's just go in," said Meadow. "The door is ajar and Ramsay's car is still out front. Maybe I can at least get us some tap water."

There was actually a good deal of activity going on inside. For one thing, June Bug Frost, a quilter, housekeeper, and cake-maker to boot, was busily sweeping the sloping hardwood floor of the living room while Miss Sissy snarled at her.

Ramsay, sitting across from Miss Sissy on a precariously creaking sofa, glanced up when the two women came in. He gave a gusty sigh of relief and stood up. While Miss Sissy barked orders at the apparently oblivious June Bug, Ramsay said quietly to Beatrice and Meadow, "I've never been happier to see you two. Miss Sissy is in quite a state."

"Did something else happen?" asked Beatrice.

"It better not have!" said Meadow darkly. "No one needs to mess with Miss Sissy twice!"

"No one messed with her *once*," reminded Beatrice. "She hurt herself chasing out a completely innocent visitor."

"No, nothing's happened. Nothing except for the fact that she's driving me crazy with all this texting. Posy had a good idea, but Miss Sissy didn't agree. Posy thought that Miss Sissy's house could use a good cleaning and that Miss Sissy wasn't in perfect shape to do it. Plus, usually, Miss Sissy likes June Bug pretty well. Not this time. She doesn't want anyone in her business, apparently," explained Ramsay.

They looked over as June Bug, now finished with the sweeping, was busily wiping down the tabletops and other furniture with lemon-scented furniture polish as Miss Sissy gnashed her teeth at her.

Ramsay said sternly, "Now, Miss Sissy. I've got to leave and do some serious police work. Under no circumstances are you to text me again unless it's a real emergency."

Miss Sissy wildly waved her hands to indicate June Bug, who was trotting placidly from the room with her rag and polish. "Emergency!" she gasped.

"Absolutely not," objected Ramsay coolly. "In fact, this house would likely have become an emergency if June Bug *hadn't* done anything about it. Why don't you settle down and let Meadow fix you a nice cold drink?"

Beatrice guessed that they'd get their cold drink one way or another. Right now she was thirsty enough to drink just about anything. And, with any luck, June Bug had already done Miss Sissy's dishes and there might be something clean to drink from.

Meadow ran off for a drink, taking Miss Sissy's level glare as a sign that a drink would be acceptable. Ramsay leaned in and said under his breath to Beatrice. "Maybe you can distract her from the whole housekeeping thing. Otherwise, we might be getting indignant texts from her all night."

"I will certainly do that, never fear," said Beatrice. Although her form of distraction would include talking about the suspects in the case. Still, Miss Sissy was going to be agitated no matter what, so best to try to get as much information as possible. "Any news? I know you and the state police have been working hard on this."

Ramsay said, "Not a lot of news, no. You'd think no one in this town lived here forty years ago. They saw nothing, heard nothing, know nothing, remember nothing. That includes me, too, although I was busy with Meadow getting ready for our wedding and trying to learn the ropes at the police department."

"You don't remember anything about Vivian either?" asked Beatrice.

"She just wasn't someone whose path I'd have crossed very often." said Ramsay.

"Which makes me very sad!" said Meadow, returning with a cold drink for Miss Sissy before disappearing again to bring more out. "She would have loved Dappled Hills if she'd known all of us!"

"Although I do remember her a bit. Unfortunately, nothing very helpful. She was a reporter of some kind for the paper. I want to say she was supposed to do fluff pieces and then surprised us by trying to uncover the hidden Dappled Hills or some such. I know that my chief at the time didn't let her ask more than a couple of questions before he sent her off with a bug in her ear," said Ramsay.

"So pushy?" asked Beatrice.

"Very. Smart and driven, too. She clearly wanted to be an investigative journalist and was trying just to get her feet wet at the Dappled Hills paper. I don't think she made a lot of friends around town, unfortunately. Plus everyone behaved a little oddly because of the fatal accident—Vivian was driving and Ida's sister died. Somehow, lots of people here seemed to take that accident personally. The general consensus seems to be that she left because she found the town unfriendly. The town *was* unfriendly to her. Unfriendly enough to murder her and throw her in the lake."

Meadow returned with two clean-looking glasses of water and a wince. "Terrible thing to think about," she said.

Ramsay nodded. "Well, I'm off to try and find out more information. Good luck with everything here." He rolled his eyes at them as Miss Sissy hissed at the hapless June Bug who scuttled by to wipe down the front door.

Miss Sissy had already drunk the entire glass of water by the time Beatrice took a sip. "Goodness!" said Meadow. "You must really be thirsty."

"All that frothing at the mouth," murmured Beatrice to Meadow as she passed by her to get more water.

Beatrice took a long sip of her own water and said, "Miss Sissy, Meadow and I have been trying to find out what happened to Vivian Hastings four decades ago. I know you remember her because you mentioned her in the hospital. In fact, you seemed to know that she was dead."

June Bug trotted past her on her way to clean the bathroom and Miss Sissy glared at her as she went by, momentarily distracted.

Beatrice gently said, "How did you know Vivian was dead? Did you see something? Did you hear something? Did someone *tell* you something?"

The old woman sighed and pulled a quilt from the back of the decrepit sofa onto her lap. She absently traced one of the squares. "Because she was nosy," she muttered. "And pretty. Boys liked her."

Beatrice frowned. Meadow came back in with the water and a questioning look on her face at Beatrice's intensity. Beatrice said, "So because Vivian was nosy and because people might have been jealous of her, you figured someone murdered her. Is that right?"

Miss Sissy said, "Not just that. She had big plans for quilting. Wouldn't have just left town. Bought a lot of quilting stuff at the shop."

Meadow gave the old woman a fond look. "I know *you* can't believe that she could. After all, quilting is your favorite activity! But Vivian might have only *wanted* to start seriously quilting. Is that really what made you decide that she was dead?"

"Course!" said Miss Sissy scornfully. "And she *was*, wasn't she?"

They certainly couldn't argue with that.

"Spent gobs of money at the quilt shop. Left it behind!" Miss Sissy shook her head until her hair started falling out of the loose bun on her head.

It did seem unlikely, when you looked at it that way.

Beatrice said, "Do you know who did it? Do you have any idea who might have killed Vivian?"

Miss Sissy looked at them furiously. "Everyone!"

The rest of the visit had involved Beatrice and Meadow doing their best to drink as much water as they possibly could before the now-short trek home. This did, of course, also necessitate a visit to Miss Sissy's sparkling bathroom, courtesy of June Bug.

June Bug finished a flurry of cleaning, apparently to ensure that she wouldn't have to be there by herself with the unpredictable Miss Sissy. Her eyes shone as she closed the door behind them on the way out. "All done!"

Meadow said, "That's the fastest, best cleaning job I think I've ever seen, June Bug. I'm going to have to have you over to my house at some point. Of course, my house wouldn't be the cleaning challenge that Miss Sissy's was." She paused to correct herself. "I mean, well, but it's cluttered."

June Bug nodded and gave a happy smile. She always liked hearing of upcoming work opportunities.

Beatrice said, "Actually, June Bug, you might be able to help Meadow and me out by giving us your thoughts on something. You've been here in Dappled Hills a long time, haven't you?"

It was hard to tell exactly how old June Bug was. There was a certain childishness to her round face and her guileless, protruding eyes. But she briskly nodded and so did Meadow.

"Oh, June Bug's been here all her life," said Meadow. "I can't think why it didn't occur to me to ask her about Vivian."

Beatrice said, "You'd have to think back about forty years, but do you remember a young woman at the time? Vivian Hastings. She would have been someone who moved here, not someone who grew up in Dappled Hills."

But June Bug was already nodding earnestly before Beatrice had even finished. "Oh yes. Yes. Vivian was a friend of mine."

Beatrice and Meadow stared at the little woman. June Bug was always in the process of *doing* something. Trotting to the next house to clean. Busily hurrying down a sidewalk to deliver one of her delicious cakes to someone. Even her quilting, which she was incredibly modest about, seemed to be industriously and hastily constructed, lovely though it was. This little woman had the time to devote to friendship then? Because she certainly didn't seem to now.

"Oh yes. Vivian was such a nice girl and very kind to me. She wanted me to show her how to quilt. I told her that I didn't really know a lot about quilting, but she didn't seem very worried about that," said June Bug. "I was just a teenager."

Because June Bug's quilts were award-winning works of art and Vivian definitely seemed sharp enough to be able to understand that.

"So you'd meet up—where? At her house?" asked Beatrice.

"It just depended. Sometimes she'd come over to my house and we'd sit and quilt for a while. Mother did, too, sometimes. She was so kind! She'd bring over Mother's favorite muffins from the bakery," said June Bug, beaming at the memory.

"Would that be the Jake Bakes Bakery?" asked Beatrice. Surely it wasn't around back then.

But June Bug was nodding her head. "That's exactly right. The Jake Bakes Bakery. Mother just loved the fact that the muffins had blueberries practically falling out of them."

Meadow said, "He was just starting out at the time. He was just a kid."

Beatrice asked, "Vivian spent a lot of time with Jake?"

June Bug nodded solemnly. "Yes. I think maybe he loved Vivian. But he was a friend to her like I was a friend to her. She'd run by and get some muffins and bring them over. Of course, when I came over to her place, I'd bring some cake. We *always* had cake in the house."

Meadow laughed. "You were probably up to your neck in cakes at that point!" She turned to Beatrice as they walked. "June Bug made Ramsay's and my wedding cake that summer. She always was the best cake maker in town."

June Bug blushed.

Beatrice said, "What did you think when Vivian disappeared? Had she, as a friend, shared any troubles or worries she had? Was there anything that made you think that she met with foul play?"

"No," said the little woman. "I thought everyone liked Vivian." Her wide eyes clouded at the thought that anyone wouldn't. "I was sad when she left. I told the police that I didn't think she would have left without saying goodbye."

"What did the police say?" asked Meadow. "It wasn't *Ramsay*, was it?"

June Bug gave a decisive shake of her head. "No, it was the older one that day. He said that people did funny things sometimes, but it didn't mean that she'd come to any harm or that she meant to hurt my feelings by leaving."

At least the policeman had had kind words for the teenaged June Bug. She must have been baffled at the loss of her friend. But she didn't seem to have much else to offer them about the time surrounding Vivian's disappearance. "Did you happen to see a stranger in town recently? You're out and about so much that I thought you might."

June Bug quickly asked, "The man with the hat?"

"The very one!" said Meadow.

June Bug shook her head again, sadly. "No, I didn't see him. Everyone was talking about him, though."

Beatrice swallowed a sigh. She was ready to be back in her house with a tall glass of iced tea and a corgi snoring beside her. If June Bug knew anything, especially considering how eager she was to help, they would already have heard about it. "Well, how have *you* been doing, June Bug?"

Meadow said, "Yes! I haven't talked to you in forever. Whenever I see you, you're always running somewhere."

June Bug, with her perennially startled expression, somehow had even wider eyes. "Busy. Running to deliver a cake, running back home to bake, running back out to clean a house, running to deliver again."

"Shouldn't you slow down a little?" Meadow clicked her tongue. "Aren't you stressed out with all that back and forth?"

June Bug gave a tiny sigh. "I need more work."

"*More* work? Are you trying to drive yourself into an early grave?" gasped Meadow.

June Bug said in a small voice, "Times are a little tight."

Beatrice said, "Maybe you could raise your rates on your cleaning and cake-baking?"

June Bug just looked worried.

"Or maybe we can scare up some more business for you?" said Meadow. She looked worried now, herself.

"Thanks!" said the little woman. And, with a cheery wave and clutching her cleaning bucket, she trotted up to a large white house, ready to start in on more cleaning.

Meadow said, "I'm tired just looking at her."

"You're tired because you just walked a huge number of miles," pointed out Beatrice.

"Still, I'm going to mull it all over. I hate for June Bug to be so busy that she doesn't have time to *quilt*."

Beatrice was more concerned that June Bug was so busy that she wouldn't have time to *sleep*.

Chapter Twelve

July 10th

I'm trying to figure out a better way to approach the problem. When I reached out before, it was assumed I was a blackmailer. Look, I might be poor, but I don't have to resort to a life of crime to make a buck or two. My thought is that maybe I could sell a freelance story to one of the bigger papers to jumpstart my journalism career. I'd love to launch myself as an investigative journalist.

A couple of fairly quiet days passed. Beatrice occasionally saw Ramsay driving past when she was out walking Noo-noo. She'd have loved to have asked him how things were going with the case, but he didn't have time to stop—he just gave her a quick wave and smile.

Beatrice didn't even hear from Meadow because she was completely engrossed in putting the finishing touches on a quilt she planned on displaying in the upcoming craft fair.

Beatrice didn't have much time either. She spent the two days setting up social media profiles for the quilters and uploading pictures she had on hand of different quilts. She did spend a few minutes searching online to see if there were any old stories from the local paper from around the time of Vivian's disappearance. She was impressed that the newspaper had carefully scanned and uploaded back editions for decades, although the task might have been made easier by the fact that the paper was only published twice a week.

Beatrice was disappointed not to see any mention of Vivian's disappearance. But then, time and time again, people she'd spoken with had really downplayed her sudden absence from the little town. It certainly hadn't seemed at the time like the momentous occasion it now seemed to Beatrice. Even June Bug had been told by the police that this was just something that happened sometimes.

The only thing that she was able to find online was a picture at the craft fair from forty years ago. Now that Beatrice had seen the picture that Jake carried around, she was more easily able to spot Vivian in a picture. In this one, Vivian was standing in front of the Dappled Hills library with a variety of quilts hanging in the background. She wasn't looking at the camera, but was instead laughing at a young man who was holding a couple of hot dogs and grinning back at her. The picture wasn't captioned, but Beatrice was able to see that, upon closer inspection, it was a younger version of Jake.

There was another figure in the picture too, but Beatrice couldn't tell who it was. She made the image on her laptop larger and stared at it for a minute. Finally she realized that it was a younger Huey in the background. You could really only see part of his face, but what was visible held a very grim expression. Beatrice printed the photo.

Her phone buzzed at her and Beatrice sighed before reaching for it. Miss Sissy had been quiet the last couple of days too, which had been a nice change. But the brief respite was apparently over. It was indeed Miss Sissy who was texting.

Car dead. Need ride.

Beatrice could only assume that the hardly-loquacious Miss Sissy needed a ride to the craft fair. She texted back, "10:30?"

Miss Sissy texted back the equivalent of a grunt with *k*.

Beatrice still had the phone in her hand when it startled her by ringing. She smiled this time, though, when she saw who it was. "Hi, Piper! How are things going today?"

"They're good!" said her daughter, a smile in her voice. "I'm just calling back to see if you wanted to go to the craft fair with Ash and me."

"It sounds good, but I've got to drive Miss Sissy there, so I'd have to meet you. And we'd perhaps have Miss Sissy as an escort," said Beatrice. "Which means, if we're eating, that we'll have to bring a good deal of extra money with us."

Piper laughed. "I remember how she eats, yes. That's no problem—we're meeting Meadow downtown anyway, since she has to drive because of the quilts and the set-up she's doing."

They arranged a time and place to meet and Beatrice, since her day had now rapidly filled up, hurried off to get ready.

It was a gorgeous day for the craft fair. Miss Sissy was waiting by the side of the road when Beatrice pulled up. "Eager to go?" asked Beatrice wryly.

Miss Sissy, who was clutching a bag and a cane, scowled at her.

"Did you bring your cell phone? In case we're separated and need to meet up to drive back home?" asked Beatrice.

But she didn't even have to ask. Miss Sissy had the phone in her hand and was, in fact, texting someone as she was posing the question to her.

"Got quilts," said Miss Sissy, nodding absently at the bag at her feet.

"For the fair?" asked Beatrice, startled. "But weren't you supposed to register in advance and show up for set-up before the fair opened?"

Miss Sissy didn't deign to answer her. And the quilts appeared to be all rolled up at the bottom of the bag. Beatrice hoped that whoever was in charge of the fair would understand. Or, at least, would be so impressed by the real quality of her quilting that they'd give her a pass.

Beatrice immediately realized that parking was going to be a challenge. It appeared that not only was the event popular in tiny Dappled Hills, but it also attracted people from other towns. Drawn by the beautiful weather and the crafts, people were looking at and buying quilts, handmade jewelry, metalwork, photography, carved wood, blown glass, and paintings.

But Beatrice knew exactly what Miss Sissy was going to head for first. The old woman was already peering out the window at the food trucks. And these weren't just any food trucks—they'd traveled here especially for the festival and offered gourmet baked goods, specialty barbeque, and homemade ice cream.

"Miss Sissy, I know you're still a little under the weather," said Beatrice, noting the cane again, "So I think I'd better just drop you off and find a place to park. Do you want to meet me at the—?"

But the old woman was apparently more interested in the food trucks than in meeting up with Beatrice. She hopped nimbly out of the car, cane in one hand and cell phone and bag in the other. Miss Sissy walked with quick determination into the crowd.

"Well, I suppose she brought her own money," muttered Beatrice. She continued craning her head to see if she could find a parking place, but just as she saw one open up, someone would be pulling into it.

Finally, after she drove several blocks away, she found something that resembled a free spot. It wasn't *really* a spot, though. That is, it didn't have any painted lines to mark it as such. But it wasn't on the sidewalk, and it was out of the way of people driving, and it seemed to really be Beatrice's only option. Still, what had made everyone assiduously avoid the spot? The rule-follower in her kept this concern in the back of her head as she hurried to meet Piper and Ash. Now she was definitely running a bit behind.

Piper and Ash didn't seem to mind, though. They were sitting on the steps of the library and eating some delicious-looking vegetable wraps. Delicious but messy. "We'll spare you a hug until after we clean ourselves up," said Piper with a twinkle in her eye. "Where's Wyatt, by the way? Isn't he usually your escort for these types of events?"

Beatrice said, feeling a little guilty, "You know, I didn't even call to ask him. I wasn't sure at first if I were going to go, then Miss Sissy called up and y'all did. I guess I've gotten into the habit of waiting for *him* to call for things."

Piper gave her a knowing look. "It's easy to do that. But maybe you can meet up with him here."

"I'm sure I saw him here a few minutes ago," said Ash, glancing around the crowd. "I think he was helping with one of the booths."

Suddenly Beatrice was hugged from behind. Meadow gasped, "Got to run for now, but I'll catch up with all of you in a little while. Quilts are selling!" And she was gone in a flash.

Ash asked Beatrice as he wiped his hands with a napkin, "Did you find a place to park all right?"

Beatrice frowned. "As a matter of fact, it took quite an investment of time. And I'm not really sure that what I ended up parking in was an official spot. It wasn't marked off by white lines. But I couldn't see that the spot served some other function, either."

Piper smiled at her, used to her mother being a stickler for the rules. "It's probably going to bother you until you move your car. Although I'll point out that you *do* know the chief of police here and likely won't get a parking ticket. You just gave his wife a hug, after all."

"But you know I don't like gaming the system," said Beatrice. Piper was right. It was going to bother her until she moved the car.

Ash was already standing up from the stair he was sitting on. "How about if I go with you? I seem to have a knack for finding parking places. It'll just take a second and then it won't be on your mind anymore. Oh, and I know some spots that hardly anyone knows about at the back of the park."

Beatrice felt relieved. "That would be great. I'm sorry—I know that wasn't part of our plan."

Piper said, "We don't *have* any set plans. That's what's so nice about today. I'll come along with you."

Piper and Ash filled her in on the craft fair as they walked. Piper had her eye on some beaded necklaces at one of the booths and Beatrice made a mental note that she should try to get one for Piper's upcoming birthday. Although Ash also seemed to be making the same mental note. He winked at Beatrice. Perhaps they could coordinate so that Piper wouldn't end up with two of the same necklace.

They found the car and got in. As Ash had mentioned, he was able to nearly immediately find a parking place down a few side streets and at the back of the craft fair.

"Ash has a gift," said Piper airily from the backseat.

Ash parked in a real parking place with actual white lines and right behind the tennis courts and public restrooms. They walked up the stairs toward the courts where there were booths of hand-smocked dresses for girls, glasswork, and quilts.

Beatrice glanced over to the other set of shaded concrete stairs farther down that led from the restrooms to the road. She frowned. "What's that over there?"

"Where?" asked Piper, squinting in the sun.

Ash said, "Over at the bottom of the stairs?" He saw it, too.

Piper said, "Oh, that? That's probably something one of the set-up crew accidentally dropped. A tablecloth or something."

But Ash was already walking over there and Beatrice followed. By the time she caught up with his long strides, he was already turning and stopping her. "I think we need to call Dad," he said grimly. "It's a body."

Piper called Ramsay and Ash made sure that no one came down from the festival to contaminate the crime scene. Beatrice got as close to the body as she could. "It's Ida Calkin," she said sadly.

Piper was hanging up the phone. "She is ... I mean, I shouldn't have been calling an ambulance, instead?"

Beatrice shook her head. "I'm afraid not. Not with her neck at that angle. And her eyes are wide open."

They all stood quietly for a moment, out of respect for Ida. Then Piper said quietly, "Ramsay is on his way over. He's just at the other end of the fair. I guess she fell down the stairs? Just a terrible accident?"

Beatrice said, "I'd like to *think* that's true, but I doubt it. Meadow and I were just talking to her a couple of days ago, as a matter of fact. She was acting as if she might know something about the Vivian Hastings case."

Piper's eyebrows shot up in alarm. "You're not doing anything with these murders, are you? You and Meadow aren't trying to investigate? It's too dangerous."

"It sounds to me from what Dad has said that someone has something to cover up," said Ash grimly. "Who knows how desperate they might be feeling? After all, they got away with murder decades ago—or *thought* they'd gotten away with it. And they've been living here in Dappled Hills, just acting like a regular, ordinary citizen. Someone upstanding, maybe. Someone with responsibilities. And all the time, they have something horrible in their past that they think no one will ever find out about."

Piper shivered. "And then that guy comes to town and starts asking questions and trying to dig up the past. They must have been so determined to shut him down and protect their secret that they killed him. And now you're saying that Ida also knew something about it?"

"It's not like Meadow and I are playing detective," said Beatrice, crossing her fingers slightly. "We're working on that history of quilting, remember? Ida was one of the original quilters who helped to set up the craft fair. I've got my camera today so that I can take a few pictures for the book. But while we were talking to Ida about the craft fair and seeing if she could help with the quilting history, she made an oblique reference to the fact that she had some sort of information."

Ash said grimly, "Which wasn't a very smart thing to do—let people know that she knew something. Do you think she might have been planning on blackmailing the person?"

"Maybe. Meadow and I couldn't help but notice that her house wasn't in the best of shape. The outside needed repair and the inside was threadbare. It could be that she decided to try and make a little income off of the information she had," said Beatrice.

Piper said, "It probably even seemed like a safe thing to do. The person she was making arrangements with, or *trying* to make arrangements with would have been someone she'd known her whole life. It would have been hard to think of them as dangerous."

"But someone who was involved in the deaths of two, now three, people *is* dangerous. It's too bad Ida couldn't have seen that," said Beatrice as Ramsay's police car, lights flashing, pulled into the parking lot near them.

Piper said, "I suppose Ida tried to set up a meeting with the killer here at the craft fair. Tried and succeeded, obviously. Although that seems risky with everyone milling around."

Ash said, "Actually, it seems like a good idea. After all, it would stand out a lot less to everyone than having him come over to her house or meeting in a remote location."

Ramsay got out of his car and hurried over to them. "So, Ida Calkin?" he asked in a tired voice.

"I'm afraid so," said Beatrice, motioning toward the body.

"Meadow is going to flip out," said Ramsay with a sigh. "She always thinks the world has come to an end when there's any hint of violence in Dappled Hills." He walked carefully over to briefly inspect Ida before taping off a large swath of area with police tape and getting on his phone to talk to the state police who would lead on the investigation.

A few minutes later, Ramsay joined them again.

Ash said, "We were thinking this wasn't an accident or a natural death. Is that what you think?"

Ramsay said in a sad voice, "I think that it's not very natural that she has huge purple bruises around her neck. No, I'm afraid she was strangled, probably from behind, and then shoved down the stairs so that she wouldn't be immediately discovered to give the killer a chance to get away."

Beatrice said, "And Ramsay, she did seem to know something about the case. That is, when Meadow and I were speaking to her about the history of Dappled Hills, she alluded to knowing something about Vivian or maybe about Oscar's death. Did you get a sense of that from her?"

She was relieved that Ramsay didn't say anything about the fact that Meadow and she were pretty obviously snooping around. It wasn't as if Ida would have said anything if she hadn't been pressed on it.

Ramsay said, "I did speak to Ida about the case, as a matter of fact. After all, she had every reason to be angry with Vivian forty years ago with that car accident. And she was very clearly still bothered by Fiona's death—it was almost as if it had just happened. She got all red in the face talking about Vivian and basically said she got what she deserved. She denied that she had any connection to Vivian's murder, of course. But I did get the feeling that she was hiding something. When I asked her if she knew anyone else who might have wanted Vivian dead, or Oscar Holland, she wouldn't look me in the eye. And she was definitely evasive. But I couldn't get anything else out of her. Typical for this case. It's been driving me crazy."

"No leads?" asked Piper.

"No one seems to have seen anything either back then or now," said Ramsay in frustration. "Who have y'all noticed at the fair today? Anyone in particular stand out?"

Beatrice sighed. "I'd have loved to have some information, but I've spent my entire time here trying to park my blasted car in a legitimate parking space."

Piper and Ash looked at each other. "I've seen Mom," said Ash with a shrug.

"Very helpful," said Ramsay, rolling his eyes. "She's about the most unlikely suspect we've got."

People were walking away from the craft fair with purchases and car keys in hand and Ramsay said quickly, "I'm going to have to make sure this area is secure. Let me know if you think of anything that might be helpful to the investigation." And he walked away, toward the crime scene.

Ash said, "He's right—this is really going to upset Mom. I guess I should try to meet up with her and tell her in person."

Beatrice said, "I'll go with you. I need to probably locate Miss Sissy, too. I'm not sure how much money she brought with her and she's likely getting hungry if she didn't bring much. Besides, Meadow has been at the fair longer than we have. Maybe she's seen something."

Chapter Thirteen

It didn't take long to find Meadow since she was in the thick of the quilt section of the craft fair and having a very good time. She'd sold several quilts and also appeared to be handing out a brochure with information on quilting in Dappled Hills that included a coupon to Posy's Patchwork Cottage store.

As soon as her customer left (and after Meadow had both introduced and bragged about Ash to this customer), Ash told her what had happened and she suddenly became serious. She glanced over at Beatrice. "This has to do with something she knew. But what could she know and why didn't she tell Ramsay about it? Oh, this is so frustrating. Do you think she made any notes at home?"

"I'm sure if she did, then Ramsay and the team from the state police will find them," said Beatrice in a soothing voice. "Although it didn't seem to be the kind of house that had a lot of extra clutter."

"No," admitted Meadow. "You're right. It was very Spartan in there. I suppose she had an idea of getting money for keeping quiet."

Ash said, "It wasn't a great idea." He leaned over and gave his mother a quick hug. "Sorry to be the bearer of bad news, but we wanted to let you know before you found out about it from someone else. I'm going to head back over to Piper now. I guess Dad is going to let the craft fair continue and just block off that one area, so we may stay for a little while."

"Stay and spend money!" ordered Meadow. "That way at least some good can come from today. The money goes to local arts and crafts programs." Ash left and Meadow gave a big sigh.

Beatrice said in a low voice as people milled around looking at quilts hanging nearby, "You spent more time at the craft fair than anyone else. Did you see anyone who we've been talking to?"

Meadow said, "Well, Ida. She was the first person I saw. I called over to her, but she totally ignored me."

"Maybe she didn't hear you."

"No, she definitely heard me," said Meadow rather hotly. "She cut her eyes over my way and then hastily looked away and kept walking. Very annoying, especially since we just saw her a couple of days ago. Maybe if she'd come over and had a conversation with me and given up skulking around, she'd still be alive now." This thought made Meadow tear up and she rooted around in her purse for a tissue.

"You said that Ida was the *first* person you saw," said Beatrice. "There were others?"

Meadow said, "I saw Huey out here. We had a conversation for a few minutes, as a matter of fact. But it would have been more suspicious if we *hadn't* seen Huey out here, if you know what I mean. Since he helped get this fair started so many years ago."

The women who were looking at the quilts moved farther away and Beatrice said, "How did Huey seem? Was he distracted or did he look worried?"

"Neither. He seemed just like regular old Huey. He was greeting everyone and acting like he owned the place, which he practically does. But maybe that's a great cover for him. Maybe it made him feel like he could get away with anything. It could have been pretty easy to be talking with someone and keeping an eye on the area where Ida was meeting him. Then, when the coast was clear, he could have hurried over there and done the deed." Meadow intoned the last bit and looked angry as if she'd convinced herself that Huey was at fault.

"Anyone else?" asked Beatrice.

"Jake is here, of course. He's selling his baked goods at a booth." Meadow nodded to the concessions and food truck area.

Beatrice looked over there and, craning her head, she could see a booth with 'Jake Bakes' painted on the outside. A throng of people milled through the area. "That sure looks like an alibi to me. There's no way he would have been able to get away from that number of people to run off and kill Ida and then get back to work."

"You'd think so," said Meadow thoughtfully. "But, as a matter of fact, that's not true. You see, all the vendors—the craft vendors, too—have an arrangement worked out. There are craft fair marshals. You've probably seen them with the bright yellow vests on."

Beatrice had. And she was very relieved that she hadn't volunteered for the job when asked. The marshals appeared to be constantly in motion in the warm sun.

"The marshals sit in for the vendors when they need a break of any kind—to get lunch or to make change, or to use the restroom. They also direct visitors to food, facilities, and parking," said Meadow.

Beatrice said, "So, in effect, Jake could have pretty easily left his booth."

"Exactly. And, if he were smart, he would have left it a couple of different times so that it wasn't obvious when he was leaving it to commit murder," said Meadow. "That scoundrel."

Meadow had the habit of shifting blame onto whichever suspect they were discussing at the time. And completely believing each one was responsible.

Beatrice said, "And how about our final suspect?"

"I've lost track," said Meadow, frowning. "We lost a main one today. I was thinking Ida was the culprit and then she goes off and gets herself murdered. Poor thing."

Her sympathies were switching back and forth, too. Beatrice said, "Gwen. Have you spotted Gwen today? Hopefully skulking around the tennis courts and waiting for Ida to appear?"

Meadow snapped her fingers. "You know, I *did* see Gwen this morning. Actually I was annoyed by her."

"Sounds likely," agreed Beatrice.

"Yes. She was supposed to be here to help me set up. Setup wasn't easy, you know. Not only did I have my own quilts that I wanted to display and sell, but I needed to help set up other quilts to hang. It took a while. Gwen volunteered to help me set everything up. I mean, *why* would you continue to volunteer your time and then not show up? It's like a sickness with Gwen. I should know by now that Gwen doesn't do what she says she's going to do," fussed Meadow.

Beatrice tried to bring the conversation back around to its original point. "So you saw Gwen here. And you told her off for not coming when she was supposed to?"

"I saw her and she didn't even stop! I called out to her and she acted as if she didn't even hear me. Honestly, the times I've been ignored today are amazing. She seemed to be in a tremendous hurry when I saw her so I'd assumed she was heading my way with an apology. But no—she strode right past the booths and kept on going. I've no idea where she was heading in such a hurry." Meadow fumed for a moment. "Maybe she was hurrying off to kill Ida without further delay."

Meadow clearly didn't have any other information besides pure speculation. Beatrice said, "Good thing you were here early, though, setting up. Otherwise, I don't know how we'd have figured out who was here or not."

Meadow said dryly, "Not that it helped much, really. It just means that everyone had the opportunity to murder Ida. Ida, who I vacillate between being very indignant with for withholding information, and feeling sorry for."

More customers came up and were waiting to ask Meadow a question so Beatrice quickly said, "But it's information, still. I'm going to head off and look for Miss Sissy. I'd planned on keeping a closer eye on her but it hasn't worked out that way."

"Well, she *does* have her cell phone now, so she probably doesn't need a sitter at these things," said Meadow as she turned to greet the customers.

It really didn't take too long for Beatrice to locate Miss Sissy. As she guessed, she was still hanging around the food trucks. Judging from the stains on her dress, she'd worked her way through the gourmet taco truck to the handmade, powdered doughnut truck. Now her eyes lit up as she spotted Beatrice. It made Beatrice leap to the instant conclusion that Miss Sissy had run out of all available funds and now needed to be spotted more cash.

Miss Sissy spryly bounded over to her. "Have money for a little food?" she crooned.

Beatrice absently fished around in her purse. "Let's see. I've got a ten. But can you talk to me for a few minutes first? I had something to ask you and it's easier to talk here than in the food line."

Miss Sissy nodded reluctantly, but her eyes cut over to the food truck she was hoping to patronize—some sort of stuffed onion thing.

"First of all, have you heard the news about Ida?" asked Beatrice.

The old woman looked back at Beatrice. She shook her head and gazed curiously at her. "What happened? She sick or something?"

"No, unfortunately she was murdered," said Beatrice under her breath. She was sure Ramsay didn't need a big crowd gathered over at the crime scene.

"Evil!" spat Miss Sissy.

"Most certainly," agreed Beatrice evenly. "But I was more interested in the *who* of this particular bit of wickedness. Have you seen or heard anything while you've been here that might help us find out who did it?"

Miss Sissy's eyes narrowed. "That man! Arguing! Angry!" She put her arthritic hands up and pawed at the air like a cat.

Beatrice sighed. She wasn't sure what was worse—Miss Sissy with no information at all, or Miss Sissy with useful information but without the means to articulate it. "What man was it? And with whom was he arguing?"

Miss Sissy's blank expression indicated that Beatrice should focus on one question at a time.

Beatrice took a deep breath. "The man that you saw earlier. What did he look like? Was he one of the people that Ramsay was asking you about? Someone who knew Vivian? Someone she talked about in her diary?"

Miss Sissy nodded enthusiastically. "Wicked!"

"Yes. What does he look like?"

"A baker!" hissed Miss Sissy.

Beatrice raised her eyebrows. "So Jake from the bakery was having an argument with someone? Is this while you were around the food trucks? Someone came up to him and had an argument at his booth?"

"No," said the old woman scornfully. "Not at the booth. Over there!" She pointed a crooked finger haphazardly to indicate another, fairly far-flung location.

"You mean? Over near the tennis courts? Near the restroom?" Beatrice couldn't imagine that Miss Sissy had had time to get over in that direction. Not with all the eating she was doing. But she was still very quick when she wanted to be. And perhaps she'd had to run wash her hands after going to the doughnut truck or something. Maybe this was the lucky break that meant the case was over.

But Miss Sissy was already shaking her head vehemently. "Not that far. Just over *there*." Now the pointing was a bit more specific and indicated the area that was decidedly on the *way* to the tennis courts and restroom, but not that far away. "He saw me. I waved at him. Wanted a muffin." The old woman's face was sulky as she remembered.

"I see. So you went to his truck. But the helper person should have been there. The marshal. To get you a muffin, I mean," said Beatrice.

"Too busy!" said Miss Sissy. "Not enough people to help. The helper was over at the booth next door."

Beatrice said, "Okay. I see. There were too many customers and not enough marshals so the marshals had to scurry from booth to booth." She felt a twinge of guilt now at *not* helping—but then sternly reminded herself that she was trying to enjoy a quiet retirement. And she had just volunteered, after all, for the quilting service project. Or had *been* volunteered, at any rate. "You wanted a muffin, it was going to take a while, and you spotted Jake the baker and tried to flag him down." Now for the big question. "Who was Jake arguing with?" She held her breath, hoping the answer was going to be Ida. And also worried that the answer was going to be Ida. She rather liked Jake.

"That old woman!" said Miss Sissy triumphantly. "The old woman!"

Now Beatrice was feeling desperate. Surely she could get more specific information from Miss Sissy before she fell into her usual mutterings and wild accusations. "Which old woman? There are so many of them here! Are you talking about Ida? The old woman who I told you has just been murdered?"

Miss Sissy was unfortunately rapidly losing interest in the conversation and looked longingly at the food truck. She did manage to nod her head vaguely.

Beatrice gritted her teeth before sweetly asking again, "So Jake the baker was arguing with the woman who's now dead. Is that right?"

More nodding from Miss Sissy.

"Did you hear anything they were saying to each other?" asked Beatrice.

"He said he had to go! Customers!" reported Miss Sissy.

Naturally, he *would* be saying that if Miss Sissy were standing there waving him on.

"Yes, but anything else? Other than that? Anything to let you know what they were arguing about?" asked Beatrice.

Miss Sissy sighed. "Old times. Arguing about old times."

And that was all Beatrice could really get out of Miss Sissy. She scampered off to the food truck with Beatrice's money and Beatrice walked over near the bakery booth, looking at Jake Hunter thoughtfully. He had a line of several people in front of him, but since muffins and croissants and other breads were easy orders to fill, the line was quickly dealt with. Once it cleared, Beatrice approached him.

He smiled at her when she stood in front of him, but there was a certain wariness in his eyes. "Hi there, Beatrice. What can I get for you today?"

"What's your favorite thing here?" she asked him.

"My *personal* favorite? That would have to be the cranberry orange muffin," said Jake, pointing to the unassuming looking muffin.

"I'll have one then, please," said Beatrice, pulling out some change to pay him with. When he handed it to her, he looked at her expectantly and she obediently took a small bite. She immediately followed that with a larger bite because it *was* very good. Jake smiled at her.

There was a lull in the crowds so Beatrice lingered at the booth, hoping for the opportunity to question Jake about his argument. "How is the fair so far?" he asked, carefully cleaning his already-pristine counter with a white paper towel. "It looks well-attended, anyway."

"It's definitely making money. Lots of people here today and, judging from the bags they're carrying, they're buying things, too." She paused and asked delicately, "I actually have a question for you, Jake."

He raised his eyebrows at this and smiled, but the smile didn't quite reach his eyes.

Beatrice took a deep breath. "You're certainly in a good mood now, but earlier I saw you arguing with Ida." She crossed her fingers. She didn't want to bring poor Miss Sissy into this, though. She'd gone through enough lately and didn't need more trouble. "I hope I didn't have anything to do with that."

Jake frowned, looking confused. "I'm sorry, I'm not following you. Why would you have something to do with that at all?"

"Oh, just the fact that when Meadow and I were in there talking to you we brought up a lot of old memories. I wondered if the old memories had been better off buried," said Beatrice with a small shrug, eyes trained on his face.

A mix of emotions crossed Jake's features. He said quickly, "You mean Vivian. But you didn't bring the memories *back* to the forefront. That's to say ... well, the memories are always there, regardless. Vivian meant a lot to me. I guess that must be obvious, since I still carry her picture around. I think about her a lot." He tilted his head and looked closer at Beatrice. "But I don't understand why you think our talk about Vivian has anything to do with Ida."

"Don't you?" asked Beatrice.

He nodded slowly. "Okay. Yes, I still harbor a lot of anger against Ida. I always blamed her for running Vivian out of town. At least, I *thought* she'd been run out of town. Then, finding out that Vivian was dead, it made me even angrier at Ida. I wondered if she had let her need for revenge take control."

"If she had killed Vivian," said Beatrice.

"Yes. When I saw her today, that's what I had on my mind. I told her I didn't appreciate the way she treated Vivian all those years ago. And told her she better keep an eye out," said Jake.

"You threatened her?" asked Beatrice.

"I wouldn't call it a threat. I just tried to make her realize how upset I was."

Beatrice said, "I'm guessing that you haven't heard the news. Since you've been busy with customers here."

Jake studied her again. Then he smiled. "You sound a little like a detective."

"Oh, I wouldn't say I'm a *detective*. It's just that I was worried I'd somehow created a problem between you and Ida. I was familiar, from my work writing the Dappled Hills history, with Ida's background with Vivian. That's all," said Beatrice. She finished her muffin, which was indeed delicious. She took a deep breath. "But what you probably don't realize, since you were busy here, is that Ida is dead."

Jake stared at her without saying a word.

"Someone ... well, I'm afraid that someone murdered her. And I'm sorry to be the bearer of grim news. Again."

"But that's impossible! I was just talking to her—arguing with her—whatever. Do they ... did Ramsay find out who is responsible?" He ran his hand distractedly through his blond hair.

"He hasn't, no. But he's investigating, of course," said Beatrice.

Jake said, "Look here. I hope I didn't leave you with the wrong impression. I did argue with Ida. I'm not saying that I didn't. But I sure didn't kill her, nor would I wish harm on her. Honestly, I felt much better about Ida after I'd given her a piece of my mind. Blown off a little steam ... you know."

"Oh, I know," said Beatrice with a smile.

His eyes went from pleading to relieved and Beatrice looked away. There was something very attractive about Jake. Hard to imagine that he was still single. In his crisp white chef jacket, he was quite a sight to behold, Beatrice had to admit. Untamed blond curls, unrepentant grin, flashing dimple and baby blue eyes.

Jake said hesitantly, "I don't know if—well, I've enjoyed talking with you, although the subject matter has completely stunk. I was wondering if you wanted to come by the bakery another time and try talking about something else." He gave her a wry smile. "I'm not handling this well, but I see you're not wearing a wedding ring. Are you attached?"

Out of the corner of her eye, Beatrice saw Wyatt approaching the booth. She took a deep breath. "I'm afraid so," she said with a smile. "But I'm very flattered at being asked."

Jake nodded briskly and said, "Well then, feel free to just come by for muffins and coffee with Meadow at any time. Cranberry orange muffins are on the menu a *lot*." He gave her a wink and then called out to Wyatt, "Hi there, minister! What can I get for you today?"

Chapter Fourteen

Leaving the booth together a few minutes later with several more cranberry orange muffins, Wyatt said with a small smile, "It was nice of you to rebuff Jake. Particularly since we haven't even had a chance to see each other lately. Good to know that you do still feel 'attached.'"

Beatrice grinned back at him. "I guess if we were technically *attached*, we'd be seeing a good deal more of each other, wouldn't we? Maybe too much. I might drive you crazy with the constant exposure."

"Never," said Wyatt quietly, giving her hand a squeeze. Beatrice felt a warm glow.

Then she sighed as the day's events pushed their way into her mind again. "Did you hear about Ida?" she asked.

Wyatt slowed his pace and turned to look at her. "No, I didn't, but then I just got here. Sorry I didn't call you in advance or we could have come together. Ida Calkin? What happened?"

"She was murdered. Right over near the stairs leading away from the restrooms and tennis courts."

"*What*?" Wyatt stopped short.

"She was murdered," repeated Beatrice in a soft voice. "I was with Piper and Ash when we discovered her. Then we called Ramsay."

Wyatt reached out to put an arm around Beatrice's shoulder and she felt some of the tension in her shoulders release as she relaxed into his embrace.

"I'm so sorry you had to go through that again. What an awful week you've had." Wyatt paused. "Did Ramsay ... well, did he seem to know what happened?" asked Wyatt.

Beatrice said, "He believed that she'd been strangled and pushed down the stairs that lead down to the parking lot."

Wyatt shook his head as if unwilling to believe what he was hearing. "Who would do something like this? A stranger to our town is bad enough, but Ida Calkin? Who could have something against her?"

"Ordinarily, I'd agree with you. But when Meadow and I were visiting Ida the other day for the quilting history, she was acting a little smug about the Vivian Hastings case. As if she knew something about it," said Beatrice.

"You're thinking that she confronted the person who was responsible for Vivian's death," said Wyatt, walking slowly with Beatrice again.

"Confronted them or tried to get them to buy her silence," said Beatrice.

Wyatt sighed. "Poor Ida. She should have been a lot more careful. If this person killed once, they were clearly ready to kill again."

"Right. But let's face it—she probably felt a sense of safety or security around them. It would have been someone she's known and lived close to for her whole life. It's hard to think of a neighbor as a dangerous killer. Although, if she had, she'd probably be alive now," said Beatrice.

Wyatt's face was concerned. "You sound as if you're trying to get to the bottom of this case. But aren't you just like Ida? Putting yourself in danger?"

"Definitely not like Ida," said Beatrice coolly. "I have a quilting history I can use as an excuse to talk to people. And Meadow is frequently with me. Killing one person takes some effort but killing two people at once is going to be pretty much impossible."

He squeezed her hand. "Just promise me you'll be careful."

"I promise," she said, giving him a warm smile. Although, if she were being completely honest, she was already thinking of talking to Huey. He was one of the more difficult suspects to talk to—at least in a completely natural way.

Which was when she caught sight of him. He was signing paperwork for one of the vendors at a table near the quilt section. Beatrice murmured to Wyatt, "Do you have any business at all with Huey?"

He said wryly, "You mean business that will give you the opportunity to casually ask him if he murdered Ida? I can probably come up with something."

They approached Huey right as the vendor walked away from the table. Huey stood up when he saw them and reached out his hand. He seemed very jovial. "Hi there, Wyatt. Beatrice. How are you liking the craft fair this year?"

"It's wonderful," said Beatrice. Then she realized she had her own good reasons for talking with Huey. "As a matter of fact, I wondered if you'd let me take your picture here. Maybe I can use it in the history as part of a 'then and now' type of thing."

Huey said in his smooth voice, "Absolutely. Of course those pictures will sadly show the Huey with more hair versus the Huey with less of it." He moved away from the table and in front of a display that held several different quilts.

"Perfect," said Beatrice. She gave what she hoped was a wistful look. "It'll be nice to try to look at today purely as a good day for the arts in Dappled Hills."

Wyatt nodded. "I know what you mean. It's hard to think of events overshadowing what we're trying to do to promote the local arts. Maybe the history will be a good way of helping people to focus on all the *good* aspects of the event."

Huey turned his head back and forth to look at them as if he were watching the action at a tennis game. Finally he held his neatly manicured hands out in front of him. "All right, I give up. Clearly you both know something that I don't. Has something happened today?" His eyes grew wide. "Nothing happened to any of the art, did it? I *always* said we should have more security here.

We're just asking for someone to come up and steal from the fair. Is that what happened?"

"No, nothing happened to the art. But something happened to Ida Calkin," said Beatrice.

Huey's eyes narrowed. "Ida. I'm trying to place her." His gaze slid off to the side of them as if he weren't quite able to look them in the eye while saying he couldn't remember Ida.

Wyatt tilted his head, thoughtfully. "You remember Ida from the church, don't you? Didn't you both serve as deacons some time ago?"

"A very *long* time ago," said Huey quickly. "Yes, that's it, of course. Ida and I did both work together as deacons. It must have been decades ago. And you're saying that something happened to Ida here at the craft fair?" He shifted uneasily. "Did she have a ... health crisis of some sort? It didn't draw a crowd, did it?"

Huey clearly was the type of person who really didn't like to attract the wrong sort of attention. He was the kind who must protect his reputation fiercely. Which made Beatrice think that there might be plenty to hide. Plenty of wrongdoing or potential ugliness that he might want to keep private. His attitude was enough to make her suspicious.

"Ida was murdered," said Beatrice. "Right here at the craft fair, yes. Not in the middle of a crowd, as you'd possibly expect. I'm sure it hasn't damaged the reputation of the fair or made people feel unsafe. But it's very sad."

Huey blinked several times quickly. "Well I certainly hate to hear that. I certainly do."

"I feel a strange sense of responsibility for the whole thing," said Beatrice. "Not that I was responsible for the tragedy, but you see, my group discovered her body. It made me feel like I'd like to find out who did this to poor Ida."

Huey nodded, but was looking away from them as if wanting desperately to throw himself into a bunch of other work that was waiting for him. "I can understand that."

"I'm sure that you've been here at the fair since early this morning. In fact, you were probably one of the first ones here since you had to set up everything. Did you see or hear anything unusual?" asked Beatrice. Wyatt stood quietly next to her, listening.

Huey said smoothly, "Well you know I wish I had some information to give you to track down who did this. It sounds as if we've got some sort of killer that's wandered into Dappled Hills and needs to wander back out of it again."

"Ramsay doesn't think it's some sort of itinerant murderer, unfortunately. He thinks it's someone in Dappled Hills," said Beatrice.

"That's hard to believe," said Huey. "Perhaps Ramsay is wrong. He *could* be wrong. At any rate, as I was saying, I *don't* have any information for you. *Or* for Ramsay, if he talks with me. I was over here near the exhibits and the craft vendors the entire morning. I never ventured my way over near the tennis courts or the public restrooms."

Beatrice's breath caught in her throat. "But I never told you where Ida's body was found, Huey. I just told you that she'd been murdered."

Huey swallowed a nearly imperceptible bulge in his throat before he gave a dry laugh. "I just assumed that's where she was found. You said it wasn't in the middle of everything. Well, that's where I've been. In the middle of everything. The only place that's *not* in the center of activity is the area near the restrooms and tennis courts. That's all."

"You didn't see anything unusual? You can't think who might be responsible for murdering Ida?" asked Beatrice. She couldn't help the irritated tone in her voice. She was just so tired of having everyone lie to her. And it was certainly clear to her that Huey wasn't telling the truth. He hadn't from the very start.

"Ida seems like such an innocent character that it's hard to imagine her a victim in a violent crime," said Huey smoothly. He put a finger up to his chin as if in quick thought and then raised the finger in the air as if something had occurred to him. "There is one thing I noticed. That's the fact that Gwen and Ida never seemed to get along very well. In fact, I want to say that I saw Ida and Gwen snarling at each other this morning while I was setting up."

This was new. Had everyone at the craft fair been at each other's throats today? "Did you hear what they were arguing about?"

"I didn't care enough to listen in, to be perfectly honest. Besides, I assumed it had to do with the usual sorts of things they argued about. Ida and Gwen have frequently served together on the craft fair committees in the past and I always dreaded it when they did. Ida thought Gwen was quite slothful, you see. Full of promises to make phone calls or to help drag out displays or to put flyers about. But then when it came down to it, Ida thought Gwen didn't follow through."

This was a common refrain when it came to Gwen. "I've heard that before about Gwen. But is that really enough to fuss over?" asked Beatrice.

Huey looked at her with surprise. "Of course it is. In a small town, *everything* is enough to fuss over. I forget, though—you're not from Dappled Hills. Where is it that you're originally from?"

"Atlanta," said Beatrice.

"Atlanta. Well then. I'm sure in Atlanta people held grudges for quite bigger things. But here in Dappled Hills, your word is supposed to be your bond. And when someone consistently forces someone else to do more work, it can create a certain ... hostility, shall we say? Oh, I think it's definitely enough to fuss over, as you called it." Huey looked pointedly at the large watch on his thin wrist. "And now, if you'll excuse me. There are things I need to do."

Beatrice and Wyatt walked away. "I think we were dismissed," said Beatrice wryly.

"Well, you probably can't really blame him. He was getting questions that made him uncomfortable," said Wyatt. "Although I hope we don't find out that he's responsible for all this. I hate to think that people we know could be involved with murder."

"I know. We always have these high hopes that it will prove to be some sort of itinerant killer who is roaming the countryside, killing people in small towns. But somehow it never ends up quite that way." Beatrice's head started throbbing and she realized she hadn't had anything to eat or drink since she'd gotten there. And she'd skimped on breakfast, too, in her efforts to get ready in time to get Miss Sissy. "Maybe I need to take a bit of a break."

"That's a good idea," said Wyatt. "This has been a pretty intense day for you. Let's visit the food trucks and see what we can find. I was glad to discover that they didn't all seem to be the typical Southern food truck choices of fried candy bars."

Beatrice said, "I know. I think I want to check out those vegetarian tacos. They looked wonderful. And maybe get some water in the process."

Amazingly, they didn't run into Miss Sissy near the food trucks. This was a good thing since Beatrice was out of cash. Wyatt and Beatrice took their plates over to a nearby picnic table to enjoy the food. As Wyatt mentioned, there were a lot of healthy options. Beatrice had decided on the vegetarian taco along with a side order of sautéed corn and black beans. Wyatt had discovered a creole food truck that served seafood gumbo and red beans and rice. They'd both gotten fruit smoothies from a juice truck. The sun was shining, they had delicious meals in front of them, and it became hard for Beatrice to believe that the morning had been so stressful and distressing.

Wyatt said, "Have you had a chance to take a look at the crafts? There's an amazing amount of talent on display over there."

"Not yet. My morning at the fair really got hijacked. There was a lot I wanted to see and I know the fair only goes on another hour or so," said Beatrice, glancing at her watch. "I also wanted to pick up something for Piper's birthday, if I can find something. Hopefully not the same thing Ash ends up getting her."

Wyatt took the last bite of his red beans and rice. "Let's take a look. I love looking at the glass, in particular."

They did look at the glass, the beautiful and delicate hues of color that the artists had imbued in the glass. They also saw some amazing quilts, including an experimental art quilt that combined applique, hand-dyed bits of cloth, and machine embroidery. The result was a playground of texture. Beatrice got closer to see who the quilter was. "It's June Bug!" she gasped. "How does she make the time to create art like this? I have all day and I can't accomplish what she can. Has she cloned herself? Are there lots of little June Bugs running around?"

Wyatt said gently, "It might be stress relief for her. She quilts to relax when she's scurrying all over town delivering cakes and cleaning houses. We didn't make our way to the dessert section of the food, but she has a selection of cakes here."

"I think I'll pick one up before I go home," said Beatrice. "Maybe we could all have cake at the service project meeting tomorrow."

Wyatt was studying a long table with handmade necklaces of semi-precious and natural stone. Beatrice eyed one that looked like a lovely match for Piper. It was a combination of copper, leather, and stones that would go well with all the neutral colors she wore. She checked it out while Wyatt studied the selection of jewelry. He reached for a necklace of turquoise stones and gave

Beatrice a shy smile. "Do you like turquoise? I was wondering if this necklace would look as wonderful on you as I think it will."

She smiled back at him and turned around so that Wyatt could fasten the necklace around her neck. There was an older woman manning the booth and she said, "You look absolutely beautiful," and handed Beatrice a mirror.

"I agree," said Wyatt, eyes twinkling.

Beatrice had to admit that the stones were beautiful and set off her platinum-white hair nicely.

"They go perfectly with your beautiful top, too," the woman quickly added.

"Sold!" said Wyatt. Then he added quickly. "If it's all right with you, Beatrice. I'd love to give this necklace to you as a gift."

She smiled at him. "I'd love that."

The woman behind the booth smiled too. And, glancing around, Beatrice saw a couple of women from the church beaming at them and giving them a happy little wave. That was certainly one thing about small-town life. You never really knew who was watching and sharing information at all times. Wyatt was frequently discussed as all the ladies from the church hoped that he'd find a nice woman to settle down with.

Beatrice was trying to decide how she felt about that settling down idea when Wyatt said, "I didn't realize that Georgia had a booth dedicated to her pet clothing. I thought she was only participating here as a quilter."

"Let's take a look. Piper already got Noo-noo a bandana from Georgia last week so I think Noo-noo's wardrobe is probably good for now. But I'd like to get something for Maisie, Posy's shop cat. I'll give it to Miss Sissy to dress Maisie in. That should give her something to do," said Beatrice as they walked toward the booth. "It's always a good idea to keep Miss Sissy busy."

Miss Sissy, as it happened, surprised them by rushing up behind them and grasping Wyatt by his free arm. "Murder!" she hissed.

Beatrice said, "Yes, poor Ida. It'll be okay, Miss Sissy. I had an idea for something you might want to do. How about if we head to Georgia's booth and you can pick out an outfit for Maisie? I think Posy's customers would eat that up, she'd be so cute. What do you think?"

A smile creased Miss Sissy's face as she considered Maisie in an outfit. Then she knit her brow and said, "Two outfits!"

"All right then. Find two," said Beatrice, rolling her eyes at Wyatt who was suppressing a smile.

Georgia greeted them happily and Beatrice and Wyatt gave her a wave as Miss Sissy immediately absorbed all of her attention as she hovered over the booth.

Beatrice saw that Georgia seemed to be in an especially joyful mood. She said warmly, "You really seem to have found your niche with the pet clothing. Not that you didn't enjoy quilting or teaching, but this seems to make you feel really satisfied. It's so good to see you so happy."

Savannah joined them in just enough time to overhear Beatrice. She said with a laugh, "The pet clothes is good, but it's not the only good thing. Tell them, Georgia!"

Georgia blushed. "I can't believe it's not all over the town already. Word travels fast."

"Yes, but this just happened last night," reminded Savannah.

Georgia looked shyly at Wyatt and said, "I was going to call you later today. Sometime after the fair. Tony and I are engaged."

Beatrice and Wyatt hurried around the table to give Georgia a hug. "What wonderful news!" said Beatrice, squeezing Georgia's hands. "I'm so happy for you."

"Tony Brock is a lucky man," said Wyatt warmly. "And it will be an honor to officiate at your wedding ... if that's what you had in mind?"

Georgia nodded. "We're not going to have a *big* wedding, you know. Something small and intimate. But we both wanted you to wed us."

Savannah said in an excited voice, "And I'm going to be the only attendant! The maid of honor. Although I'm trying to convince Georgia that little Smoke would be adorable in a kitty tux as a ring bearer."

"That would be a sight to behold," said Beatrice with a smile. She was happy to hear that Savannah was being so positive about her sister getting married. For a long time, Savannah had been very possessive over her sister's time.

As if reading her mind, Georgia said quickly, "And Savannah's not only helping me out with the ceremony, but business has been so booming for me online that I've hired Savannah to help me with the accounting and other parts of the business. She's been so busy that I don't think she's even had a spare minute."

Miss Sissy appeared to have come up with some possibilities for Maisie. She held them up high and shook them at Georgia. Georgia and Miss Sissy started a conversation on the merits of the individual outfits.

"Do you think Maisie the cat will *like* wearing crocheted cat sweaters?" asked Wyatt doubtfully. "Is she the kind of cat who will tolerate that kind of thing?"

"She's a very *patient* cat. And she's absolutely devoted to Posy and Miss Sissy. I'm guessing she's the kind of cat who will wear anything they want her to wear," said Beatrice with a shrug. She peered closer at the sweater that Miss Sissy was holding up and examining. "I see. So it's more of a sweater on the back and on the front it allows the cat's legs to be free. It looks like a cape that's attached."

"Was there anything else that you wanted to see after this?" asked Wyatt.

"I did want to pick up that cake from June Bug, since you mentioned she was here. I like to give her business when I can and it might be fun to have a cake at the meeting tomorrow evening," said Beatrice. "But after that, I think I'm probably ready to head home. For one thing, I think Miss Sissy will have completely eliminated my budget for the craft fair by then."

Chapter Fifteen

Beatrice felt lucky to get out from Georgia's booth with only two purchases. Miss Sissy had quite the spring in her step as they walked away, no doubt contemplating Maisie in her new wardrobe. Wyatt held Beatrice's hand as they headed to June Bug's cake booth.

Beatrice felt the need to set expectations for Miss Sissy. "I know June Bug's cakes will look delicious, but we're *only* getting one cake and it's for the meeting I've got tomorrow."

Miss Sissy said, "Meeting? I want to go."

Wyatt said thoughtfully, "I guess with all the commotion lately, Meadow must have forgotten to ask you, Miss Sissy. It's a service project for the hospital—baby quilts. And I'm creating meditations for each of the meetings. You're certainly welcome to come. It was just an oversight that you weren't invited—you were in the hospital still when we were setting it all up."

"Humph," said Miss Sissy. She was clearly piqued at not being in on the ground floor. Or else she was simply wanting cake.

June Bug's eyes danced at them as they approached her cake booth. She was cheerfully assisting three customers at once. One seemed to be asking a question about the calorie count of her cakes (Beatrice had to wonder if anyone would think luscious butter-icing cakes could be low-calorie), one appeared determined to pay for her cake in pennies, dimes, and quarters and was counting them out into June Bug's plump palm, and another was asking June Bug if she could bake a red velvet groom's cake for an upcoming wedding in another town.

Beatrice was dismayed to see that these cakes, beautifully crafted and labored over, were being sold for a mere eight dollars apiece. June Bug should be pulling in at least double that. In fact, Beatrice couldn't help but wonder if perhaps June Bug were *losing* money on her cakes—not just with the lost time when she could be performing a job as a housekeeper, but because of the cost of her ingredients. The little woman was always so busy and in such a rush that she might not even have time to think about her pricing strategy.

Finally the customers left with their cakes and questions answered and Beatrice, Wyatt, and Miss Sissy walked up. Miss Sissy's eyes were huge as she studied the cakes in front of her, but she heeded Beatrice's warning and didn't try to get a cake all for herself.

"June Bug, these look delicious, but you should be charging much more for these cakes!" said Beatrice.

The little woman, as usual, looked startled with her round, buggy eyes. "Really?" She frowned at her creations as if they'd disappointed her by devaluing themselves.

"Really," agreed Wyatt. "But it probably was a good way to get more exposure for your work. There were lots of people here from other towns. And I did overhear that you were getting an order for a groom's cake."

"I hope you didn't quote them a price?" asked Beatrice, alarmed.

"Not yet," said June Bug slowly.

"Good. Because you need to charge a good deal more than you are here. Plus you need to factor in your travel costs," said Beatrice.

"How much do you think I should ask for one?" asked June Bug in flustered concern.

"I'm not sure," said Beatrice. "But I'll try to find out. And if I can't, I know who to ask. Jake the baker."

"Do you think he'll want to help answer a question?" asked June Bug doubtfully. "He makes cakes, too. Maybe he wouldn't want to help me get business."

"I have a feeling Jake gets plenty of business. At any rate, he's a resource if we need one. But please don't quote a price until we get a good idea how much groom's cakes are going for!" said Beatrice.

June Bug nodded, looking relieved. "A little extra money would be a good thing."

"And it should be relatively easy to find out. Probably if I do a search of local bakery websites," said Beatrice. This reminded her of something else and she clapped a hand to her head. "Oh, for heaven's sake. I just remembered I'm supposed to be setting up all these social media accounts for the guild. I got started with it and then I got distracted and never came back to it."

This made June Bug look even more startled. "Is that bad?"

"It's not bad exactly, but it's not like me. When I say I'm going to do something, I like to do it. It's just a testament to how busy it's been lately and how much I have going on. I shouldn't have really *agreed* to do the social media set up," said Beatrice with a sigh.

"Why did you? Just to be helpful?" asked Wyatt.

"No, I think I did it because I was railroaded into it. Which is never a good reason to take something on. Still, it's a good cause. I just need to create a chunk of time to get it done," said Beatrice.

Miss Sissy, whom Beatrice had supposed completely engrossed in helping choose a cake for the service meeting, gruffly chimed in. "I'll help."

There was a long pause while Beatrice struggled to figure out what Miss Sissy meant by this. Was she alluding to the fact that she was presently assisting in choosing a cake? That she would help at the service project meeting by quilting for the hospital? Or was she for some reason making reference to something completely different? Beatrice decided to assume that her volunteering to help was for one of the things she knew the old woman was already helping with.

"Yes, you've been a tremendous help, Miss Sissy. Wyatt, did you know that Miss Sissy is going to be part of our service project? She's coming to the meeting tomorrow evening. Not only that, she's picking out one of June Bug's delicious cakes for our enjoyment at the meeting!"

June Bug and Wyatt smiled at Miss Sissy. Miss Sissy scowled back at all of them.

"No!" she said, in great irritation. "I'll *help* you."

"With what, Miss Sissy?" Beatrice asked this with some trepidation. She felt she was already getting entirely too much help from the old woman.

"With the social media!" spat Miss Sissy, glowering.

Beatrice's heart sank. Wyatt appeared to be hiding a smile and June Bug simply looked bewildered.

"Do you know much about social media?" asked Beatrice. She'd learned it didn't pay to be too direct with Miss Sissy. You never wanted the old woman to get her back up and be defensive. "Are you sure you'd be interested in seeing me set up accounts on the *computer*?" She put some stress on the last word. After all, Miss Sissy didn't even possess a computer. Did this interest all date back to her sudden possession of a cell phone? Did this mean that Beatrice was going to be investing in some sort of computer for Miss Sissy?

Miss Sissy gave her a furious look. "I can *help*!"

"If you want to, Miss Sissy," said Beatrice stiffly.

Wyatt quickly inserted, "Do we know what cake we want for the meeting tomorrow?"

As Wyatt discussed the pros and cons of chocolate cake versus carrot cake with Miss Sissy, June Bug gave Beatrice a sympathetic look. "Been a long day?" she asked.

"It certainly has! Although I've had a nice time visiting with Wyatt," said Beatrice with a small smile.

June Bug's large eyes fell on the turquoise necklace around Beatrice's neck. "Your necklace sure is pretty."

"Thanks! Wyatt saw it at one of the craft booths and thought of me." Beatrice fingered the smooth stones.

June Bug's face was wistful. It made Beatrice wonder if, despite all the time spent running around and the time she spent in other people's houses, if June Bug weren't lonely.

She changed the subject. "I saw your art quilt when Wyatt and I were walking around. June Bug, it was *amazing*."

June Bug's face lost its wistfulness and lit up. "Do you think so?"

"I *know* so. And I hope that you didn't devalue it by putting a low price on it." The thought had just occurred to Beatrice and worried her. That quilt must have taken a lot of loving work on June Bug's part.

She shook her head. "I didn't even want to show it. Meadow made me though, and she set the price. Took care of the whole thing."

That was good news indeed. Because if Beatrice knew one thing, Meadow understood about the value of money. Usually her time was spent in the process of saving it and squeezing her budget, but she was also able to see the value in her art and price it accordingly and shrewdly when the time came.

Beatrice suddenly realized that June Bug had been at the fair the entire day and might have seen something. Although that was a pretty big *might*, considering how busy she'd been. "June Bug, did you hear that there was a tragedy at the park here today?"

June Bug's eyes somehow managed to get wider.

"It's Ida. I'm afraid she was murdered," said Beatrice quietly.

"Evildoers!" snarled Miss Sissy, proving that despite looking at cakes, she still had an ear open.

"Awful," said June Bug fervently. And then, "I wish I could help you. I'm trying to think if I saw anything suspicious, but I just don't think I did." Her brow furrowed in her efforts to think of something useful.

"As far as people who were here," continued Beatrice in her quiet voice, "did you happen to see Jake leave his booth? Or Huey walking around?"

June Bug nodded fervently. "Both of them were walking around." She looked worried. "But I didn't see them doing anything wrong. Huey was trying to help get the vendors and the crafters all set up."

"Did you, perhaps, see Huey heading in the direction of the tennis courts? Near the restrooms?" asked Beatrice.

June Bug's face was a study in concentration. "Yes. Yes, actually, I think I did, Beatrice. He was walking over there quite briskly, I thought. It was at a point where I was looking for him, as a matter of fact. I needed his help making change. When I finally saw him, I noticed he was walking quickly away from me, so I just crossed my fingers that I wouldn't get anyone who wanted a brownie. In fact, just to make it easier on me, I concealed the brownies."

Beatrice studied the counter. "Did you remember to put them back out again after you made change?"

June Bug flushed. "Oh dear!"

Not only did Beatrice give June Bug a lot more than the asking price for the triple fudge chocolate cake Miss Sissy finally decided on, she also quickly changed the prices for the remaining cakes so that the next group of shoppers would pay a fairer price for their goods.

Beatrice was ready to leave the fair at this point. The morning had given her a good deal to absorb and she also had the service project and the social media on her mind. Wyatt gave her a parting hug as Miss Sissy scowled like a gargoyle at him until he left in his car.

On the way back, Miss Sissy hissed, "Help you!"

"Yes, all *right*, Miss Sissy! As I told you, I'm happy for you to help out. Do you want to come by tomorrow morning? Noo-

noo is always glad to see you. You could help me set up the profiles."

Miss Sissy waved wildly in the passenger seat, indicating some sort of dissatisfaction with Beatrice's words. But Beatrice wasn't catching on to her subtext, whatever it might be. She resorted to giving Miss Sissy limited choices, in the hope that she could elicit some form of agreement from her. "Would you rather me pick you up in my car tomorrow morning? Or would you rather walk?"

Miss Sissy glared at her. "I can walk!"

"Oh, I know you can. You walked quite a ways today at the fair and I live just down the street from you. That's fine, then. Come over whenever you please tomorrow. I'll take any help I can get." Beatrice could only hope that Miss Sissy would be more responsive by that time.

The rain beat hard on the windows as Beatrice fixed her coffee the next morning. When she opened the door to let Noo-noo out, the little dog gave her a reproachful look, choosing to wait until the rain had subsided.

"Don't have to go that bad, do you?" asked Beatrice. "I can't say I blame you. I wouldn't want to go out in it either. And I don't think Miss Sissy will. I'll keep an ear out for a text message. Probably one that says 'get me!'"

After coffee and a breakfast of honeydew melon and yogurt, Beatrice decided she'd try to knock out some of the quilting for the baby quilt. She got more done in a shorter space of time than she'd thought. At this rate, she'd be ahead of the rest of the group and the service project was supposed to be a joint endeavor ... a communal activity. Beatrice put the project down and instead took a look at what they had for the history so far.

A rapid ringing of the doorbell made Beatrice jump and caused Noo-noo to explode into a frenzy of barking. She hurried to the door and found a drenched and angry-looking Miss Sissy.

Beatrice flung the door open wide and ushered her in. "Miss Sissy! What on earth?"

"Said I'd help," said the old woman sullenly as she walked in.

Noo-noo stared, agape, at her. Ordinarily the corgi would be flopping on the floor to have her belly rubbed, but apparently Miss Sissy was too wet for Noo-noo.

Beatrice found an old beach towel in her linen closet and hastily wrapped it around Miss Sissy.

"Isn't cold!" pointed out Miss Sissy. But Beatrice noticed that she pulled the beach towel closer around her anyway.

"Still. When one gets as wet as you did, it's easy to get chilled. Why didn't you call me? Or text me? It's occasions like this that warrant a text message! If I'd known you were ready, I'd have driven you over," fussed Beatrice.

Miss Sissy shrugged an emaciated shoulder, quickly losing interest in the conversation. Her beady eyes swept the den until she saw what she was looking for. "Computer!" she said exultantly.

"That's right. We can get started on those social media accounts, if you want to watch what I'm doing," said Beatrice. "But don't you want some food or a warm drink?"

Miss Sissy opened her mouth to automatically reject her suggestion, but then reconsidered before she spoke. "Food?" she asked.

A few minutes later, Beatrice returned with a steaming bowl of hot buttered grits and a large cup of coffee. "This should warm you up," she said. "And you can eat while I set up the accounts."

Miss Sissy thrust a cloth tote bag at Beatrice and Beatrice took it from her in surprise. She hadn't even realized she was holding anything. Beatrice peered inside. "What's this?" Inside was a battered (and rather damp) manila envelope.

Beatrice opened it cautiously and saw a bunch of old photographs in various stages of dilapidation. She walked across the small room to a brown leather chair and sat down, holding the pictures under the light from a nearby lamp. Finally, impatient with herself, she put her reading glasses on and looked at the pictures again.

There was a tremendous stack of them and they all showed old quilts and old quilters. There were some from the inside of Posy's shop, some from craft fairs from years past, and some of people she recognized. There were quite a few where she *didn't* recognize the quilters. She turned to look quizzically at Miss Sissy, nonchalantly eating her grits.

"Said I'd help," she reminded Beatrice.

"Yes, but somehow I thought you meant you were going to be helpful with the social media." Now she realized that Miss Sissy had said no such thing. She must have meant that she'd supplement the history and, yes perhaps, the social media pages with old photographs that showed the past of the guild. Beatrice felt guilty that, in a way she'd shortchanged Miss Sissy. She was so used to her frustrating erratic behavior that she hadn't had the imagination to think of her at a time when she'd been younger and had interests and had participated fully in the community. This especially bothered Beatrice since she was very cognizant of her own very different past that involved living in a large city, engaging and networking with a variety of people in a fundraising capacity, and of photographing, showing, and promoting art.

Surprisingly, these photographs were quite good. And not just a *tepid* quite good. It wasn't just that Miss Sissy hadn't chopped off the tops of her subjects' heads or that she hadn't included her thumb in any of the pictures. She had a very good eye as a photographer. Her sense of framing her subjects, the angles at which she shot, and the strong images she captured, all spoke of talent. What was more, she had a good number of pictures, which meant that she was in the habit of carrying her camera, loaded with film, *with* her when she went out. These pictures were taken long before the days when people always carried a camera because they always had their phones.

"Miss Sissy, these are ...well, they're very good. Thank you for bringing them." The old woman inclined her head in response and Beatrice continued. "It seems to me that you must have enjoyed your photography. What made you stop?"

Miss Sissy grunted. "Didn't like the new cameras."

"What? You mean the digital ones?"

The old woman nodded.

"I can understand that they would be off-putting. In fact, I can *really* understand because I felt the same way when it was time for me to make the switch to digital for my work at the museum. I was very resentful about it, as a matter of fact. But then I realized that they had an upside, too. I could take as many pictures as I liked without wasting film."

Miss Sissy seemed to be absorbing this thoughtfully.

Beatrice said, "At any rate, I'd like to scan some of your pictures to include them in the book. I'll make sure you get full credit and that you get all the pictures back."

Miss Sissy's eyes had gleamed at the idea of photo credits, but shrugged at the mention of getting the pictures back. Beatrice supposed that, since Miss Sissy had clearly crammed the photos nonchalantly in a bag, she wouldn't exactly be missing them while they were at Beatrice's house.

Beatrice started trying to sort the pictures. She decided to put the ones with especially beautiful quilts or photographic composition in one pile, pictures of people she recognized in another. As she glanced through the photos, she stopped abruptly. It was a picture of Vivian.

This picture seemed to be a candid shot because neither subject was looking at, or seemingly even aware of, the camera. Vivian and Huey were beaming at each other, love showing in their eyes. Beatrice studied the picture thoughtfully before carefully setting it to one side in a different pile.

"Computer work," said Miss Sissy impatiently.

"Oh, so you *do* want to watch me set that stuff up? I wasn't sure. All right, let's put the computer on the kitchen table so that you can sit beside me. Even better, you can help me pick out some of your photos to use on the accounts. We can load pictures into the libraries of the sites to make the accounts more interesting," said Beatrice.

Miss Sissy raised a dubious eyebrow at this. "For the book."

"Oh, I know the photos are for the book. But they also might provide a real sense of continuity for people interested in quilting's place in Dappled Hills."

Beatrice showed Miss Sissy how to set up social media accounts while the old woman looked on, yawning from time to time. But she did better picking out interesting pictures to scan and upload. Apparently, Miss Sissy still had a good eye.

Surprisingly, the process seemed to go a lot faster with Miss Sissy there. Maybe that's because her presence meant that Beatrice had to stay completely focused on the task at hand. There was no getting distracted by social media or realizing that the dishwasher had stopped and needed to be unloaded. There was only the somewhat tedious process of putting up backgrounds or covers on the accounts, uploading profile pictures, and setting up notifications.

"Okay, so that's all set. Let's scan and upload the pictures you picked out," said Beatrice as Miss Sissy pushed the pile of photos across the table to her. Again, the process seemed to go a lot faster without distractions and with Miss Sissy looking on.

"There. That will have to do. I can always tweak it later. Of course, someone needs to *post* on the account, but no one said that I had to be the one to do that. They only said that they needed me to set it up," said Beatrice. She noticed a slight defensive edge to her voice and pressed her lips tightly together.

Miss Sissy just watched her, stony-faced.

"Oh, I guess there's one more thing I should do. Tag and friend some of the quilters online. That way they can share the accounts and lend them some visibility. Let's see whom I can find online with just a casual search," said Beatrice.

Beatrice wasn't especially surprised to see that some quilters didn't appear to have much of a social media footprint at all. Others appeared to have quite a lot of accounts—Piper, for one. Beatrice tagged and friended Piper on behalf of the new accounts and crossed her fingers that her daughter had the time to notice and share them.

Then she got to Gwen's profile. Gwen was online, but she apparently didn't pay much attention to what was happening on her profile. Maybe she had the same lackadaisical attitude toward her social media that she had with her volunteering. And Beatrice's breath caught and she narrowed her eyes as she studied the profile. Surely Gwen would have untagged herself if she'd been online and seen this post. Because of one of Gwen's friends had tagged her in a picture. It was, again, a candid shot. Gwen seemed oblivious to the camera and was walking with great determination in front of a large brick building. The person tagging her said, "A rare Gwen sighting in Lenoir!"

The sign in front of the large brick building said *Oak Haven Retirement Community*. The date of the photo was a couple of weeks before Oscar Holland's death. Could Gwen have been visiting Oscar's dying mother?

Chapter Sixteen

July 20th

I wrote last time that I wasn't sure anyone in this town really liked me. Now I can emphatically say that that's not the case. But is anything on earth ever really simple?

Now I've got Huey—someone I really care for but have some concerns about—who is very interested in me. At the same time, I've got Jake. Jake is certain he's fallen madly in love with me. All I can say is that it sure doesn't take long for Jake to fall in love. But I know he's telling the truth. I can see the way he looks at me. I have such a great time with Jake—as a friend. And I really need a friend in Dappled Hills. I need someone to go to the movies with or go swimming with or just to hang out with. But am I leading Jake on if I keep doing things with him?

Miss Sissy left during a lull in the weather. Beatrice spent an hour looking through her photos and mulling over proof of Gwen in Lenoir. She didn't want to overreact to it. It might mean nothing, after all. Perhaps Gwen had a friend at the same retirement home where Mrs. Holland had lived. After all, they were all at the age where friends or loved ones were living in assisted living. Still it was very coincidental. Most Dappled Hills residents chose to live in a more local facility, like Mountain Vistas, which was right outside of Dappled Hills and not on the other side of Lenoir, like Oak Haven.

Besides, Gwen did look so resolute in the photo, so determined. Beatrice decided that the best way to handle it was to ask Gwen about it and see her reaction. She made a mental note to do that at the meeting that evening.

She also wanted to ask Huey about that other photo—the one in the stack that Miss Sissy brought over. For someone who'd originally professed not to even remember Vivian, he certainly looked cozy with her in the picture. He'd said that he'd been too old for her. It hadn't appeared in the picture that he'd felt that way at the time. And Vivian's journal entry that she read right after Miss Sissy left made it sound as if he were especially keen on Vivian. Unless Vivian lied. But who lied to their diary?

A peremptory rap at her door made her jump, and poor Noo-noo leap to her feet. Was this Grand Central Station? She peeked out the side window and saw a rather self-conscious looking Huey there, glancing around as if he might be seen visiting Beatrice's cottage. Why? Because people would talk? Or because he wanted no witnesses? Was Huey dangerous? It seemed ridiculous to think so when he seemed so innocuous.

Beatrice dropped back from the window, feeling oddly conflicted. Here she'd been, ruminating on how guilty Huey seemed and now he'd shown up at her house. She felt a little uneasy about letting him in, but felt silly about not answering the door. There was no hard evidence against him, after all.

She decided to play it on the safe side. She quickly texted Meadow. *FYI, letting Huey in my house for visit. Still a suspect, though.* At least that way, if she somehow mysteriously disappeared, Meadow could give Ramsay a lead.

Beatrice opened the door and Huey smiled at her. Now he looked a bit apologetic. "I'm sorry. Is it too early to visit?"

"Not at all," said Beatrice coolly. "I've been up for ages." She opened the door wide.

Huey shook off his large umbrella, carefully laying it down on Beatrice's front porch before walking inside. He glanced around. "This is very nice. I'm not sure I've ever been in here." He took in the overstuffed gingham armchairs, the cheery scattered rugs, and the comfy sofa. And the artwork. His eyes lingered long on the paintings Beatrice had hung, the glasswork in the built-in bookcase. The pottery.

"You've got quite the eye for art. Or maybe your husband did?" asked Huey.

Beatrice smiled at him. "Thanks. I was a curator at an art museum. In my spare time, which wasn't much, I managed to find art at local craft fairs."

Huey settled into one of the armchairs. "Did you find anything yesterday?"

Besides a body? Beatrice said, "I wasn't really looking. Well, that is to say, I wasn't looking for anything to *buy*. We get to the point, don't we, when we simply don't have the room for everything we like. I did pick up something for my daughter as a gift. I purposefully bought a cottage to limit my art acquisition."

"Very smart," said Huey. His expression indicated that he was a little surprised at Beatrice's expert background. Good. She liked keeping people guessing.

"You're not here to discuss art, though. At least, I'd be surprised if you were," said Beatrice. She sat down in an armchair across from Huey.

"That's right." Huey hesitated for a few moments as if trying to figure out how best to express his thoughts. "You see, when we were talking at the craft fair, I ... well, afterward, I started feeling concerned that perhaps you'd gotten the wrong impression of me."

Beatrice raised her eyebrows. "In what way?" she asked steadily.

"I could tell you were skeptical of my story," said Huey rather stiffly.

"Your story?" asked Beatrice.

"Yes."

"Which one? The one where you insisted you couldn't remember Vivian and then said you were far too old for her? Or the one where you claimed not to know anything about Ida's death, but realized she was found near the tennis courts?" asked Beatrice dryly.

Huey opened his mouth and then shut it tight. His gaze drifted over to one of Beatrice's favorite paintings—a rustic cabin in a wooded setting. It was done by an untaught, natural artist and the artist's love of his world came through the canvas. It had the effect of relaxing Beatrice and it seemed to relax Huey, too.

"You're reading too much into both of those things," he said. Beatrice noticed that one hand was gripping the armrest of his chair until his knuckles were white. Maybe he hadn't gotten as relaxed by the picture as she thought.

"I did know Vivian, as I've already mentioned. She was what I'd term *a friend*." His delivery was as rigid as his posture in the soft chair. "Unfortunately, she appeared to have some sort of schoolgirl crush on me." He waved his hand vaguely.

"She wasn't a schoolgirl," said Beatrice. "She was a young woman, starting out in the world. With dreams of being an investigative journalist. Interested in quilting. Someone who knew what she wanted." Her voice was brusque with irritation. The more time she spent with Huey, the less she liked him. She couldn't help but wonder what the pretty, talented, young Vivian had seen in him.

"All right, if you want to be exact about it. She wasn't a schoolgirl. But she may as well have been one. She was naïve and inexperienced in the world. Maybe she *thought* she knew what she wanted, but she didn't. Do any of us, when we're very young? At any rate, she was infatuated with me. When she saw me out shopping downtown or out doing yardwork, or whatever I was doing, Vivian would always stop by to talk to me." His face flushed with the memory. Whether it was an embarrassed flush or a pleased one, Beatrice couldn't tell.

"And that bothered you, clearly," said Beatrice.

"It certainly did," said Huey sharply. "I was engaged at the time."

"Oh, so now it all comes out." Beatrice surprised herself at her combative tone. Huey was definitely getting under her skin. "You were engaged. You were probably pleased by Vivian's attention, but you couldn't afford a scandal. You had aspirations, didn't you? You later became a mayor and then a state representative. Small town gossip wouldn't have fit into that plan, would it?"

"No, it wouldn't," snapped Huey. "That's why I told Vivian. I told her that she had to stop the nonsense. I was engaged and she was creating a problem for me. I didn't want people to talk. That was it. I didn't want them to talk and they *always* talk in Dappled Hills. Even though I was simply a meager bank manager at the time and not making any money ... I still didn't need that kind of trouble."

Beatrice nodded thoughtfully as if seriously considering this information. "You're saying that Vivian's pursuit of you was unwanted and you rejected her."

"That's correct," said Huey, relaxing a little in relief. "Correct."

Beatrice smoothly stood up, walked the short distance to the kitchen table, picked up a photograph, and handed it to Huey before sitting down again.

"Somehow," she said softly, "it doesn't appear to me that her romantic attraction was unwanted."

Huey stared silently at the photo. At the much younger version of himself with Vivian. Then he sighed. He put the picture carefully down on the table beside his chair. His gaze drifted away from Beatrice, resting lightly on the cabin painting before scanning again the other works of art that Beatrice had hanging. "All right," he said. "I was attracted to her, too. Who wouldn't be? She was lovely, smart, and outgoing. But I was a man of honor. I'd made a promise to my fiancée and I wasn't going to jilt her."

"Is it jilting when you're engaged? I thought jilting was only at the altar," mused Beatrice.

"At any rate, I wasn't going to end my engagement to Francine. Period. And I did just what I said I did. I told Vivian that she had to stop trying to spend time with me—that tongues would wag, otherwise," said Huey.

Again, Beatrice wondered what the attraction could have been for Vivian. Huey sounded so self-righteous when he spoke about matters of honor. She said, "Vivian's disappearance must have been very convenient for you. So convenient that you didn't think to tell the police."

"Certainly not. I assumed her disappearance had something to do with my rejection of her," said Huey.

Huey seemed oblivious to the ego implicit in the words. "You didn't ask the police whether there was any cause for concern when she disappeared?" she pressed. "But you were friends. More than that, she was someone who you felt some attraction for. And you didn't report her disappearance as worrisome?"

"As I just said, I thought she was just trying to save face—that she'd decided to leave town instead of risking further embarrassment," said Huey with a shrug.

"You thought Vivian would give up the relationships and the budding journalism opportunities and the new quilting craft she was learning to save face," repeated Beatrice. It seemed unbelievable to her.

Huey looked away again. "I only felt a sense of relief that an uncomfortable situation had been avoided."

His mention of an *uncomfortable situation* reminded Beatrice of Vivian's journal. There was one question she needed to ask all the suspects. A question that had arisen from her reading Vivian's journal. "When Vivian first met you, did she say you looked familiar? That she felt as if she'd known you before?"

Huey's eyes darted back to Beatrice and he tensed up again. "What do you mean? Why would I look familiar to Vivian? She was a stranger to Dappled Hills and I grew up here."

"Oh, I don't know. I only wondered if perhaps she'd mentioned something like that," said Beatrice.

Huey's eyes narrowed. "I don't know what you're referring to."

Beatrice moved on. "Going back to Vivian's disappearance. At some point after she left town, or had appeared to leave town, you got married. Is that right?"

Beatrice's cell phone chimed at her. Was it Meadow getting back to her? A quick glance at the phone told her it was Miss Sissy instead. "*Vile!*" Perhaps Miss Sissy was aware that Huey was her visitor.

"I did get married to Francine, yes. We had many happy years together before her death some time ago from cancer." His words weren't infused with feeling at all. Beatrice wasn't sure if that was because he genuinely felt nothing or he'd practiced his short speech about his wife's death to *keep* from feeling an unwanted emotion.

"I'm sorry to hear that," Beatrice said softly. "I lost my husband years ago, too. It's something you never really ever get over."

They sat for a moment in quiet reflection.

Then Beatrice said, "What about the other bit? Ida? When you told me you didn't realize she was dead and then you clearly knew where her body had been found?"

Huey's jaw was set firmly. "I told you the truth about my time at the craft fair. I was very busy helping with the set-up. I saw Gwen and Ida squabble, but didn't think much about it." He hesitated. "I *did* know that there was trouble near the tennis courts, but that was only because I'd started heading that way to make use of the ...um ...facilities. I stopped when I saw Ramsay heading toward a figure on the ground. I saw you and some others gathering around. I didn't even know who it was so, yes, I was genuinely surprised to hear it was Ida. After all, I'd just seen her a little earlier."

"You didn't try to see if you could help. You, with all your years of public service," said Beatrice in a scoffing voice.

Huey held his hands up, a flash of anger in his eyes. "What help could *I* provide? Ramsay was already on the way. I felt that surely, anyone in need of medical attention would get more assistance from the chief of police than from a retired mayor."

Beatrice was now very tired of speaking with Huey. He was defensive and still seemed to be stonewalling. And now that it was once again pouring down rain, it was the perfect time for him to make his departure. She gave him a brittle smile. "Well, now you've told me your piece. Thank you for coming by." She stood up, pointedly.

Huey, however, leaned forward in his chair, a study in intensity. Noo-noo, sensing something amiss in the atmosphere, walked over to sit beside Beatrice, leaning protectively against her.

Huey said, "That was part of what I wanted to say, yes. But the rest is even more important. I need you to stop poking around in this matter."

"Excuse me?" Beatrice took a small step backward as if to create more distance between herself and Huey.

"That's right. Just let the police do their jobs. Think of it— perhaps your pursuit of information for this history you're writing or for some prurient interest of your own resulted in Ida's death," said Huey in a grating voice.

"Ida's death resulted because someone decided she knew too much," said Beatrice.

"Stop now," repeated Huey. "For the good of Dappled Hills. There is no place in a quilting history for this rather tragic chapter." Huey's face, partly in the light, partly in the shadow, looked threatening to Beatrice and she felt a chill go up her spine.

Noo-noo suddenly leapt to her feet just seconds before Meadow exploded into the cottage, sopping wet and barely holding an equally-wet and baying Boris.

Chapter Seventeen

Huey sprang to his feet, eyes huge and mouth agape.

"Hello and good morning!" bellowed Meadow. Boris, with more energy than Beatrice had ever seen him, lunged at Huey on his leash before shaking vigorously to get the rainwater off himself and successfully onto Huey.

Huey gave Meadow a dour look and Boris a wary one. "I can see that it's time for me to go. Take care, ladies. And Beatrice, mind what we were discussing." The last sentence still held that ominous tone.

Meadow's voice was fake-jolly with its own overtone of warning. "Boris will be hurt if you don't tell him bye, Huey. I know you like dogs, considering that German shepherd of yours. Did you know how often Boris here is at Beatrice's? He *loves* spending time here. Sometimes he'll even have a sleepover here. He *adores* spending time with Noo-noo."

Noo-noo tried to contradict this statement by hiding behind Beatrice's legs and looking with concern at the hyperactive Boris.

"Bye, Boris," croaked Huey as the beast leaped against his leash at the man. He opened the door and surveyed the sheets of rain pelting down before picking up his umbrella and heading stiffly away.

Beatrice felt her whole body relax as Huey left. She felt a sudden affection for Boris and rummaged in her kitchen for treats for both him and her long-suffering corgi. Meadow tried to soothe and calm her great beast.

Beatrice gave the dogs the treats and then settled back into her chair, feeling now very tired although it was still early in the morning. She said, "Meadow, how did you get Boris into such a frenzy? He acted like one of the hounds of the Baskervilles with Huey."

Meadow beamed at her. "Wasn't he dangerous-looking?"

"Very alarming!"

Meadow said, "I did fire him up. When I got your text message, I made Boris chase me around the house a bit. Then I gave him some sugary treats. So what you see before you is a very hyperactive animal."

"He certainly is!" said Beatrice, watching as Boris was still pacing around the cottage. With any luck, all of that energy would wear off soon. "Do you need a towel? Or two or three? Sorry for making you come out in the rain like that."

"That would be *perfect*. And—of *course* I was going to come out in the rain. You were in a potentially dangerous situation and you needed backup! Boris makes for great backup," said Meadow.

As Beatrice hurried back to get an old beach towel for Boris and a better towel for Meadow, she agreed fervently that Boris certainly did make for great backup. He looked a lot more menacing than he actually was. Although she had a feeling that he would leap into action if he felt his owners or friends were threatened. As would Noo-noo! It was just that Noo-noo was a fraction of Boris's size.

As Meadow was drying herself and Boris, Beatrice made more coffee. Finally they settled comfortably with their hot drinks in the living room as both dogs fell asleep.

Meadow demanded, "Tell me what happened. Every bit. When did you first start feeling as if you were in danger?"

"I felt uneasy about even letting him in, as a matter of fact. I was mulling over the case. Miss Sissy came by early this morning to help me out with some projects, you see," said Beatrice, feeling this was a necessary conversational tangent to take.

"Miss Sissy was here, too? Wow, you've had quite the crowd of visitors this morning. And *help*? From Miss Sissy? On which of our projects, dare I ask? Has she messed anything up?" asked Meadow.

Meadow was clearly feeling very protective over the projects in general. Beatrice said, "No, she didn't actually touch anything. She wanted to share some old photos with me to include in our history. I thought they'd also be good on the social media sites, so I uploaded a bunch there."

Meadow lifted an eyebrow. "I'm impressed. So she was really being pretty helpful. But why did that make you uneasy about letting in Huey? He's not someone who I'd ordinarily put in the dangerous category."

"Miss Sissy's photos included a picture of Huey with Vivian. They seemed a lot friendlier than we'd been led to believe," said Beatrice. "In fact, I think they might have been in love."

She retrieved the photo and handed it to Meadow. Meadow squinted at it, finally taking off her red framed glasses and putting on some reading glasses she had on a chain around her neck. "I need bifocals," she muttered. She studied the picture again with her glasses on, holding it carefully under the light to see it better.

"Yes," she said firmly. "They were in love. No question. And Huey practically denied even knowing who she was. Unbelievable."

Beatrice said, "It's not only that. Huey has been tripping up over his own words. He told me that he knew nothing about a death at the craft fair. Then he proceeded to tell me exactly where Ida's body was found. I was just a little nervous inviting him in, that's all."

"What was his excuse for being here?" demanded Meadow.

"Nothing. He had no excuse at all. He told me he was there because he thought I'd gotten the wrong idea from him—his misstatements, I suppose. But he was definitely warning me. There was no question about that," said Beatrice. "Let's just say that I was glad that you and Boris showed up when you did."

"So Huey and Vivian," said Meadow thoughtfully. She made a face. "Somehow I just can't picture it."

"He was a good deal older than she was, I'm guessing," said Beatrice. "Was he even good-looking?"

"Well, sure he was! Here, look at the picture again." Meadow handed the photo back to Beatrice.

Sure enough, there was an attractive twinkle there. And Huey sported an athletic build and good hair. Good hair at the time, anyway. Beatrice said, "I see that he was. Maybe not quite as nice-looking as Vivian, but still attractive. He told me that he was engaged at the time and wasn't free to date Vivian. I don't really understand why he didn't just remove himself from the engagement and start his relationship with her."

"No, I guess you *wouldn't* understand that, since you're a newcomer to Bradley," said Meadow thoughtfully.

Beatrice sometimes felt that she would be forever a Bradley newcomer—even if she'd lived there for decades—simply because she wasn't a native resident.

"Huey, you see, was a man of big plans. Big ideas." Meadow was clearly settling into her role as storyteller. "He had every intention of making it big—either in business or in politics, or both. But the thing was, he needed a little bit of capital to get there."

"Huey needed money?" asked Beatrice. "But he seems so affluent now."

"He *is* affluent now. But that's because he was married to Francine, who was rolling in money. He used that money to make even more money. Everyone knows you have to have it to make more of it," said Meadow.

"I thought he went off to school. A nice school," said Beatrice, frowning.

"Oh he did, he did. But his parents were in major debt, putting him through school. No wonder he didn't want to break off his engagement with Francine," Meadow said with a sniff.

Beatrice said, "Do you think that, if he's telling the truth and really did break up with Vivian, that she didn't handle it well?"

"You mean, maybe Vivian tried to encourage him to cancel his engagement to Francine? Marry her instead?" asked Meadow.

"Right. Maybe she created something of a problem for Huey. He loved her, she loved him. But he *needed* to marry Francine," said Beatrice.

"Francine and he had a good life together," said Meadow with a shrug. "Maybe they weren't wildly in love, but they made it work, you know? But—you're asking if he might have felt desperate enough to do something to Vivian. Would he have done that if he loved her?"

"I think if he felt desperate enough, he would have. Because, believe me, he seemed desperate a few minutes ago and he really conveyed a sense of urgency to me," said Beatrice.

"I've known the man all my life. But how well do you really know people?" asked Meadow. "And he's a politician, to boot."

"*Was* a politician," clarified Beatrice.

"Once a politician, *always* a politician," said Meadow.

Beatrice mused, "I thought he was especially odd when I asked him if Vivian had seemed to recognize him. You know, since her journal mentioned someone seemed very familiar to her."

"Did he say that she *had* recognized him?"

"No, but his face seemed to give him away. Or maybe his expression was surprised and upset because he realized that I must have either talked to someone who knew Vivian had mentioned recognizing someone, or else I must have somehow seen that journal," said Beatrice. "After that, he really seemed intense and rather ominous to me."

Meadow said, "You really should tell Ramsay that. Maybe I should tell him."

"No, he has enough to worry about with these murders," said Beatrice. "Whenever I see Ramsay, he always looks so exhausted, like these cases are just wearing him down to a frazzle."

"Oh, well, you know Ramsay. He loves nothing better than to be sitting at home with a glass of wine and a collection of T.S. Eliot. When he's on a case, he's not sleeping regular hours or eating at regular times, and he's just generally stressed out. At least we know that the investigation won't take forever. I hope," added Meadow fervently. "It does tend to turn our lives upside-down."

"Has Ramsay said anything about the case? Any news that he shared with you?" asked Beatrice.

"He said that Ida hadn't been dead for long when she was discovered, but we knew that already, didn't we? She'd been seen having arguments and whatnot. And she was indeed strangled," said Meadow, absently putting a sympathetic hand to her own neck. "Apparently from behind. And then shoved down the concrete stairs for good measure."

"Did Ramsay think that a man would have to be the murderer then?" asked Beatrice with a frown. "In terms of needed strength to commit the crime?"

"No. He didn't seem to think it would take a whole lot of strength to knock out an old lady like Ida. Not with the killer feeling desperate. And clearly, the killer is desperate. Who kills in a public place like that? With all those people around?" clucked Meadow.

"Either someone who's desperate, or someone who has gotten away with murder once before and is over-confident," said Beatrice.

After Meadow left, Beatrice spent some time uploading Miss Sissy's old pictures online and scanning them to use for the quilting history. Noo-noo was looking longingly at her, so she acquiesced and they had a lovely walk. The rain had ended and the sunlight was streaming determinedly through some of the black clouds that were still around. A beautiful rainbow was visible in the heavens and Beatrice felt her spirits uplifted. This was an especially good feeling, since it had been a fairly discouraging and worrisome morning.

When she and Noo-noo got back home, Beatrice planned out the meeting for that evening. That is, she planned what she was going to ask Gwen. *If* Gwen were there. She wanted to ask her about her argument with Ida before Ida's death. And she most definitely wanted to ask her about the picture she'd seen online putting Gwen in Lenoir around the time of Mrs. Holland's death. Was Gwen friends with Mrs. Holland? What did Mrs. Holland tell her, if so?

Beatrice decided to walk to the meeting that night since she could fit everything into a tote bag. The air outside surprisingly wasn't humid, despite the rain. She wasn't sure how long the meeting tonight was going to run, so she put a flashlight in the bag, just in case. By the time she'd put a small water bottle, the quilting materials, the flashlight, and a couple of other personal items in the tote, she wondered if maybe she shouldn't just drive. But despite the stroll with Noo-noo earlier, she felt she could still stand to stretch her legs, so she decided to walk to the church.

As usual, she was a few minutes early. She saw Wyatt locking the sanctuary doors and heading to the steps that led to the basement room where the meeting was. He smiled when he saw her, and then said sympathetically, "Have you recovered from yesterday?"

"I did recover from yesterday. Although today requires further recovery."

She explained to Wyatt how her day had gone so far and he shook his head. "Please, please keep safe, Beatrice. I'd hate to think Huey or anyone else is capable of doing you harm, but I've been surprised by enough people to know that anything is possible. I think it's best to prepare for nasty surprises but still try to think the best of people."

Beatrice said, "Oh, I totally agree. As a matter of fact, I texted Meadow to make sure that she knew what was going on. She was alarmed enough that she and Boris came over as backup."

Wyatt grinned at her as they walked into the basement room. "I wish I could have seen that."

"It's one of the very few times I've ever wanted to hug Boris," admitted Beatrice.

Wyatt turned on the lights and started getting the room set up and pulling out his notes for the devotional. Beatrice pulled out all of her quilting supplies and water and waited for the quilters to arrive.

Before long, the room was full of women—showing each other their quilts, sharing pictures on their phones, and catching up with each other. Meadow gave her a quick wave as she came in and before long, Georgia pulled her into conversation.

Beatrice, as a rule, was quieter than the other ladies and tended to find a spot to sit down that was a little farther away from everyone else. As it happened, Gwen was apparently the same way. Gwen walked through the door, head bent, looking at the floor, and immediately moved as far away from everyone else in the room as possible. That put her right next to Beatrice. Which was exactly where Beatrice hoped she'd be. As usual, Gwen was something of a mess—mussed up iron gray hair, shapeless top over equally-shapeless polyester slacks, and lipstick on her teeth.

"Hi Gwen," said Beatrice in a friendly voice as Gwen started setting up.

Gwen, who had barely registered the presence of another quilter there, startled a bit. Her face reflected disappointment as soon as she saw it was Beatrice. Her gaze fell longingly on a seat at the other side of the room but it was clearly too late to make that change.

"Good to see you here, Gwen," said Beatrice. "And I think it's a nice tribute to Ida that we're all gathered here."

Gwen's face grew instantly suspicious. "What do you mean by that? Ida wasn't part of this service project. Should have been. But wasn't."

"Oh, I just mean that we're showing how resilient the quilting community is, that's all," said Beatrice. "After all, Ida was a part of that community for a long time. Isn't it so tragic about her death?"

Gwen said nothing, staring straight ahead as if she hadn't even heard Beatrice.

"I was wondering if you'd seen anything that could help Ramsay track down whoever did such a horrible thing," continued Beatrice in a friendly tone as if Gwen had been actively engaged in conversation with her. "I did hear that you and Ida were having an argument at the craft fair."

This did elicit a response. A splotchy red flush rose up Gwen's neck and she turned her head to look at Beatrice. "Ida was simply in a bad mood. She was picking fights with everyone."

"But what was the argument *about* that she picked with you?" pressed Beatrice. The room was starting to fill up and the quilters were settling down. Her window of opportunity was closing. She had the feeling that, if she visited Gwen at home, the woman likely wouldn't open the door to her.

"Just small-town stuff," snapped Gwen. "Ida thought I'd slighted her in some way. She was always ridiculously thin-skinned and thought everyone was out to get her. She seemed to think that I believed I was *better* than her."

But the look of smug satisfaction on Gwen's face seemed to indicate that Gwen had indeed thought that.

"I see. So it wasn't anything to do with Vivian Hastings?" asked Beatrice innocently.

Gwen's smug satisfaction disappeared to be replayed by an annoyed expression. "No. It had nothing to do with Vivian Hastings. And, if you knew what was good for you, you'd stop nosing around in something that happened long ago. It's riling up a lot of past anger, if you ask me. That's probably what got Ida killed."

Beatrice raised an eyebrow. "Really? I was under the impression that what got Ida killed was someone who thought she knew too much. Someone who needed Ida gone."

Gwen seemed determined to ignore her, staring ahead again with very little emotion on her face.

People were starting to take their seats, and Beatrice wanted to finish her questions while Gwen was still somewhat off-kilter—before she had the opportunity to build up her walls and defenses after the meeting. Beatrice asked quickly, "Was Vivian connected to your recent trip to Lenoir?"

This time Beatrice got a reaction. Gwen's face lost all its color and she swung her head back around violently to stare at Beatrice. She stuttered, "How do you know I was in Lenoir?"

"It was easy. I saw proof of your visit on social media while I was busy setting up accounts for the quilters," said Beatrice. "There's no point denying that you were there."

Gwen appeared to be trying to regain her composure. "Well, of *course* I was there. I go up there all the time to see an old friend of mine who used to live here in Dappled Hills."

At that moment, Meadow broke away from Georgia and caught what Gwen was saying. "Really? Who?"

Gwen blinked rapidly. "Excuse me?"

Meadow's already-loud voice got even louder. "I said *who*? Who do you visit? Or whom, I guess. Whatever."

Gwen's face was furious. "No one you'd know," she said, scornfully.

"Oh, I'd seriously doubt *that*," said Meadow, putting her hands on her hips.

Beatrice broke in, "You were in Lenoir seeing Samantha Holland. Did she ask you to come? Did she have something on her mind?"

"Or," said Meadow sweetly, "did you visit another Dappled Hills resident? I'd dearly like to follow up with any of the older souls that I used to know here, so I will pester you unrelentingly for his or her name and phone number until you produce it."

Meadow was, of course, completely serious. That's *exactly* what she would do and Gwen knew it. Gwen's lips tightened into an angry line. Maybe Gwen could have gotten away with telling *Beatrice* that the person she was visiting in Lenoir was no one that Beatrice would know. But she certainly couldn't tell Meadow that. Meadow, if anything, knew even more people than Gwen did. And Meadow would also know if the name Gwen gave was a friend at all to Gwen.

Gwen hissed, "All right. I did see Sam Holland. Is that a crime? I see her from time to time."

"When was the last time you saw her?" asked Meadow innocently.

"Not as recently as it should have been," growled Gwen.

Beatrice said, "She called you and asked for a visit? Or you just up and decided to go?"

"I up and decided to go. End of story," said Gwen.

"Sam Holland died soon after that. And then her son came to town and visited you and was killed soon after *that*," recited Beatrice.

Gwen said angrily, "I had nothing to do with any of that! It has nothing to do with me."

Beatrice said, "What did Samantha Holland tell you, Gwen? It sounds as if she knew she was at the end of her life. Perhaps she had a guilty conscience."

Gwen's eyes narrowed. "Sam Holland was a good woman. She had nothing to feel guilty about."

So intense was this conversation that Beatrice was startled by the appearance of the wizened Miss Sissy, who stuck her face in the middle of their huddle and furiously said to Gwen, "You! What did you do?"

Meadow must have brought Miss Sissy with her to the meeting. Beatrice felt a mixture of guilt that she'd forgotten to follow-up on bringing the old woman to the service project meeting along with delight at Gwen's shocked reaction and immediate reactive silence. Wyatt was asking everyone to join him in starting the meeting in prayer. Gwen had really been saved by the bell.

After Wyatt's prayer, Miss Sissy was completely placid again. Then followed a period so soothing that Beatrice felt all the accumulated tension leave her neck and shoulders. Wyatt's devotion on daily pressures and scriptural relief seemed especially targeted for Beatrice. The women worked steadily on quilting the 12" square preemie quilts. Both the work and the words had a very relaxing effect on Beatrice. She hadn't realized how stressed she had been until some of that stress was relieved.

At the end of the meeting, as Beatrice was packing up her notions and other supplies, she turned to speak to Gwen once more. But she found that Gwen had already slipped away. Clearly, she hadn't wanted to chat anymore with Beatrice. Beatrice wondered if she'd be at the next meeting or whether she'd find a convenient excuse to miss that one or, perhaps, all of the *other* meetings and just complete her quilt at home.

Meadow came up to Beatrice. "So the bird has flown the coop," she said, pursing her lips.

"Is that private eye talk?" asked Beatrice with a grin.

"Who knows? I don't read private eye books," said Meadow, laughing. "Come on, I'll give you a ride back. I need to take Miss Sissy back anyway. That way you don't have to schlep your stuff back home in the dark."

"I did bring a flashlight," murmured Beatrice, but she allowed herself to be led away by Meadow.

"Bye, Wyatt," hollered Meadow and he gave them a wave and smile since he was surrounded by quilters wanting to talk with him for a few moments.

As they walked out to Meadow's van, Beatrice asked Miss Sissy, "When you were talking to Gwen earlier, she was really startled by what you said to her."

Miss Sissy gave Beatrice a surprised expression of her own.

"Don't you remember?" pressed Beatrice. "You said that Gwen *did something*. What were you referring to?"

Miss Sissy glowered, remembering now. "Mean to that girl. That dead girl."

Beatrice assumed she meant Vivian, since Ida could certainly not be considered a girl in any way. "Mean? How was she mean?"

"Threatening!" Here Miss Sissy demonstrated the concept of threatening, in case Beatrice couldn't visualize it. She mimed someone rearing back with a snarl from an oncoming threat. In the process, she managed to resemble an overacting silent film star.

"Anything *specific*?" asked Beatrice.

"Yes, come on Miss Sissy," cajoled Meadow. "You can do better than that. Reach back in your memory. Gwen was angry with Vivian. What did she say to her?"

"Said she'd *kill* her! Kill her if she didn't stay away from him!" Miss Sissy nodded her head emphatically and the hair in her bun fell out completely, swirling around her shoulders in the brisk breeze like a witch.

Meadow and Beatrice exchanged glances as they got into the van. "I guess *him* is her husband. That doesn't sound very good. We should tell Ramsay that." Meadow said in a louder voice now that the engine was running and Miss Sissy was in the back of the van, looking at the old woman in the rearview mirror. "You should have told Ramsay that when he was asking you questions, Miss Sissy!"

Miss Sissy responded by shaking an arthritic fist at her driver. She muttered again, "She said she would *kill* her! Stay away from him!" Miss Sissy's anger then seemed to fizzle out and she slumped in exhaustion in the backseat.

Meadow pulled into Beatrice's driveway and said, "First stop!"

Beatrice said in a low voice, "Do you think you can handle Miss Sissy on your own? She seems sort of ... spent." They both turned to see Miss Sissy who appeared to be falling asleep now.

"Oh, yes. Yes, I've got it handled. I have chocolate in my purse. It's easy to lure Miss Sissy with chocolate, you know. You look about that tired, yourself, Beatrice," said Meadow, giving her a concerned frown. "Why don't you go inside and get ready to turn in?"

"I may just do that," said Beatrice. She did feel very worn out and in need of some sleep. "Or maybe I'll quilt for a little while and then try to sleep."

Meadow said, "The quilt will wait! Get some sleep!" And with that proclamation, she hit reverse and shot back out of Beatrice's driveway.

Noo-noo was happy to see her and she spent a few minutes on the floor giving the little corgi some love. Then Noo-noo got a determined look on her face, a look that Beatrice recognized all too well as the dog scampered off to locate a tired, worn lovey that was still somewhat in the shape of a chicken. Beatrice obediently threw the chicken doll across the room for Noo-noo a few times before letting her out once more. She decided to take Meadow's advice and turn in early. Before she headed to the back, though, she took out her phone and read another of Vivian's entries. This was the last one she'd written.

July 31st.

This is going to sound completely paranoid, but I feel very uneasy about my safety. Mittens, let's be honest, is a sweet cat but she's not much protection. Maybe it's the dislike from some of the residents, maybe it's just some of my interactions, but I can't help but feel like I'm in danger.

I've got to shake it off. Tonight I'm going to really try and relax. I'm going to put all my worries out of my head. I'm going to watch junk on television while eating ice cream. There's no way I could feel anything but better after that.

Feeling somber, Beatrice now was completely exhausted. She headed back into her bedroom, got ready for bed, and climbed gratefully into the soft bed that was piled high with quilts and down-filled pillows.

Beatrice was jolted awake by Noo-noo's sharp, urgent barking around midnight. Beatrice flung off the covers, grabbed her robe, and stuck her feet into a pair of slippers, rushing out to see what was the matter. The corgi, still barking frantically, looked relieved at seeing Beatrice, but continued to bark, pointing herself at the back door.

Beatrice hurried up to the door and warily looked out the window. At the sight of orange and red flames rising up and billowing black smoke, her heart started pounding in her chest.

Chapter Eighteen

She grabbed the dog along with her leash and harness, lifting the corgi with some difficulty, and stumbled out the back door and around the side of the house to the front.

Her horror turned into relief as Ramsay swung into the driveway in his police cruiser. He didn't even close the driver's door as he jumped out of the car and sprinted toward Beatrice a lot faster than she'd thought he could move. "I need the fire department here," he yelled into his two-way radio.

"Beatrice, you okay? Good—get back. Way back." He grabbed the garden hose from the side of the house and sprayed the flames. Beatrice heard sirens approaching as she carefully put Noo-noo into her harness and leash.

As soon as the firefighters started attacking the fire, they dispensed with it quickly. Ramsay sat with Beatrice and Noo-noo in his police cruiser. He was completely winded, gasping from the running, worry, and smoke and seemed absolutely exhausted.

While he worked to catch his breath, Beatrice said, "I'm sorry you were working so late, but I am *so* glad you happened by. Noo-noo and I thank you from the bottom of our hearts."

He smiled a tired smile at her and seemed now to have enough breath to talk. "No thanks are needed. I was so glad to help. But what I'm more curious about is the *why*. This fire was no accident."

"I had a feeling it wasn't," said Beatrice softly. "The porch would be an odd place for an accidental fire to start. There isn't any wiring under there."

"Exactly. What's more, I smelled gasoline when I was up there spraying the flames. I'm pretty sure that you didn't pour gasoline on your front porch and set it alight, so that tells me that it was arson. What's more, this is a felony because it was an occupied building."

"Very occupied," said Beatrice with a shiver. "If it hadn't been for Noo-noo's barking, who knows? I might not have made it out. I was so tired from the day that I might have slept right up until a dangerous point ... or even past it. So you and Noo-noo are my heroes."

Ramsay waved aside her accolades, still thinking it through. "Avoiding loss of life is the most important thing, of course, but I don't even think you're going to have extensive damage to replace. Well, there'll be a bit of water damage, but the fire is already extinguished. Still—it's going to be a pain getting the repairs made. Let's move on to who might have done this. Is somebody out to get you? Furious with you?" Ramsay's face, always so kind, was even kinder and more concerned than she thought she'd ever seen it.

Beatrice just kept rubbing Noo-noo's soft fur lovingly as she said, "No, this wasn't fury. This, I think, was a warning." She explained to Ramsay what she'd found out so far, catching him up on Huey's flip-flopping on details and Gwen's trip to Lenoir at a critical time.

Ramsay listened, very serious. "Someone must think you're getting close to the truth. No one, I notice, is setting *my* house on fire."

"But investigating is your job. And that's not what people do in this country—intimidate the police. Not most of the time, anyway," said Beatrice.

"Or maybe they're simply feeling secure that I'm not particularly close to wrapping up this case," said Ramsay wryly. "Maybe I'm not asking the right questions, like you are."

"Whoever did this, they were just trying to scare me. I don't think they were trying to *kill* me," said Beatrice. There was, she noticed, a note in her voice that sounded as if she sought reassurance from Ramsay on this point.

"They didn't do a good job, if that was their goal. But it's still serious. Who do you think, if warning you off was their focus, wanted you scared off the most?" asked Ramsay.

Beatrice's mind immediately flew to Huey and his visit the day before. He had certainly been very deliberate. Would he have set her house on fire, though? She said, reluctantly, "Well, Huey came out here to personally warn me against stirring things up. Although I can't somehow see him doing something like this."

Ramsay sighed. "I'll make sure to question our top suspects. I know I should warn you against being involved and point out the danger, but you're smart enough to have already figured this out. So I'll just arrange for some overnight backup for you. Want Boris to spend the night?"

That didn't sound like much of a reward for the heroic Noo-noo. "No, that's all right. Noo-noo was able to get the job done." Noo-noo laid her head against Beatrice's leg, hearing her name.

"All right, then I'm calling Piper," said Ramsay resolutely.

Beatrice winced. "Getting a call from you in the middle of the night will scare her to death."

"I'll get right to the point and won't scare her a bit," said Ramsay as he dialed the number.

Piper came immediately over, carrying a small overnight bag. By the time she'd gotten there, the firefighters were finishing up. Beatrice thanked Ramsay and the firemen profusely and followed Piper inside.

Piper looked intently at her mother. "You're okay? Really okay?"

"Really okay. It scared the life out of me when I saw the flames, but when Ramsay and the firetruck got here so quickly it really helped me to calm down," said Beatrice. "Noo-noo was amazing and woke me right up with her barking."

"Thank goodness for that!" said Piper fervently, reaching down to hug the corgi who licked her nose when Piper got close. "Are they ...well, are they thinking it was some sort of weird electrical fire? Did they have an idea what might have caused it?"

Beatrice sighed. This was the part she wasn't looking forward to. "I'll tell you all about it. Can we have some wine while we talk? Luckily, there doesn't seem to be any water damage inside—I guess that massive door and the stone exterior really helped."

Piper opened a bottle of wine and they sat down in the living room. Beatrice, a little chilly from stress, pulled a blanket over herself. "Now talk," ordered Piper.

Beatrice gave Piper as much of a watered-down and boring version of events as she possibly could. It still apparently sounded alarming though, as was evident by Piper's wide eyes and exclamations throughout the story.

"Mama, you must stop investigating these deaths!" said Piper after Beatrice had finished.

Beatrice gave her a helpless look. "I'm not really *investigating*. It's more a matter of asking pertinent questions."

"Whatever you want to call it ... can you just stop it?" asked Piper.

Beatrice said, "I'm not trying to worry you, sweetheart. But you have to understand that I can't make that promise." She hesitated as Piper slumped a little in her chair and then said, "How about if I promise you that Meadow and I will be joined at the hip when it comes to asking any questions?"

Piper sighed and said sadly, "I think that might be the best I can hope for." She finally gave her mother a smile. "Besides, it will amuse me to see you and Meadow joined at the hip."

They laughed and Piper added, "I think that you must be trying to make Dappled Hills more lively. Although I don't think this is the right way to go about making sure that your life here is as exciting as it was when you lived in Atlanta."

Beatrice reached out and held Piper's hands in her own. She said sincerely, "I love Dappled Hills. I don't want life to be like it was in Atlanta. I love the change of pace and I love being near you. I wouldn't change a thing."

Now Piper's eyes grew misty and she nodded.

Beatrice continued briskly, "Now, enough about me. Tell me how things are going with *you*. How is protecting your free time going?"

Piper said, "It's a work in progress. But the best part is that I'm trying to be more intentional with what I take on. And I'm trying to be more intentional about my free time. I'm so busy, it's almost like I have to plan my free time the same way I plan the rest of my day. So I've brainstormed a list of books I want to read, a list of movies I want to watch online, and even make a note of what days I want to take a walk and get a little exercise."

"That sounds like a very smart idea," said Beatrice. She wondered if something like that might help her curb her own sense of restlessness a little bit.

"It's been very helpful the last couple of days. Before, it was almost like I felt drained after my free time because I spent the time just aimlessly checking social media or my email or randomly watching whatever was on television," said Piper.

Beatrice said, "Has it helped you at all with finding time to spend with Ash and developing your relationship?"

"Well, it's early days. But I decided that it would be smart for us to approach our time together the same way," said Piper.

"They used to call that 'quality time'," said Beatrice wryly.

"Which is exactly what I want it to be," said Piper quickly. "That's the end goal. I want our time together to be fun and to help us learn more about each other. So I shared my list of books and shows with Ash and asked him if he were interested in doing a mini book club or watching one of the movies with me. There was a lot more crossover appeal than I would have thought. So now we've got tomorrow night set up as a movie night with me bringing takeout and we'll watch the film online."

"Genius!" said Beatrice. "I'm going to have to steal this idea to do it with Wyatt. I'm also kind of curious to see what kind of movies he's interested in watching. And the days where you're spending some of your free time walking?"

Piper was nodding. "That's right—I put them up on an online calendar and shared the calendar with him. He'll join me on the days he can."

Beatrice beamed at her daughter. "I think we should make a toast to that. New beginnings!" They clinked their glasses.

Beatrice said, "I'm going to try to do the same thing you are. Be more intentional about my time and, once these projects are out of the way, protect my free time."

Piper glanced at the clock. "Right now I think you'd be smart to protect your *sleep*. If I know Meadow, as soon as she gets up in the morning, she's going to head over here. Ramsay is sure to tell her first thing, of course, or she'd be furious with him. She's going to want to see with her own eyes that you're okay."

Beatrice glanced at the clock and saw to her surprise that it was already three a.m. "And you've got to teach tomorrow. Ugh. I'm so sorry, Piper, you're going to have a fraction of the amount of sleep you need to have tonight. You should be fast asleep in your own bed at home by now." She stood up.

Piper gave her a long hug. "I wouldn't have wanted to be anywhere else but with you tonight."

A few hours later, Piper had gotten up and ready as quietly as she could in the tiny cottage. She whispered a goodbye to her still-dozing mother when she left. "Have a good day, Mama. Be careful. I love you. Be sure to sleep in ... I'm putting a note on the door to say that no one can disturb you until after ten."

It was a good thing that Piper left the note because Beatrice slept until slightly past nine. She was surprised at how refreshed she felt when she woke up. She called the insurance company to report the fire and damage, first thing. She got ready and was fully dressed and fed when Meadow tapped at her door right at ten.

Meadow was solemn at the door. There was no Boris with her this morning, but she gave Noo-noo a lot of hugging. "Is it visiting hours?" she asked, voice muffled as she buried her face in Noo-noo's fur. She looked up at Beatrice, subdued and eyes teary.

"It's visiting hours," said Beatrice with a smile. She followed Meadow's gaze out the still-open front door at the charred wood of the porch and the sadly destroyed porch chair and cushion. "It could have been worse."

"It certainly could!" said Meadow furiously. "Ramsay told me this morning that the fire department's preliminary findings are that it's arson with a gasoline accelerant of some kind."

"That would explain the faint odor of gasoline," said Beatrice with a sigh.

"Arson. I'm feeling very *vengeful*," said Meadow. "I want to investigate. Do you feel the same way, or are you feeling warned off, as you were meant to feel?"

"I'm angry," said Beatrice slowly, assessing her feelings. "I'm also feeling a little cautious, but more just determined to find out who was behind this. Behind *all* of it. And doing it in a safe way. I told Piper that I'd stay joined at the hip with you—a buddy system, isn't that what they called it in Scouts?"

"I'm a buddy all right," said Meadow grimly. "Woe to the person who tries to do either one of us harm. And by that, I mean Huey."

"Huey?" asked Beatrice. She was a little dubious. "I don't know. Arson? He's also sort of the obvious choice. I do want to talk to him and find out what he was doing last night, though. But I also want to know the same from Gwen and Jake. I've been pushing all three of them and one of them obviously was pushed over the edge."

"What's our next step, chief?" asked Meadow, a lighter tone in her voice. Beatrice could tell that she was trying to lift her spirits and she felt a warmth toward Meadow for it.

"Although I want to find out who set the fire, I think I *most* want to find out what Samantha Holland might have told Gwen during her visit," said Beatrice.

"Well, you know she's not going to cough any information up. She totally stonewalled you last night. And that was with both of us working on her. I don't think she's going to be any better today, especially since she's got her defenses up now," said Meadow.

"I agree with you. Do we know anyone else who was close to Sam? Maybe someone who's even living at the retirement home that she lived at?" Beatrice reached for her phone, ready to make a call.

Meadow pursed her lips. "I'm not really sure. I definitely knew Sam, but I didn't know her well enough to be able to say who her friends were." She snapped her fingers. "Posy! Posy would know, for sure."

Beatrice dialed Posy's number and, fortunately, she was available to talk. "Let's see," said Posy slowly. "Who did Samantha hang out with? I want to say that Rita Tremaine was a good friend to Sam. Yes. They'd come into the shop together and chat for a while in the sitting area. Of course, Rita moved to Oak Haven some years ago. Her children live on the other side of the country and she needed a little extra help."

Beatrice said, "Thank you, Posy. You've been super-helpful."

Posy added quickly and with a worried tone to her voice, "And are you all right, Beatrice? Someone was telling me this morning that you had a fire at your house last night! Is that true?"

Beatrice suppressed a sigh. Living in a small town meant that you kept no secrets. "Thanks for asking, Posy. I'm just fine. Very minimal damage."

When she'd hung up she said to Meadow, "Rita Tremaine. Lives at Oak Haven."

"Let's go," said Meadow grimly, picking up her purse.

Beatrice drove to Lenoir this time and much more sedately than Meadow had during their trip to see Miss Sissy. The temptation was there, however, to be distracted and she had to pull her focus back to the road.

She heard a text message notification on her phone and Meadow picked it up to peer at it. "It's Miss Sissy. She's rambling ... something about cat clothing?"

"Oh, for heaven's sake. I can't believe I forgot to give her those. And I can't believe Miss Sissy forgot to grab them! Miss Sissy picked out some clothes for Maisie that Georgia had made for the craft fair. I have them in the same bag as Piper's necklace for her birthday. I guess Miss Sissy just got distracted and forgot to get them."

"Well, we *are* talking about Miss Sissy," said Meadow dryly. "She really lives in a constant state of distraction."

"I know, but I've seen her a couple of times since then and neither one of us has remembered the cat clothes," said Beatrice. "It's just been so busy."

"And scary!" said Meadow. "I still can not *believe* that someone would intentionally set your home on fire."

"It's okay," said Beatrice. "It was scary, but it's over and now I've moved on mentally to the tedious insurance part of the ordeal. I'm okay. Noo-noo is okay."

But the mention of Noo-noo fired Meadow up again. "The idea of someone wanting to *hurt* Noo-noo! That brave little dog!" She dissolved into tears again, fishing out a tissue and loudly blowing her nose.

After what seemed like an interminable trip there, Beatrice parked at Oak Haven with some relief. It looked like an old-fashioned retirement home—definitely not one of the new and luxurious places. This one was boxy and multi-story and had lots of red brick. The landscaping was attractive, though, and there were many residents out walking or reading on benches, or playing checkers on a screened porch nearby.

They checked in with the front desk to find out Rita's room number. The middle-aged woman who worked behind the desk raised an eyebrow at their question. "Does she know you're coming?"

Beatrice and Meadow looked at each other. "No. We didn't have her number; we just knew that she was a resident here."

The woman said, "I'll give her a quick call to make sure it's okay." She turned away from them to use the phone.

Meadow said in her stage whisper to Beatrice, "Do you suppose we look very threatening and dangerous? She had to phone Rita to make sure she'd receive us as guests!"

"More likely that she wants to make sure Rita is available in her room and not in the dining hall or in the shower or taking a nap or whatnot," said Beatrice.

The woman turned back around. "Mrs. Tremaine is available," she said. "Room 219."

Chapter Nineteen

Beatrice and Meadow navigated the winding hallways to find the elevator and Rita's room. When they lightly knocked at the door, she answered, wearing a pristine, conservative nightgown and robe with her white hair pulled back in a chignon.

"Oh!" said Meadow. "Rita, we're sorry. We should have called first, but I didn't have your number." She gave the older woman a hug. "It's been a long time. This is Beatrice Coleman, a friend of mine."

Rita greeted Beatrice with a curt nod and then said to Meadow, "No need to apologize. This is my usual attire. At this point in my life I figured, who really cares? I'd rather be comfortable."

She led them into a small room with a loveseat backed in front of a window, a bed against another wall, and an armchair in a corner. Rita sat in the armchair that was turned cattycornered to the loveseat and Beatrice and Meadow sat on the loveseat. The walls were a very institutional white, but Rita had hung up some cheery paintings to try to make the place homier.

Although Rita had stated that she didn't really care about upholding her looks anymore, Beatrice wondered if that were really true. She got the impression that she *did* care. Rita wore carefully applied but natural makeup, and the chignon was something of a work of art.

"Mind if I smoke?" asked Rita. It was apparently a rhetorical question because she was already pulling out a cigarette and lighting it.

"Um, is that allowed?" asked Meadow dubiously. "There were signs on the way up ... lots of signs."

Rita rolled her eyes at her and took a deep draw on the cigarette. "Don't be a goody-goody, Meadow."

Beatrice was no fan of smoking, but this barely qualified. Rita sat closely to the open window and fanned at the blue smoke to diffuse it. No matter what she said, she clearly didn't want the staff to know what she was doing.

Meadow moved on. "I'm sure you're wondering why we're here," she said brightly.

Rita shrugged, still intent on her cigarette. "Good works?" she asked.

"No, as a matter of fact, we were trying to find out some information," said Meadow. "Somewhat related to someone you knew. Samantha Holland."

For the first time, a light of interest shone in Rita's eyes. "Sam."

"You were friends?" asked Beatrice carefully.

Rita's expression grew tired. "Yes. We were. She passed away recently. It's the worst thing about living in this place—having your friends pass away and then being forced to make new friends. Funerals all the time." She waved a thin hand to illustrate the repetitive nature of life there.

Beatrice tried to gently move on. "What we're most interested in is Sam's past. You see, her son—maybe you know him— Oscar?"

Rita nodded. "Oscar. She loved that boy. Always talking about him, showing pictures."

"Unfortunately, from what we can gather, during her last meeting with him shortly before she died she told Oscar something and most likely *gave* Oscar something. He felt a duty to check into it and went to Dappled Hills and started asking questions. These questions led to his death," said Beatrice, watching Rita's reaction to her recitation of events.

Rita's eyes grew wide. "Wait a minute. You're saying that *Oscar* is dead, too? But how? He wasn't old like us. Some sort of accident?"

"No accident. It was murder," said Meadow darkly. "It wasn't Oscar's time to go."

Rita's mouth formed a thin, grim line as she considered this. Then she said, "Then it's good that Sam passed away when she did. It would have killed her to have something happen to her boy. Sam was more like a sister to me here—best friend I've had at Oak Haven. I'll help you any way I can, although I don't know what information I've got to help you. But for Sam's sake, I'll answer anything. She'd want me to help you find out who was responsible for Oscar's death."

Beatrice nodded. "Did you ever hear her talk about someone from long ago—decades ago, really. Someone in Dappled Hills named Vivian Hastings?"

"Oh yes. Not only that, but *I* knew Vivian Hastings. I wasn't always at Oak Haven, you see." A slight smile played around her lips. "Right, Meadow? I wasn't always old."

"You certainly weren't," corroborated Meadow. "Were you a friend of Vivian's?"

"I wasn't really a friend, but I spent a bit of time with her, mostly because I was a friend of Samantha's. She was a nice girl, a rather *driven* girl. I think Vivian had plans for her future, plans to make something of herself. The only thing was that she was trying to do that in Dappled Hills. That wasn't the best town to execute those types of plans." Rita took another pull on her cigarette. "In a small town, when you're pushy, people push back. Residents of small towns are nosy enough without having an aspiring journalist there, being even nosier. When I think of her now, I think of her asking questions, her head tilted just so (Rita demonstrated), and her notebook always in hand."

Beatrice said, "Did you hear the news about Vivian, then?"

Rita nodded curtly. "That she's dead? Oh yes, I heard. I do get the papers, you know. An old body isn't such a daily occurrence that the papers in Lenoir wouldn't report it, you know." She paused, studying the smoke she was fanning out the window. "Sad. Those plans of hers came to nothing."

"Did Sam talk much about Vivian?" asked Beatrice. "About life in Dappled Hills at all?"

Rita said, "She wasn't a huge talker, our Sam. At first she didn't say a thing about her past. It was all about what table in the dining hall was the best and who had a car and where a nice place for a picnic lunch might be. But over the years, she grew a lot more reminiscent. Reminiscent and regretful. We'd sit in the tall-backed rocking chairs overlooking the courtyard here. We'd look at the roses and Sam would tell me all her worries. It was almost a confessional."

"What *was* on her mind?" asked Meadow. She coughed a little. Smoke especially bothered Meadow, even the tiny bit that was wafting her way. Rita fanned more out the window.

"For one thing, Vivian had told Sam everything that was on her mind. It didn't bother Sam at the time. She was a strong woman and certainly strong enough to have someone else use her as a confessional. Over the years, I believe it started worrying her, this information that she held. It meant a lot to Sam that Vivian trusted her not to tell anyone her thoughts and secrets. But after so many years, it wore on Sam. She knew, in return, that she could trust me not to say anything." Rita looked straight at Beatrice. "But now we know that both women are dead, one of them long-dead and under mysterious circumstances. The time has come to talk."

Beatrice and Meadow both leaned in slightly, not wanting to miss a word.

Rita seemed to be enjoying their rapt attention. "For one thing, your former mayor and former state representative?"

"Huey?" asked Beatrice and Meadow in chorus.

Rita nodded. "That's right. Huey. He was a bank robber."

Beatrice's jaw dropped and Meadow's eyes grew round and wide.

"Doesn't look the part, does he? It was some sort of youthful indiscretion, I suppose. He was away at school, apparently. Vivian lived in Boston, which was where the robbery took place. In fact, her aunt worked at the bank and was there when it was held up, so Vivian took a lot of interest in the case. The police had released sketches of the suspects and she recognized him right off the bat," said Rita.

Meadow said in a breathless voice, "So Huey is loaded with money he took from a *bank*? I mean, I knew his family didn't have a lot of means—that's why he had to marry into money. But stealing?"

"If people in Dappled Hills had known that, he certainly wouldn't have ended up representing them in the state house. He'd have been in jail. His entire life would have been different," said Beatrice.

Rita stubbed out her cigarette as Meadow gave an audible sigh of relief. "Yes, he would have had a different life. And yes, he'd have been in jail. But no, he *isn't* loaded with money. I guess the bank robbers got freaked out at some point. The money had dye packs in it and the dye packs exploded, making the money worthless. They ditched it in a dumpster. I suppose Huey went on with life as usual, pretending that nothing had happened, returning to school and then back home after graduation."

"Wow," said Meadow. She and Beatrice sat back and thought this over for a minute.

Beatrice said, "So Vivian knew. She recognized him from when she was in Boston where her aunt worked in the bank. She was hoping to become an investigative journalist and build up her credentials. She had a story land practically in her lap. And she told Huey, or at least hinted to him that she was aware of his past. Maybe she thought she could end up with a job writing for a big newspaper with her expose. At the time, Huey was probably already something of a rising star. He was about to marry someone well-respected in the community and he was, ironically, a bank manager."

"I just don't understand why her aunt didn't try to track her down after Vivian disappeared," said Meadow with a frown.

Rita said, "Her aunt died before Vivian moved to Dappled Hills. She was completely alone in the world."

"So that's Huey's secret," said Meadow. "I'll be dog-gone. I guess that wraps everything up, then. He didn't want Vivian to tell his secret. Complicated by the fact that they were obviously completely in love with each other. Such a mess. Then, when Oscar came to town, he started asking uncomfortable questions and had to be silenced."

"And Ida?" asked Beatrice, lifting a quizzical eyebrow.

"Clearly she knew something. Maybe Vivian confided in her," guessed Meadow.

"Very unlikely. Ida hated Vivian, remember?" asked Beatrice.

"Okay, then. Maybe Ida knew something about *Oscar's* murder. Maybe she spotted Huey lurking in the woods or something. Huey had to get rid of her, too," said Meadow.

"Maybe. But I'd like to hear our other possibilities," said Beatrice. "Because I'm thinking that Rita knows even more. Besides, why would Sam have asked Gwen to come see her if this all had something to do with Huey?" asked Beatrice.

Meadow said, "And how did Sam end up with Vivian's journal?"

"The other possibilities?" Rita asked Beatrice. "You mean in terms of people who might have wanted to get rid of Vivian?"

Beatrice nodded. "Did Sam talk about why anyone else might have a grudge against Vivian?"

Rita said, "Well, you mentioned Ida, so I suppose you know about Ida's anger against Vivian for the accident. Vivian confided in Sam how she feared Ida. She thought that Ida could turn everyone in the town against her."

"But Ida's dead," said Meadow pointedly. "So I don't think that she's the one we're looking for." Rita looked surprised and Meadow said, "Oh, I thought you'd have seen *that* mentioned in the papers, too. Yes, she was murdered."

Rita sat back in surprise and Beatrice added, "We think she must have known something about either Oscar's murder or Vivian's death. Perhaps she tried to blackmail someone about it and they were desperate enough to silence her."

Meadow said angrily, "They must have been so relieved when poor Vivian suddenly disappeared. After the welcome they gave her, she *should* have wanted to leave."

"And that's why no one found out what happened to Vivian until decades later," said Beatrice. "Some were glad to see her gone and some just felt as if they understood why she might have left. No one dug a bit deeper to ensure that she really had left Dappled Hills. And she had no family to follow up with the police. And it sounds as if she left her things there, which would have seemed suspicious to me, anyway."

Rita said, "There was one person who *did* dig a little deeper. Sam did. As you're saying, she also understood why Vivian might not have felt welcome in town and decided to leave. But she was unsettled by the fact that there were things left behind. Not a lot, though ... the apartment where she was living was furnished and Vivian had brought only a few bags with her. Sam kept going to Vivian's to see if she'd maybe just left for an impromptu vacation and had returned home. The first time she'd gone by Vivian's house, there were some things strewn around carelessly ... just sort of the poor housekeeping of the young. On a subsequent visit, though, some of those things were gone."

"Gone?" echoed Meadow. "You mean, someone had broken into Vivian's and taken some of her things?"

"We'd gotten a hint that someone might have wanted to make it appear that Vivian had disappeared of her own volition," said Beatrice. "This seems to reiterate that. Someone took enough of her belongings so that it appeared she'd moved, and likely disposed of them."

Rita said, "I think Vivian was likely killed in her home and whoever did it also took her things and disposed of them at the same time. Maybe they're in the lake, as well."

Meadow made a face. "What were Sam's thoughts on Gwen? Or your thoughts on her?"

"We talked about Gwen a good deal. She was ... what's that word? Sort of a 'frenemy.' Sam spent a good deal of time around Gwen because of quilting, but Gwen was never someone who acted like a loyal friend. She had her own reasons for disliking Vivian, too," said Rita.

"None of which she wants to share with us, though," said Beatrice. "Although we understood that she felt Vivian was after her husband. Miss Sissy told us something she'd overheard about that."

Rita rolled her eyes. "As if her husband were some prize catch. But Gwen obviously felt differently."

Beatrice said, "On another subject, how did Sam end up with Vivian's notebook?"

"Sam decided that, regardless what had happened to Vivian, she would *not* want everyone in town pawing through her notebook. Sam said that Vivian was practicing her writing and observation skills. Hoping to make it as a reporter. That notebook had a lot of private stuff in there. Vivian had given Sam a key to her place because one time Vivian *did* go out of town and asked Sam to take care of her cat for her."

"But she didn't this time," said Beatrice.

"Exactly. Which is another reason why Sam was suspicious that maybe Vivian had met with foul play. She walked right in and got the notebook, meaning to hold onto it until Vivian asked for it back. Of course, Vivian never did." Rita looked at her packet of cigarettes as if she'd like another one."

Meadow said quickly, hoping to distract Rita from smoking again, "Was the cat inside then? With no food? Poor kitty!"

"No, it was an outside cat for the most part, although Vivian took care of it. She kept the cat food inside, though," said Rita.

"It seems to me as if that notebook would have been the first thing someone took," said Beatrice. "After all, from everything we've heard, she was always writing in it. It's not like no one knew it existed."

"Apparently, Vivian hid it whenever she didn't have it with her," said Rita. "I guess she didn't trust her landlord to come in and find it and spread gossip all over town. At any rate, it was in her pillowcase. Sam kept it all these years for Vivian."

Beatrice said, "Did you know that Sam invited Gwen to visit her not long before she died? Do you have any idea what that might have been about?"

"From what I understood, because Sam didn't talk a lot about it, she wanted to ask Gwen about Jake," said Rita.

"Jake? What—like something she knew all those years ago about Jake was weighing on her conscience and she wanted Gwen's opinion on it?" asked Beatrice.

"I don't really know. That's at the very end of Sam's life and she was doing poorly. Her son was here a lot and I wasn't seeing as much of her as I had. All I know about Jake is that he was great friends with Vivian and seemed to really care about her. They were always together. Vivian told Sam that Jake became despondent that Vivian wouldn't date or marry him. He threatened suicide." Rita pursed her lips disapprovingly. "Maybe she thought Gwen knew something about that or that Jake had somehow told Gwen something about it."

Beatrice and Meadow stared at each other. Beatrice said slowly, "Do you think it was a murder-suicide attempt, then?

That Jake killed Vivian because he'd been rejected and meant to kill himself?"

"But couldn't go through with it?" asked Meadow.

Rita shrugged and reached for another cigarette. It was all she knew.

Chapter Twenty

As Beatrice and Meadow left Oak Haven, Meadow said, "So what's our next move? And what are your impressions from our conversation with Smokin' Rita?"

Beatrice said, "I think we should speak to Huey first. After all, it he technically had the most to lose if Vivian were planning on writing a story about his connection to a bank robbery up north. And he had been very threatening to me. I want to see what he has to say about the fire."

"And your impressions?"

"I'm just glad we went. But there's a lot to absorb there. We knew Jake was serious about Vivian, but not to that extent. And Gwen breaking into Vivian's duplex apartment sounds really odd, too," said Beatrice.

Meadow said, "Let's go to Huey's house first, then. And he better let us in, or I'm forcing the door."

Meadow was so angry and indignant that Beatrice was positive she meant every word. "With any luck, he won't allow his German shepherd to come after us."

The rest of the drive to Huey's was quiet, each one thinking about what Rita had told them. As Beatrice pulled into Huey's driveway, she said, "Looks like he's home."

Huey's visage was a mask of fury when he opened the door and the German shepherd, picking up on his master's feelings, looked equally angry. He had a restraining hand on the dog's collar as he hissed at the women, "I thought we were done with information for the history. And I thought I told you, Beatrice, that you should leave any investigating alone or you would pull Dappled Hills apart."

Meadow's eyes narrowed and her hands balled into fists. Her voice was shaking with anger as she spat out, "Oh, this has to do with a bank robbery, not the history. Although I think it would provide a very interesting footnote for our book. In fact," she turned to Beatrice, eyes flashing, "since Huey is giving us such a poor welcome, we'll just go back and add it into the history."

Beatrice nodded coolly. "The book is sure to be a bestseller if it includes something salacious. I don't know why that sales tactic didn't occur to me before."

Meadow said, "Of course, I'd feel an obligation to tell Ramsay before the book is released. After all, I can't live with a lawman and not share the fact that a longtime respected resident is nothing more than a bank robber. Can't wait to see his face when I tell him!"

Huey turned quite white and he quickly said in a broken voice, "Come in. Let's talk about this inside."

Beatrice raised her eyebrows. "Will you put your dog away first? The poor thing is wound up right now and I don't fancy being bitten."

Huey briefly disappeared, German shepherd in tow, and put the dog into an interior room of the house where the women could hear it intermittently barking with frustration. He returned to them moments later, wordlessly ushering them inside.

His mind must have been moving at a frantic pace because when they took seats in his living room, he appeared to already know what tack to take with them. He immediately told them, "I'll confess. I was part of that rather notorious bank robbery when I was in college. It feels like a lifetime ago, but I think about it every single day. Not a day goes by when I don't see the frightened faces of the tellers and the other customers. It's been weighing on my conscience for decades."

Beatrice said, "Is that why you were so determined to keep me from digging into the past? Because I might discover your crime?

Is that why," she leaned closer, pinning him with her eyes, "you set my house on fire last night? To scare me?"

Huey's mouth dropped open, his face shocked. "What? Believe me when I say that I know *nothing* about that. I'll admit that I didn't want you to find out that I was involved with the robbery. But that's only because I wanted to confess on my own terms and of my own volition. I would never dream of destroying the amazing art in your house and I would *never* intimidate by using something as dangerous as fire."

"But you'd rob banks," said Meadow, voice stern.

Huey held up both hands defensively. "Point taken. But it wasn't a violent crime. Our guns weren't even loaded. No one was harmed, only frightened. And I didn't even profit from the crime because we dumped the money along the way since a dye pack exploded all over the cash. It was a stupid thing to do, a college prank, and I deeply regret it. I've spent my entire life trying to make up for it and pay my dues to society through service."

Meadow glanced around at the expensive furnishings, a derisive look on her face. "Yes, I can see that you live like a monk."

Huey ignored her and continued, "I've never done anything remotely like it since that long ago poor decision. I certainly never killed Vivian over it, much less Oscar and Ida. And I've never set a fire in my life."

Beatrice said, "You cared about Vivian, didn't you?"

Huey's eyes reflected his exhaustion and sadness. "Yes. Yes, I did. But I was already engaged when I met Vivian. I would never have hurt her, although I did discourage her from disclosing what she knew. I didn't want to go to jail—I admit it. And, in my own mind, I could do more in terms of reparation to society on the outside than I could ever accomplish being locked up."

They couldn't get anything else out of Huey. As they left, he told Meadow to let Ramsay know that he wanted to speak to him.

Meadow said, "Imagine that. I wonder what's going to happen to Huey after he confesses?"

"I'm sure there's probably some sort of statute of limitations on a crime that took place so many years ago," said Beatrice. "Although it will probably relieve his mind a good deal. I can't understand how he was able to keep a secret like that for so long. Not even telling those closest to him and then allowing the whole town to put their trust in him as a bank manager, mayor, and representative!"

Meadow nodded. "It's nuts. But let' s move on. I don't want you to spend another night in that house without this case being wrapped up. Who's next? Gwen or Jake?"

"Let's talk to Jake first. We might have more luck with Gwen if we have some of the preemie project fabrics with us—that would be a better excuse to visit. Otherwise, I'm not sure she's going to let us in the door after the meeting last night."

"Then Jake it is," said Meadow as she climbed into the passenger's seat. "To the bakery. I only hope it's not busy there. I hate to accuse someone of arson and murder in front of a bunch of pastry-seeking customers."

Fortunately, they learned there was something of a lull at the bakery. Jake was busily wiping down the already fingerprint-free glass display case. He gave them a quick smile as they came in. "Good morning, ladies! Or, actually, good afternoon," he said, glancing at the clock. "Somehow the fact that noon has come and gone has escaped me."

Meadow put her hands on her hips. "Jake Hunter! Where were you last night when Beatrice's house was set on fire? Did you have something to do with that? Were you trying to scare her off of this case because you don't want us to find out that you killed Vivian because she'd rejected you?"

Jake's eyes grew wide and a red flush climbed up his still-handsome face. "Meadow, what are you talking about? Beatrice's house was on fire?"

Beatrice said, "Someone set a fire at my house last night. We're guessing it was a warning to me to stop asking questions."

"I was here until midnight last night," said Jake. Beads of sweat popped up on his forehand and he absently grabbed a napkin to dab them off.

Beatrice said, "That's odd for a baker, isn't it? I thought bakers got up early to bake for the day."

"It *is* odd," said Jake hurriedly. "But I needed to catch up on bookkeeping. And I needed enough time to really plan out where I'm going from here. All your question-asking has made me think about what's important. I remember when my relationships meant everything to me. Now all I do is spend time working. I buried myself in my work right after Vivian disappeared and I've never really surfaced. I've done well here and now I'm ready to stop."

Meadow gasped. "You're going to retire? But who will fill your shoes?"

"Not my problem," said Jake, giving her a regretful shrug. "After doing my bookkeeping last night, I realized that I have enough to not only retire but to travel some. Maybe meet someone to spend the remainder of my life with. It's definitely time."

Beatrice said, "So you were here. At the time of the fire. Although no one can verify that, I guess."

"Exactly my point. I need someone in my life—for alibis and everything else," said Jake with a small smile. "And no, I didn't kill Vivian because she rejected me. I was devastated that she rejected me, but I wouldn't have hurt a hair on her head...or, for that matter, on Oscar Holland's or Ida's. And arson isn't exactly my thing."

Meadow said, "So after Vivian, you *never* pursued love again. Never. Because that's a total tragedy, Jake. You're a nice guy, a smart guy. You run your own business. It's just really sad."

"I felt love like I had for Vivian only happened once in a lifetime. So why even try?" said Jake with another shrug.

Beatrice said thoughtfully, "But I'm guessing there were women who *did* try. For all the reasons that Meadow just stated."

"And the fact that you're fairly easy on the eyes," added Meadow.

Jake was clearly trying to be modest. "From time to time. But I could always seem to dispatch them pretty quickly. Most of the time." He made a face.

Beatrice said, "Who in particular has been hard to get rid of? Anyone with a bearing on these murders?"

Jake shook his head with a small smile. "I'm not one to kiss and tell."

"But you didn't kiss them, did you? You just got rid of them. So why *not* tell?" demanded Meadow.

Jake just continued to shake his head.

They asked a few more questions, but Jake, although cheerful and eager to help, couldn't provide any additional ideas. Beatrice and Meadow thanked him, bought a couple of muffins, and headed on their way.

Meadow said, "I don't even feel like that visit was very helpful. Let's head on to Gwen's house. If I'm very threatening, maybe she can give us some kind of information. Jake was being pretty evasive. But the fact that Sam was talking to Gwen about Jake tells me that Gwen should know *something*."

"All right. But first, let's run by your house and get those quilting materials so she'll have a better chance of letting us in the house," reminded Beatrice.

When they got to Meadow's she jumped out of the car. "I'll be right back," she said breathlessly.

But she wasn't right back. Beatrice checked messages on her phone and read a news story and eventually just turned the car off.

When Meadow finally *did* appear, she had Ramsay in tow. He was holding the remains of a sandwich and had a very determined expression on his face.

"This sounds like trouble, Beatrice," he said uneasily.

"What part of it?" asked Beatrice.

"All of it. Or, at least, whatever Meadow has filled me in on. You had a house fire last night. You've got around and asked the people who are most likely to have set it if they were responsible." He shook his head.

"But she had me with her," protested Meadow.

Ramsay finished off his sandwich, gulped it down, and said, "To be completely frank, Meadow, what good do you think that does Beatrice? What would you do if she were threatened?"

"I'd find a way to stop them, don't you worry," said Meadow.

"That's all well and good and I appreciate the fact that you're both trying to be careful. But if it's all the same to you, I want Beatrice to stay as our guest the next few days. Noo-noo, too."

Meadow, who'd been looking peeved at Ramsay's unusual protectiveness, immediately brightened. "A sleepover! Boris will love that. And I will, too. I can cook all sorts of sleepover type foods and plan big breakfasts. We can stay up late giving each other manicures and watching scary movies."

Beatrice gave them a weak smile. Staying at home in her cozy cottage seemed like heaven in comparison. But she saw that Ramsay was absolutely determined. "All right," she said. "Thank you. That sounds like a good plan."

"What it sounds like is a *safe* plan," said Ramsay, turning away now that he was satisfied with the direction the conversation had headed.

"But Ramsay, we still want to talk to Gwen," said Meadow. She held up a bunch of fabric. "On pretext of quilting the preemie quilts."

Ramsay nodded. "That's perfectly fine. Go ahead and wrap up your questioning. Then, Beatrice, if you don't mind, go on and pack up for coming over—whatever you and Noo-noo need. It'll relieve my mind."

He tread heavily back to the house and Meadow made a face at Beatrice as she got into the car. "Sorry about that. He doesn't usually interfere. Although he's right to be worried about you, Beatrice. I'm worried, too. I think I forgot how worried I was when I got so mad."

"It's okay. It's nice to be worried about," Beatrice said with a smile.

Meadow said, "Just remember to let Piper know you're staying with us for a few days or else she'll be worried sick when she calls your house and no one's there."

"Okay, will do. Although usually she does call my cell phone," said Beatrice. "But first, let's head over to Gwen's house before Ramsay changes his mind and forbids us from going!"

Beatrice drove right over and parked in the driveway. Meadow said thoughtfully, "Maybe you better wait in the car while I get positioned inside. Then I can wave you in. I'm worried she's going to look out the window, see you out there, and just hide."

"That sounds good. Although, to be honest, I don't see her car right now," said Beatrice, peering at the driveway.

Meadow said, "I think sometimes she parks in the garage. So she might still be here. I'll try." She grabbed all the supplies, wrenched open the car door, and strode purposefully to the front door.

A few minutes later, she shrugged and returned to the car. "I guess you're right—she's not there. We can try again later today, I guess. Maybe she went out to run some errands."

"Or maybe her car is in the garage and she's hiding from us," said Beatrice with a sigh.

"Either way, she can't hide from us forever. We're in a service project together every few days, after all! Let's try back this afternoon," said Meadow.

"Honestly? I'm thinking I need to go home and put my feet up for a while. Despite the late start, I didn't have as great a rest last night as I could have," said Beatrice.

"Well, of course you didn't!" said Meadow indignantly. "Your sleep must have been absolutely rife with nightmares. Which is why it's such a good idea that you're staying with us. I wasn't sure about it at first, but the plan has grown on me. My Ramsay is a genius!"

"He certainly is," said Beatrice with a small smile. "A very wise and kind man."

"All right. So we'll just have you drop me off home, I guess? Then check on Noo-noo, put your feet up, pack, and I can run by and pick you and Noo-noo up," said Meadow. "Around suppertime. That way I can cook for you. You look as if you could eat a few fattening meals." Meadow eyed her friend's slender figure.

"That's a matter of opinion," said Beatrice dryly. "But I love your cooking and that sounds perfect."

"Unless," said Meadow, eyes narrowing thoughtfully, "I should just come in with you now, help you pack, and you keep driving us to my house. You could always put your feet up in my guest room."

Although this sounded like a perfectly reasonable offer, Beatrice knew the loud reality of Meadow's house. The phone and doorbell were constantly ringing, Boris the dog spent a lot of time in joyful barking, and Meadow's voice had a way of carrying. Particularly in the lofty acoustics of the converted barn.

"Thanks for the offer, but I think a few minutes at home will do me good. It's just two o'clock in the afternoon—not a scary time of day at all. I'll be over before you know it," said Beatrice.

Beatrice fed Noo-noo and they took a brief walk outside. When Beatrice came back in, she sat for a few minutes and looked through more of Miss Sissy's old pictures. She sighed. She'd forgotten again to get her those cat clothes for Maisie. Maybe Meadow could drop her by there before she drove her to her house.

Beatrice paused at one picture. It showed a younger Gwen with someone who presumably was her husband ... a man with black hair and brown, piercing eyes. Gwen wasn't as dumpy as she was now—she was attractive in her own way with a determined chin and high cheekbones. Beatrice studied the picture a bit longer. There was something there in the old photo—something she felt must be significant that she wasn't quite catching.

Finally, her own tiredness overtook her. She gave up with the photo and headed back to her room to kick off her shoes and lie down for a while.

Sometime later, Noo-noo's barks woke Beatrice up. She listened hard to determine what was upsetting the corgi.

Chapter Twenty-One

Then she heard it ... a light tapping on the door. She slid off the bed and padded into the living room, feeling disoriented after the nap. A quick glance at the clock showed it was 5:45 and that she'd slept much later than she'd intended. Beatrice groaned. She should have set an alarm.

She carefully looked out the window to see who was outside her door. It was Gwen, carrying what appeared to be a tremendous pile of clearly vintage quilts. A peace offering? Had she gotten over her pique from the quilt meeting then?

Beatrice hesitated only for a second. She did still need to speak with Gwen. And she *was* bearing quilts, apparently for the history. Just to be on the safe side, she hurried into the kitchen and reached into a drawer for a knife, which she stuck into her pants pocket which was covered by the rust-colored tunic top she wore. Then, still groggy, Beatrice opened the door.

Gwen said levelly, "Sorry about last night."

Beatrice shrugged, keeping a tight grip on the door in case she wanted to slam it. "Most people would feel defensive when faced with uncomfortable questions."

Gwen blinked steadily. "Still, I was rude. Thought about it last night and realized I had some quilts that might be helpful for your history. If you want them, that is."

Beatrice relaxed a little. For Gwen, this appeared to approximate an apology.

It was only after Gwen had stepped inside and adjusted the quilts that Beatrice froze. Because Gwen carried a gun.

Beatrice carefully pushed down her panic and said coolly, "So it's come to this. It's pointless, Gwen. Ramsay is already on your trail. Are you really going to kill the whole town to keep your secret?"

"No one knows," said Gwen, a fierce glint in her eye. "The only ones who even had a hint are gone, as you will be soon."

"Starting with Sam Holland," said Beatrice. "Although that was really just luck on your part, wasn't it? She'd been worrying about Vivian's disappearance for decades and, at the end of her life, tried to convince you to confess. That was it, wasn't it?"

There was no reaction from Gwen, and Beatrice suddenly realized the significance of the old photo of Gwen and her husband. Her voice was strong as she said, "Oh, Rita thought that Sam believed Jake was behind it all. But what Sam guessed was that you had gotten rid of Vivian *for* Jake. You were in love with him. Vivian even alluded to it in her journal—that you felt 'his blue eyes bewitched everyone, including her.' I'd thought you were jealous of Vivian because you thought she was after your *husband*. But your husband had brown eyes, didn't he?"

This time there was a flicker of surprise in Gwen's face that Beatrice had figured this out, before her expression was shuttered again. "Well, I was young and foolish," said Gwen. Her voice, almost friendly, sent a chill up Beatrice's spine. Noo-noo, sensing her mistress's alarm, stayed protectively at her side. "I had a very simple idea that if Vivian weren't around, I might be able to convince Jake that we could be a couple."

The wistful tone in her voice was at odds with the fact that she was discussing coldblooded murder.

Beatrice said, "And Jake had no idea, did he? No idea that you had eliminated what he's always thought of as the love of his life."

Gwen said flatly, "I was stupid. It made everything worse. Maybe if he'd spent more time with Vivian he'd have finally gotten sick of her. But when she disappeared, he got even more obsessed with her." She muttered again, "It made everything worse. Finally, I just gave up on him. Gave up on everything, pretty much."

"Vivian let you in her house one night. She didn't think you were dangerous. But you were. You killed her—with what? A hammer? A fire poker? Then you disposed of her body and some of the things from her house. You typed a short note with her typewriter to make it appear she'd purposefully left town. Covering your tracks," said Beatrice, trying to keep her voice level and keep the shakes out of it.

Gwen gave a short laugh. "The girl didn't have much to get rid of! I picked up a few of her clothes and things and tossed them in the lake after I'd weighed them down."

Beatrice continued, "But you didn't think about the notebook. Why would you? It was really only incriminating to someone who had a secret."

Gwen looked only mildly curious at this.

"Huey, for instance, would have loved to have gotten his hands on it. But I'm guessing that the mentions of you wouldn't have been alarming to you, even if you *had* known about it. Sam thought the notebook was key, but it wasn't, really, was it? Sam read it, saw a lot of mentions of Huey and Jake in there, and she wanted to enlist your help to find out if maybe Jake had something to do with Vivian's disappearance. You must have been so surprised to hear her ask about him. To hear her be so suspicious of him," said Beatrice.

Gwen kept staring at her. Noo-noo kept a watchful eye on her every movement.

"But you didn't want anyone poking into the past. You discouraged her, didn't you? Didn't take the notebook, didn't offer to help find out any information. And then she gave it to her son, Oscar. She sent Oscar to find out what he could in an effort to keep this sense of guilt and growing concern at bay. She thought Vivian had been murdered and it weighed so heavily on her mind that she felt someone needed to find out what had happened to her," said Beatrice.

"Poor Oscar," said Gwen, an odd smile on her face.

"You must have been horrified when he came by your house, determined to ask nosy questions about Vivian," said Beatrice.

"What worried me was that he'd definitely come to the conclusion that she had come to some sort of violent end," said Gwen. "He was the sort of person who was very pushy. He asked a lot of really piercing questions, and he wasn't going to give up. He was a real terrier. What was more, he surprised me so badly when he confronted me that I accidentally revealed that I knew Vivian was dead. Which wasn't common knowledge, obviously. As far as anyone in Dappled Hills believed, Vivian had gotten bored with the town and decided to move on."

"I think, what's most difficult to imagine," said Beatrice, "is that a woman of your age would be able to take down a man Oscar's age."

Gwen took a step forward and Noo-noo gave a low growl. Gwen said, "It wasn't at all hard. Not when I could tell by his expression that he knew. Because he did. He knew Vivian was dead and he knew that I knew something about it. He had to be taken care of."

Beatrice moved her hand slowly to feel for the knife. But weren't there jokes about bringing a knife to a gunfight? She said, "How exactly did you manage to take care of him? It seems like he should have been both faster and stronger than you."

Gwen said pleasantly, "What I had going for me was the element of surprise. He was very deep in thought, you see. I saw him right after he left seeing Miss Sissy. I think he'd been upset by his encounter with her. He looked ... disheveled. I came up behind him ... I had a hammer I'd brought with me. Since there were so many houses around, I didn't want something like the report of a gun going off."

"A good idea," said Beatrice fervently, eyeing the gun.

"I called Oscar's name. He stopped, frowned, turned around. I hit him with the hammer with both of my hands on the hammer, as hard as I could, swinging from behind my head." She shrugged. "It was easy."

Beatrice swallowed. Noo-noo, still not understanding the atmosphere in the room, but not liking it, stayed alert, eyes wide open.

"I see. Very clever of you to use the element of surprise," said Beatrice softly. "And Ida? She knew something, I suppose."

Gwen squeezed her lips shut into a tight line. "Ida *thought* she knew something. She'd always thought she knew something."

Beatrice said, "She suspected even when back when Vivian died?"

Gwen nodded. "She did. She'd spotted me over by the lake ... after. I was damp from the water. Ida was out walking her dog. She looked right at me, didn't say a word, and then kept right on going."

"But then, she wouldn't really have been upset about Vivian's death, even if she'd known for certain what had happened to her," said Beatrice.

"She was no fan of Vivian's," agreed Gwen cheerfully.

"Which served you well for many years," said Beatrice.

"She didn't really *know* anything," snapped Gwen. "She knew Vivian had disappeared. She saw me, damp with water from the lake. What she knew was circumstantial."

"I'm sure the look on your face when you spotted Ida was probably pretty telling," murmured Beatrice.

Gwen refused to take the bait, choosing to glare at her instead.

"But then something happened, didn't it? Ida got old and poorer. Meadow and I were both surprised at the condition of her house. Who knows—maybe there was even an underlying medical condition now that needed treating? At any rate, there was more than just the long-ago circumstantial evidence and a mysterious disappearance. Now there was also a murder ... a real, out-and-out murder of someone who Ida knew was asking a lot of questions about Vivian," said Beatrice.

Gwen repeated, "Ida didn't know *anything*."

"She knew enough to blackmail you though, didn't she?" asked Beatrice. "Except it didn't come to that. Because you didn't want to pay out. You had no *intention* of paying out. It was a lot more economic to simply kill Ida. What's more, getting away with murder the two previous times had made you feel cocky. You were filled with confidence, thinking you weren't going to get caught. You made arrangements to meet Ida at a time and a place where you were both going to be in attendance, anyway—at the craft fair. You had a perfectly legitimate reason to be there, didn't you? And what if you'd killed Ida at her house? Maybe someone would have spotted you going out or going in. The craft fair was the perfect cover."

"Oh go on," said Gwen, raising an eyebrow. "Since you've got it all figured out."

Beatrice took a deep breath. "Although Ida did make you mad enough to engage in a public argument, didn't she? Was she talking about the deal you were making? You told her you'd meet her over by the tennis courts and restroom. She didn't suspect a thing. You paid her. She turned her back on you ... after all, you were someone she'd known her entire life. And you, you were furious, weren't you? Ida had the gall to try to threaten you. She signed her own death warrant. You strangled her with the strength from that fury. Then you gave her a shove so that she fell down the stairs."

"And I took my money back," said Gwen wryly. "You didn't mention that part. And you neglected to mention how much hassle you've brought me."

"I think you've brought me more hassle," said Beatrice, motioning to her front porch. "After all, you tried to burn my house down."

"And clearly did a terrible job," said Gwen. She raised the gun.

Beatrice, feeling the unwanted sense of panic rising again said quickly, "Did you mean for it to be a warning? Or were you trying to kill me?"

"Oh, I was trying to kill you," said Gwen. "And if that hadn't worked, I figured you'd be scared off at the very least. Shows what little I know. Now I'm back to finish the job."

Which was when Beatrice's cell phone started buzzing.

"Ignore it," hissed Gwen.

Beatrice said in a reasonable tone, "Gwen, you don't want to do this. It's broad daylight."

"That hasn't stopped me before," said Gwen with a cold smile.

"And there are people coming and going. All the time. Busy place."

"Doesn't seem that busy to me," said Gwen.

"Someone will have seen your car here," insisted Beatrice.

"I didn't drive. I walked here and I didn't see anyone on the way over. Maybe everyone has been napping ... like you were," said Gwen.

Now Beatrice's phone rang and it was a tone she recognized—Piper. She'd forgotten to let her know of her plans to stay over with Meadow and Ramsay and she was probably trying to check in and see how she was doing after her scare with the fire last night. Beatrice fought back tears thinking that it might be Piper who would discover her body. That thought made her want to keep fighting and not give up.

The phone rang again as Gwen lifted the gun to hold it in front of Beatrice. Beatrice gripped her knife, preparing to dive down and slash at Gwen's legs at a second's notice.

Which was when there was suddenly a loud crash against Beatrice's front window—a wild, ghostly looking creature that screeched a terrifying yowl.

Gwen gasped, turning and pointing the gun at the new threat. And Beatrice, who'd been waiting for any distracted moment, dove at Gwen with the knife. Taking a deep breath, she sliced into Gwen's gun-holding arm. Gwen screamed, dropping the gun, which Beatrice immediately kicked under the sofa. Noo-noo bit Gwen's leg hard, making her scream louder and shake her leg to knock off the little dog.

In the meantime, the wild, ghostly creature had flung open the front door and launched herself at Gwen, assisting in the melee. It was Miss Sissy, angrier than Beatrice had ever seen her. Gwen had no hope of getting the gun from under the sofa with Miss Sissy clawing at her and Beatrice yanking frantically at Gwen's legs.

The grand finale was Meadow and Ramsay at the door, there to pick up Beatrice and Noo-noo, or so they thought. Ramsay's expression, decided Beatrice, was something that she would always remember. His jaw looked like it might hit the floor, his eyes huge, his hand automatically moving to his gun as he surveyed the loose gun on the floor, Miss Sissy scratching and clawing furiously at Gwen, Beatrice using all her strength to pull Gwen's legs, and Noo-noo biting wherever she found skin.

"Freeze!" yelled Ramsay at Gwen.

Gwen froze. Beatrice backed away with a relieved sob from Gwen and Noo-noo reluctantly backed away to join her, still keeping a watchful eye on Gwen. Miss Sissy continued her snarling, scratching rampage until Ramsay gently pulled her away from Gwen. Beatrice put her arm around Miss Sissy, startled to see a tear trickling down her wizened cheek.

Meadow's temper, however, was just getting started. "You!" she bellowed at Gwen.

But Ramsay, knowing Meadow was beyond indignant this time, stopped her by raising a hand. "Please," he said. "It's time for me to read Gwen her rights."

It was some time later. Beatrice wasn't sure how much time had passed, but she was glad that she'd had that long nap. Meadow had taken over her kitchen and poured them all wine. Miss Sissy, who'd come over for the cat clothes that were now secured safely on her lap, had enjoyed plenty of the wine and was now snoring on Beatrice's sofa. Wyatt and Piper had both come by to make sure for themselves that Beatrice was all right.

"I'm absolutely fine," assured Beatrice once again as Piper asked her for what seemed like the twentieth time. "But I love y'all for asking. I don't have a scratch on me."

"Which is more than Gwen can say," said Meadow with a snort.

Wyatt raised a quizzical eyebrow. "Gwen sustained a few injuries in the struggle?"

"I'll say!" said Meadow. "Between Beatrice's knife wound and Noo-noo's bites and Miss Sissy's scratches? I think Gwen is going to take a little time to heal. And she'll have all the time she needs in jail."

Beatrice said, feeling fondness for her friend, "And Meadow's still mad at her."

"I sure am! Look what she did. Killed three people and tried to kill another? Set fire to a house?" Meadow broke off, shaking her head in amazement. "It's hard to imagine all that happened in this one small town."

"And not just that," said Beatrice. "I'm guessing Ramsay has had a very long day."

"Yes, with Huey. He just decided to get a statement from him and will forward it to the authorities up north," said Meadow. "There may a statute of limitations or something, as you mentioned earlier."

Piper and Wyatt just stared at her and Meadow waved her hand. "Too much to explain tonight. I'll give you the rundown later. As for this ... this thing with Gwen? Ridiculous. I could have told her forty years ago that she didn't have a shot with Jake. I mean, seriously."

"It was all for Jake's sake?" asked Piper with big eyes. "Jake the baker?"

"Yes," said Beatrice. "Although he didn't know anything about it. He was completely oblivious. Vivian's disappearance actually likely served to make him *more* obsessed with her instead of less obsessed. It's all really very sad. I can only hope that Vivian is at peace." She carefully didn't mention the connection she felt with the young woman—the connection that reading Vivian's thoughts in her journal had provided. She didn't want to get in trouble with Ramsay ... or for that matter, Piper and Wyatt. And, now that the investigation was over, she was going to delete Vivian's private musings from her phone for good.

"And now," said Meadow sadly, "we've found out that Jake isn't going to be Jake the Baker any more. He's going to retire and move away and find something different to see and do."

Beatrice snapped her fingers. "That's it! June Bug! June Bug could take over Jake's bakery. Instead of scurrying all over town trying to deliver cakes and clean houses, she could stay in one place, focus on one thing, and take over an already-established business."

"Brilliant!" beamed Meadow. "Does she have the money to do it, though?"

"I can try to help her, starting out," said Beatrice.

"Me too," said Meadow.

Wyatt and Piper were also nodding. "I think everyone would like to give June Bug a hand," said Wyatt. "She works harder than everyone I know. And we'd all be sure to come to a June Bug bakery. Maybe she can make the cake for Tony and Georgia's wedding, too."

Meadow glanced at the clock and said sadly, "Does this mean our sleepover is canceled? I was looking forward to it."

"Maybe another time," said Beatrice. "I have a feeling I'm going to enjoy the feel of my own bed tonight. But let's plan some fun things on the calendar. All of us! I'm ready to lighten life up a little bit. And Piper taught me to be more intentional with my free time. I'd like to try it."

Wyatt smiled at her. "And we can't wait to fill your calendar."

Sign up for Elizabeth's free newsletter to stay updated on new releases:
   http://eepurl.com/kCy5j

Other Works by the Author:

Myrtle Clover Series in Order:
Pretty is as Pretty Dies
Progressive Dinner Deadly
A Dyeing Shame
A Body in the Backyard
Death at a Drop-In
A Body at Book Club
Death Pays a Visit
A Body at Bunco
Murder on Opening Night
Cruising for Murder (2016)

Southern Quilting Mysteries in Order:
Quilt or Innocence
Knot What it Seams
Quilt Trip
Shear Trouble
Tying the Knot
Patch of Trouble (2016)

Memphis Barbeque Mysteries in Order (Written as Riley Adams):
Delicious and Suspicious

Finger Lickin' Dead
Hickory Smoked Homicide
Rubbed Out

And a standalone "cozy zombie" novel: Race to Refuge,
written as Liz Craig

About the Author:
Elizabeth writes the Southern Quilting mysteries and
Memphis Barbeque mysteries for Penguin Random House and
the Myrtle Clover series for Midnight Ink and independently.
She blogs at ElizabethSpannCraig.com/blog , named by Writer's
Digest as one of the 101 Best Websites for Writers. Elizabeth
makes her home in Matthews, North Carolina, with her husband
and two teenage children.

Where to Connect With Elizabeth:
Facebook: Elizabeth Spann Craig Author
Twitter: @elizabethscraig
Website: elizabethspanncraig.com
Email: mailto:elizabethspanncraig@gmail.com

Cover Design by Karri Klawiter

Acknowledgments:

Thanks most of all to my family; especially Coleman, Riley, and Elizabeth Ruth.

A special thanks to Karri Klawiter for the cover design and Judy Beatty for her careful editing.

And thanks as always to the writing community for its support and encouragement.

Thanks!

Thanks so much for reading my book...I appreciate it. If you enjoyed the story, would you please leave a short review on the site where you purchased it? Just a few words would be great. Not only do I feel encouraged reading them, but they also help other readers discover my books. Thank you!